BLACK DART

Jacob Hawes

Yugo Publishing

CHAPTER 1

M Y LEGS WOBBLED, DRIVEWAY gravel crunching and crackling uncomfortably beneath my bare feet. There was a chorus of car doors closing behind me. More crunching. Crackling. Snap-crackle-popping of rocks against boot heels.

Ahead, a bird whistled pleasantly, as if in greeting. Exactly what kind of bird, I couldn't tell. Mainly because there was a black bag over my head.

I had no idea where I was. There was a nice, calm, gentle breeze, though. I could hear trees swaying around me.

The sun warmed my forearms, my feet, and the back of my neck. It came and went, replaced by what felt like, by contrast, frigid cold.

My head felt light and woozy, as if at any point I might lose consciousness. Dark spots bled in an out of my vision, like phantoms.

Being up all night was doing things to my brain. Not to mention being abducted.

Not to mention that, before being abducted, I'd spent the last several weeks in Aberdale Rithium Rehabilitation Center.

It's a prison with lipstick. Don't let anybody tell you otherwise.

You've likely seen it before, probably in some ad trying to convince you it's such a great use of taxpayer money.

It's got these tall, bleach-white walls surrounding it. There's a giant gate, guarded twenty-four seven. Cameras are everywhere. They're these little black half-bulbs that almost look aesthetic, part of the architecture.

Most of my time was spent in a locked room not unlike a cell—despite the attempts at homey furnishings.

Every day I was escorted down hallways packed with these rooms. I'd leaned, peering through the windows on each door—desperately searching for some new visual stimuli in my surroundings—only to discover that every room looked exactly the same, down to the smooth plastic vase next to every bed.

Always sunflowers in those things. Couldn't hurt to switch things up a little. With such a rigid routine and environment, any change at all would have been more than welcome. Waking up and seeing red roses in that vase would have knocked me flat.

Speaking of...

There it was. That musty smell, with just a hint of pine, like a torn branch.

Hands gripped my arms on either side, steering me like a rudder. My wrists were ziplocked together behind my back, so all I could do was lean into it and try to stay out of the way of those heavy-sounding boots. Ouchie.

"Excuse me, I have to ask. Is that...sunflowers I smell? Because I freakin' hate sunflowers."

The hands on my left gripped tighter. A voice next to my ear hissed. "Do you feel like you're in a position to ask questions?"

I gulped. "So, tulips, then?"

I should have seen it coming. It hit my ear like a dumbbell. I staggered sideways, my hearing popping in that ear, the surface area around it throbbing, signaling the onset of what would probably be a nasty bruise.

The guy on my right put a hand on my shoulder, propping me back upright. "Hey. We need him conscious." His voice was rough, husky.

"Does he look conscious, to you?" The one on my left shot back.

"Guys, guys, please don't fight over me."

I felt a twitch on my right, and a battering-ram jab into my gut.

I heaved.

Please don't throw up. Please don't throw up...

"What the hell is wrong with you?" Leftie said. He seemed both pissed and oddly concerned for me at the same time.

"What can I say," I said, gasping. "I have issues with authority. Honestly, I kind of blame my mother—" I felt the cold, familiar, ring-like texture of a gun barrel against my right cheek, pressing the rough fabric of the bag against the side of my face.

So that's how it was.

I decided to stop talking.

The henchmen, after pausing a moment, possibly to have some exchange I couldn't see or hear, marched me forward, off the spiny gravel and onto a walkway of smooth, loose pebbles that parted slightly underneath my feet.

How the hell did I even get into this?

Perhaps it was the lack of sleep, but things were hazy, out of focus. And not just because the fabric pulled tight against my face left nothing but muddy shadows in my vision.

CHAPTER 2

I RETRACED THE LAST twenty-four hours. Normally the type of mental exercise I fell back on when I couldn't sleep, but that was because average day-to-day events are so boring and menial that you couldn't possibly go over them and stay awake. It's actually a great trick. You lay back and stare up at the ceiling. *"Well, this morning, I woke up, then I put on my socks, then I think I brushed my teeth—"* By that point, your brain checks out, ushering you into unconsciousness.

Like I said, great.

As far I could remember, yesterday had been one of those days.

Well, it had been at first. It had started, before my eyes were even open, with the green musk of a soaked sunflower stem. So that wasn't new.

Then there had been a knock on the door, signaling the arrival of a "certified professional". In this case, a short man who looked me over through small lensed glasses perched near the end of a sloping, hooked nose. He'd made a few quick scribbles on a pad, before rolling a cart into the room. He'd handed me a couple plastic cups, two or three colored pills in each one. Wouldn't want to take them all at once and choke, I guess.

The drug administrator had rolled the cart out of the room, clicking the door shut behind him, and for what felt like an eternity I'd laid back against those white sheets—which wrapped a white mattress, on a white bed frame, standing on a white tile floor, surrounded by walls blanketed in grainy-white wallpaper, with a white plastic vase on my left soaking a solitary sunflower whose petals were...yellow—and waited for the drugs to kick in.

Sometimes the effects weren't all that noticeable in the short term. One of the pills—I could never figure out which one—seemed to make me feel stoic and indifferent. More agreeable and suggestive. At least for most of the day.

The pills that were supposed to fight the Rithium withdrawal symptoms actually worked, but occasionally they had some severe side effects. It was maddeningly unpredictable. Some days, I would be perfectly comfortable, no pain or difficulties at all. Others, I would black out, only to find myself on the floor, convulsing, bars of pain gliding across my body like electric shocks.

When I was deemed fit for it, most of the daily activities involved mandatory physical exercises, as well as participating in phony, pretentious lectures held in the wooded garden area.

The best sense I could make of it was that the general public saw Rithium as a psychologically addictive escape from reality. So to keep public approval of these government-funded facilities high, every aspect of their functionality had to play nice with that perception.

That was why they had us out on the grass, doing calisthenics and yard work. Getting us "back in touch" with ourselves, and nature, whatever that means. That is, it doesn't really mean anything, but it looks good on the news. A nice, open shot of some Senator strolling through the garden, past young men doing yoga on the grass, shaking hands with the head manager.

It was all a charade, and not just because they had doped us up every morning and night. I grew up on a farmhouse in Montana, surrounded by hilly country—a flat, farming valley in the middle of a sort of mountain slope cul de sac. That had been "real", for as much as that word means anything. Getting up at four in the morning to milk goats, feed and water the animals, cleaning out pens, rotating sprinklers. Going on hikes in the mountains. That had all been real. It had been my way of life.

As for the specially deposited grass and the transplanted trees, enclosed by smooth, high walls the color of polished bone—well, there wasn't anything real about it.

But it wasn't for my benefit. Or anyone else in rehab. It was for the public.

For roughly six years now, Rithium had been condemned by the Catholic Church and the United States government, as well as soccer moms everywhere. It was an epidemic that needed to be stomped out.

We weren't just criminals, though, being punished. In the eyes of the people, we were "victims". We just needed help. The type of help that Aberdale provided. This way, they can feel superior, patting themselves on the back. Aren't they good to help those who are less fortunate.

Honestly, I can't speak to whether I'm a victim or not. I'm certainly a criminal.

Here's what I do know.

Rithium is illegal. It is addictive. You have to be in touch with dangerous people in order to even access it.

And it is one hundred percent worth it.

A thought that echoes in my brain at the same time I find myself being escorted into a building with a bag over my head, so maybe I'm not the best judge.

CHAPTER 3

"**W**ATCH YOUR FEET," RIGHTIE said.

I could hear a door open ahead of me, over the *plik* and *plok* of us stepping across the pebbles, like giants in a ball pit.

When the door closed behind me, I could intuitively tell that this wasn't a particularly fancy or luxurious place. It was a homey one. I felt like I was back visiting my grandmother's house in the city, stepping across the thick, fluffy carpet. Only instead of laying back in a soft, engulfing LA-Z-BOY recliner, looking at colorful binders filling the bookshelf against the wall, I was being forcefully escorted, a gun barrel prodding painfully into my side.

Wordlessly, they yanked me forward.

A grandfather clock ticked away somewhere near the entryway.

A fireplace spat and crackled somewhere in a room off to the side.

With every step my toes sank into the spongy carpet, entangled by the fuzzy fibers.

Suddenly, the caravan came to a halt. The hands holding my arms felt like they were connected to rigid pillars.

"What's the holdup?" I said, without thinking.

Instead of hitting or threatening me, one of them—Rightie—said, "Stairs."

It occurred to me that I could use this to my advantage. Ever fall down a flight of stairs? It's enough to distract you, slow you down for a few moments. Long enough for a captive to wrench off his blindfold and get away. I've seen it in the movies.

Still, the blindfold posed an issue. How could I leverage things to my advantage if I couldn't see what I was leveraging?

Needed to even the playing field.

"We'll just have to take it slow," Leftie said, and they began to pull me forward.

"Or," I chimed in, "we could, you know, get this thing off my head?"

The only response was silent hesitation. One of my feet was planted firmly on the top step, the other hanging out over what could be an abyss, for all I knew.

"Look," I said. "You guys are obviously professionals. You—" I winced as Rightie jabbed his handgun painfully into my vulnerable side. "—somehow managed to abduct me from a secure government facility. I'm not even sure exactly how. I know you're probably looking forward to the part where you put me in a seat in front of your employer before dramatically pulling the bag off my head, but if we could dispense with just the one part of that—"

My head whipped back as the bag was forcefully removed. The fabric and seams scraped my face, giving my cheek what felt like rug-burn. Strands of my hair were caught, painfully snapping off my scalp.

I blinked. I was facing a long, downward set of carpeted stairs, turning, going who knows where. My eyes, accustomed to an entire day in darkness, protested against the round light in the ceiling of the stairwell.

The pressure on my arms disappeared, unexpectedly. I tottered, but regained my balance.

Until a thick, divoted boot sole pressed against the small of my back, shoving me forward, into infinity.

Well, not infinity, exactly. Unless infinity is the amount of time it takes to fall forward onto a flight of stairs. Or just enough time to think, *"Shoulda seen that one—"*

My shoulder hit the steps first. My hands were still zip-tied behind my back, so there was no way to try and cushion the impact.

It was more painful than I thought it was going to be. Or at least more than I had time to imagine while I was in free fall.

I hit my nose on the sharp corner of a step and kept going, slamming my side, followed by my knee, and a dozen other places.

By the time the world righted itself, I was curled up against the wall, at the corner halfway down the stairwell. My cheek was flat against the cold, bumpy texture of the wall. I had the aching sensation of a dozen different bruises sprouting throughout my body; enough that I likely wasn't aware of them all.

Boots stomped slowly down the stairs above me, every *thump* accompanied by a slight creaking reverberation.

I tilted my head.

"Whoops." The man said smoothly, stepping toward me. He wasn't looking at me.

He had to be Leftie. His hair was neat, smoothed over in a fashionable way, with only a little bit of shine. He walked right past me like I wasn't even there, jerkily adjusting the flaps of his suit jacket as if to knock some small, clinging thing from it.

It made sense, really. I had asked to be able to see where I was going, and he had given it to me. But not without warping the situation, to show he was in control.

Cute.

Rightie followed behind, and he was exactly and uncannily what I had imagined.

If Leftie's footsteps were tremors in the stairwell, Leftie's were full-on earthquakes. He pounded from step to step, descending on me like a Saint Bernard.

Underneath a coarse-brown Carhartt jacket, his gut strained against a plain T-shirt, protruding over and on top of a belt that was holding on to his blue jeans for dear life. That belt was also somehow responsible for a handgun holster at his inner thigh, as well as another holster that seemed to be holding a cellphone. Not all heroes wear capes.

He stopped and looked down at me, running a hand over the scratchy, receding stubble on the top and sides of his head.

"Yeah," he said. "You're gonna have to get up on your own there, buddy. Upsie daisies."

I flexed my elbow, stifling a groan. I was beginning to feel that these people weren't my friends. You know, just beginning.

A part of me had hoped that the secrecy of the bag over my head had been for my sake as well as my captors. A quickly dissipating thought, and perhaps a naive one to begin with, but again, everything was a little fuzzy.

The possibility these people were trying to help me, even if there were other interests at play, was part of what kept me calm during our little road trip. That and it wasn't the first time I'd been in situations like this. It came with the territory.

As I leaned against the wall, pushing myself to my feet, I couldn't help but think of the definition of Survivor Bias. *"I've lived through every other gunpoint encounter before, so obviously I'm going to survive this one...right?"*

"I said get up." Rightie said.

"Get him over here," Leftie said, voice echoing weirdly from the room he'd stepped into.

"I'm not going anywhere." I said, heart thudding, lungs working. "Not until I...have a word with my lawyer..."

I wasn't scared. I'd dealt with punks like these before.

I wasn't scared. It was gonna be fine. *It was gonna. Be. Fine.*

Rightie gripped his gun like he was about to whip it out.

"Okay!" I said. I leaned, palm pressing against the cold, lumpy texture of the wall. "I'm getting up."

The stairwell led to a garage, big enough to fit two or three cars. It was empty, except for three metal folding chairs scattered in the center and a folding table against the far wall with a coffee machine and an upside-down stack of styrofoam cups on top, an orange extension cord running out from underneath. Rightie stood next to the folding table, hands in his pockets, studying me distantly. There was also a black duffle bag underneath the table. I tried not to imagine what was in it.

The garage door was closed. It looked sturdy, secure.

Leftie walked around past me, grabbing one of the chairs and banging it loudly as he adjusted it, gesturing for me to sit.

I sat, deciding not to mention that a cushion on that seat sure would be appreciated.

The place smelled of coffee and motor oil. And the penny-lick odor of blood, but that was probably just my bruised nose. I wiped the blood coming out of my nostril on my shoulder sleeve.

"Coffee?" Leftie said. He was perched like a statue, hands still in his pockets. His face was placid, enigmatic.

"Am I leaving here in separate bags, or what?" I said, then found that I was biting my tongue.

Nice. Give them ideas. Great job, Kit.

"Eh, sounds messy." Leftie said. "I'd rather move you, first. I like to avoid messes. Which is part of why you're here, but it also means I don't like to shit where I eat."

Reassuring.

"This your place, then?" I said. "I like it. It's...homey."

"One of my places," Leftie said, speaking casually. "It's a safehouse, of sorts."

"Might want to keep that information a little closer to the vest." I said.

"Oh, I'm not worried about it." Leftie said. "We're either going to be friends, or we're going to be enemies. And if we're enemies, it won't be for very long."

"I try to avoid relationships with unhealthy power dynamics. Like the kind where I get held at gunpoint and kicked down a flight of stairs."

That got a little smirk from Leftie, which was unsettling more than anything. There was a wound-up tension behind his eyes that looked like it could blow at any moment, despite how composed the rest of his body was.

Behind him, Rightie was walking over to the folding table, reaching for a cup. His back was to the both of us as he set his cup underneath the coffee machine spout. As he flicked the lever, the smell of coffee intensified, and the garage echoed with trickle and sputter sounds, making me viscerally aware of the fact that I had not peed in over twenty four hours.

"You don't even know how it happened, do you?" Leftie said.

He seemed way too happy about that.

But that was what I'd been trying to figure out earlier, wasn't it? Retracing my steps and all that.

I woke up. Sunflower. The guy with the drugs. Laying on the bed, waiting for the pills to kick in. And then...

I stiffened. Somewhere in the dark and dusty attic of my doped up, underslept mind, a light flickered on.

"Assholes. You drugged me."

Leftie shrugged noncommittally.

I probed my mind, tripping over splintered memories that before now hadn't had any context or grounding, no relevance or reason to exist.

I must have been only half conscious when it happened. I remembered being wheeled on a gurney out the back of an ambulance, oxygen mask over my face. They'd rolled me out onto some freeway, slamming and sliding across asphalt toward a black SUV.

Of course. It's always a black SUV. If there was an APB out on all black SUV's, organized crime would be done for.

Then there'd been a needle in my arm; painful, biting. Injecting something. They propped me up in the backseat of the SUV, shutting the door behind me. Child safety lock on that thing.

Once they were in the front seats, they revved the engine, leaving the gurney lying sideways on the road behind them.

Had they spiked my meds, intercepting me on the way to the hospital?

"Picture this scenario," Leftie said. "We roofie you, so you forget any of this ever happened. We leave you, say, on the side of the road somewhere. The police find you. You end up back in Aberdale, filed away, prescribed new meds, kept on an even tighter leash."

My jaw clenched.

It was a strange thing. Usually I wasn't one for violent thoughts—outside of virtual reality, anyway. But I slowly found myself developing a self-righteous desire to off this man.

"Alternatively," Leftie went on, "Here's another scenario; one I actually find a bit more compelling. Imagine that everything I just described has already happened to you. Spiking your drugs, kidnapping you. Using you for our purposes. We've already done all of this before." He crossed his arms. "You just don't remember."

I bit the inside of my lip. It was warm and tasted the way rust smelled.

I held Leftie's iron gaze, not daring to show weakness.

Ringing loud and clear, clanging through my memories like a bell, was the voice of one of the glorified yoga instructors at Aberdale. I could practically feel the tickling grass underneath me as I stretched, my eyes closed, taking in the instructor's words.

"You are not a victim."

But maybe I was, wasn't I? My parents dying in a collision, being taken in by my aunt—I hadn't chosen that. It was something that had happened to me.

When I'd first become a Rithium user, I'd had no idea just what it was, or that in a matter of months it was going to be illegal in most countries. I hadn't realized it was brain-altering, or chemically addictive. All I'd known was after a long period of mostly death, it was the only thing that made me feel alive.

I decided not to give Leftie the pleasure of responding. Just because I was a victim didn't mean I needed to act like one.

There was a tense moment of quiet, interrupted by Rightie loudly slurping his coffee in the corner.

"Good stuff," he said.

"It was in the bargain bin." Leftie said, annoyed, eyes still fixed on me. He suddenly stepped away from the table and pulled a small roll of black duct tape out of the deep pocket of his dress pants.

Rightie continued to slurp his coffee in the corner, but he was watching carefully, with one hand on his gun.

Leftie stepped around behind me, putting me between him and the coffee-sipper. "Hands behind you, through the back of the chair."

Rightie nodded at me, tapping his gun assuringly.

I balled my fists and put them behind me. Leftie ran a zip tie around my wrists and pushed them against each other, zipping them tight. He moved quickly and efficiently, taping my legs and lower torso to the chair. It was kind of strange, though; he left my upper torso and arms untouched by the tape. Not that I was about to complain.

He stepped back, tossing the leftover roll of tape onto the table. There was an awkward silence following this, as both my captors seemed to relax visibly. They were clearly waiting for something. Or someone.

I wriggled a little, adjusting against the tight constraints of the tape. "So, what now? Twenty questions?"

No answer.

"I could start," I said.

There was a loud whirring sound. Light beamed in from under the slowly rising garage door, a bright bar slowly moving it's way across the cement floor. Warm sunlight blasted the inside of the garage.

CHAPTER 4

I SQUINTED.

A brightly backlit silhouette of a girl stood in the opening. The edges of her light-blond hair beamed, glowing like tendrils of light. She wore big, dark aviator sunglasses, with shiny frames. Her hair was pulled up into a messy bun. I have no idea how girls do that, but it looks like both chaos and order at the same time.

She wore a white t-shirt and a pair of denim jeans. She was cute, and seemed close to my age. In another time and place I would have been interested. But at the moment I was...a little busy. Might even use the phrase "under duress".

She held out her hand palm up, like she was holding a sandwich. Holding a sandwich in my direction.

"Guys," she said. "You broke him."

"He'll live." Leftie said.

"*Such a fucking edgelord,*" she muttered. Her hands went back to her hips. "Where's the stuff?"

Coffee still in hand, Rightie nudged a black bag underneath the foldable table with his boot.

The girl cocked her head. "That's the table?"

"You said to get a table."

"Yeah," the girl said, "But it's for—you've got coffee on it!"

Rightie shrugged. "And? We've been up all night."

"Come on, guys!" The girl said. "You know what it's for. It needs to be...stable."

With slanted eyes, Rightie splashed the rest of his coffee out onto the cement and tossed the styrofoam cup. He grabbed the table with both hands and wiggled it. Coffee sloshed out of the top of the coffee maker and splattered across the surface of the table, running off of it.

"See? Stable."

"Great." The girl said, arms folded. "Now go get some soap, we need to sanitize it, now."

Rightie swaggered past her, toward the stairs. "Always acting like you're the boss."

"*Apparently, I need to be...*" she muttered. She turned on Leftie, who was still leaning against the table. "Get those hands out of your pockets. Go get a drill and some zip ties."

"My lady," Leftie said. He sauntered toward the steps, square-toed boots clacking on the cement, echoing in the space. You'd think he was on the way to broker a billion-dollar deal.

"Get that smirk off your face." The girl said, watching him go.

She stood in the middle of the garage, seemed to take a deep breath. Then, the girl turned on me, like a turret swiveling toward a new target. She leaned forward, hands on her knees, face level with mine, affording me a generous view of her cleavage—one that I exerted a good deal of self-control not to take advantage of. Any situation can always get worse. Instead, I held my gaze with hers.

My jaw was tight. I tried not to blink. *Go on. Look. See all there is to see. Just a junkie in over his head.*

Her face was placid, focused. Then, several emotions seemed to travel across her expression. I didn't know what it meant, but I had the feeling it wasn't good. There was a sense of recognition, there. Or at least bias, like she had already decided who I was, what I meant.

Then, it passed, and she straightened, apparently done sizing me up.

"Wow, they really did a number on you," she said. "What the hell did you say to them?"

I sighed. "Nice to meet you, too."

The other two had drugged me, kidnapped me, and beat me. Somehow, I had felt safer with them than I did alone with her.

Thankfully, Rightie soon returned with a roll of paper towels and a bottle of cleaning spray. He unplugged the coffee machine and moved it off the table. He sprayed the table down and wiped it.

The sound of Leftie's boots announced his return. He held a battery-powered drill in one hand and a cylindrical container of zip ties in the other. Following the girl's instruction, he drilled four holes in the table. Two pairs of holes, each pair several inches apart from the other.

The girl picked up the black bag and put it on the table. She pulled a pair of blue nylon gloves out of the bag and put them on. They made loud snapping sounds as she pulled them tight.

"Bring him over." The girl said. As the two henchmen stepped toward me, she was rummaging around inside the bag.

Maybe it was the drugging and lack of sleep, but up until this point I had been watching the table activity with a level of absentminded dissociation, like it was happening to somebody else. It hadn't clicked that this was specifically relevant to me. But there was something about those gloves and the holes that got my attention.

"Guys. What's happening?" I said. "Guys?"

They were moving quickly. Rightie leveled his gun at me.

"Guys, we've had some good times, haven't we?" I said, glancing at the uncomfortably close barrel of Rightie's handgun. "Remember when you guys threw me down the stairs? That was...classic!"

"I remember it like it was five minutes ago." Leftie said. His voice was cold, distant and focused. He began sliding me toward the table.

At what point I'd started sweating, I wasn't sure, but I suddenly felt abnormally wet. Cold beads clung to my forehead like barnacles.

A lifetime ago, my aunt—Eva to most, but always Evelyn to me—used to have me throw out the dead mice that stepped onto the sticky traps in the barn. Sometimes it happened while I was out there, working. There was something so disturbing about it. Partly because the death sentence wasn't instantaneous, like with snap traps. It was a process. A process made worse by the fact that the mice didn't understand what was happening to them. They would shriek and wriggle, further trapping themselves, sometimes breaking their own limbs and back in the process.

Once my chair was against the table, there was a snap as Leftie cut the zip tie he'd used to bind my wrists not long ago. He duct taped my left arm to the chair. My right arm was grabbed, laid flat and palm up on the table, in between the drilled holes. From under the table, Rightie ran zip ties up through the holes, zipping them, pulling them deep and tight into my skin, holding my arm against the table.

The girl rummaged in the black bag and pulled out a small leather pouch. Inside was an array of small scalpels.

A gutteral sound came out of me—something between a panicked scream and a low growl. I felt a burst of manic energy. I pulled. I wriggled. I was wriggling.

"Hold him!" The girl barked.

The other two pushed against the table, pinning it to the wall.

I was panting fast, exasperated gasps. Each gulp of air felt like it was coming in through a straw.

I pulled, as if I could wrench my arm free. It wouldn't budge.

"I'd try not to budge so much if I were you," the girl said. She leaned over the table. The scalpel hovered near my arm-flesh, like an orbiting satellite, then descended, then made contact. It sank easily, like hot metal parting a bar of butter.

Molten pain lanced through me. There was no way to categorize it. It was beyond getting punched, or kicked around, or convulsing on a tile floor—

We interrupt this regularly scheduled program to bring you a message from Kit's forearm—

"JESUS!" I screamed. "JESUS FUCK!"

My eyes never left the blade. It moved slowly, delicately, forming a small slit in the middle of my forearm. Blood welled quickly, like a waterfall bubbling in the rocks. It ran down the side of my arm and pooled on the surface of the table.

"I think I'm gonna hurl," Rightie said. His hands fidgeted on the edge of the table, as if to avoid the approaching tide.

"Just don't do it on the table." The girl said. Her brows were furrowed in tense, focused lines. She set the scalpel off to the side and grabbed a curved pair of tweezers out of the leather pouch. She lowered the curved end toward the gash in my forearm, like a crane being lowered into an oceanic ravine. Only there wasn't any valuable wreckage in there. Just...me.

What the hell is she...

Pain cut that line of thought off, again. It was sore and excruciating. The tip of the tweezers dug around inside the incision, searching.

"Tanya." Leftie said, warningly.

Tanya?

"Tanya" shot him a deadly look.

"That's a lot of blood." Leftie said.

"Silly me," Tanya said. She held up one of her elbows. It was caked in a layer of blood, like a shiny, red velvet glaze. There were splotches of red on her gloves, her forearms, even a small spot on her left cheek. She looked like a painter. "I guess I hadn't noticed. Do you want to keep distracting me, or should I go ahead and finish this?"

Leftie went silent.

I was starting to feel lightheaded. I couldn't tell if this was from the blood loss or the fact that I was starting to pay attention to the blood loss. Or the fact that I was panting like a dog in the midday, summer sun. I could hear my own yelps and ragged breaths echoing back in the tinny space.

Was no one else supposed to hear this? Wouldn't there be neighbors or joggers wondering what the hell was happening inside this garage?

Then the tugging sensation happened. It was a pulling, scraping feeling, and it didn't feel much better than what had come before. No sir, not at all.

Tanya yanked, and the tweezer tips emerged from the incision, holding something in its grasp. Blood gleamed across the surface of it. It was flat, thin, and rectangular, with little grid-like protrusions. Some kind of...computer chip?

My feeling of lightheaded uneasiness grew.

It was such a small object, nickel-sized in diameter. But to my eyes—I watched as Tanya gently set it flat on the surface of the table, glinting like a blood-drenched doubloon—it seemed enormous. Such a massive thing to be oblivious about, to not remember.

Who... why...

My neck lolled. Darkness cut in on my vision, like a hole opening. I fell in.

CHAPTER 5

I WAS UNCONSCIOUS FOR a day and a night. I later discovered that I was the only one in the house who slept soundly during that time. The three took shifts, took turns checking in on me, watched and waited.

Tanya moved from room to darkened room in the house, wandering like a ghost. Eventually she opened one of the top floor windows and stepped out onto the shingled roof. She let her hair down, leaned back, and smoked pot under the stars.

Rightie had found a plush, comfy LA-Z-BOY—not unlike the one at my grandma's house—and sank into it. His fingers ran along a bookshelf in the living room until he found something that piqued his interest. He plopped the volume open in his lap, muttering and reading quietly to himself.

Leftie made a concerted effort to sleep(which, in my personal experience, doesn't work). He threw off the covers and ended up wandering the house. He found the open window, where Tanya was blowing plumes of pot-smoke. They were tiny, inconsequential streams of smog, evaporating immediately into the night. Tanya saw him, passed the bong. They smoked and talked. What about, I don't know. Actually, looking back, I probably do know. I just don't like to think about it.

Meanwhile, I was in a tunnel. Up ahead, I could see light, and a subway platform. My aunt and grandparents were there, leaning against the platform railing. They waved and beckoned to me.

I was limping. Stuck, really. Something was holding back one of my legs. A manacle, with a long, black chain. It ran along the floor of the tunnel, rattling and clanking on the metal tracks, winding its way like a snake into the darkness behind me.

I took a wide step and held up my manacled leg, pulled. The chain went taut. It hovered at waist height, like a power line coming out of the blackness, connected to nothing.

I yanked, harder this time, and there was a yelp, coming from somewhere there in the dark. Something pulled back, threatening to throw me off balance. I took a step back, planting both feet on the ground.

Back somewhere in the tunnel, light bloomed. It cascaded along the ceiling of the tunnel. Something was eclipsing the source of the light. It was round and solid, and took up most of the width of the tunnel. Still, the light crawled, steadily illuminating the path behind me. Shadows peeled back, like the sun rising at the crest of a hill. And I could see what the chain was connected to.

It was my best friend, Oscar. He'd been an almost constant part of my life after the move to Montana.

"KIT!" He yelled. Both his hands were manacled together, connected to another length of chain that wound further back. He gestured behind him, further into the tunnel. "Kit, help!"

Wherever that light was coming from, it seemed to be getting closer, pulling back the curtain of dark, until I could see where Oscar's chain led. It was connected to Oscar's sister, Jackie. Another big presence in my life, at one time. Wherever Oscar and I went, Jackie seemed to tag along, with a naive, puppy-like interest in whatever we were excited about at any time. She always did seem to take after her brother.

Her hands were also cuffed together, with another chain running behind her. She had this confused, plaintive look on her face. Her eyes were on me. Like I was supposed to do something.

"Kit!" Oscar yelled. "The key!" He pointed.

A bronze key hung from a hook on the tunnel wall, just three paces ahead of me. It was a large, old-fashioned looking key, pocked with rust.

I took a step forward. Once again, the chain went taut. Both Oscar and Jackie seemed to be trying to make room for me, pulling tight against their chains, with no progress.

The tunnel began to shake and rumble, echoing with the clunking, humming sound of a train on the tracks. A loud horn blared warningly as the light grew brighter, the vibrations came closer.

The boulder-like structure obstructing the tunnel was now clearly visible. A giant hunk of rock not unlike the one that had chased Indiana Jones through a cave somewhere in the recesses of my childhood, only this one was flat on the bottom, and didn't seem like it was about to go rolling anywhere. Beams of light shot through the cracks above and around it, so bright and sharp that it seemed the light itself might split the rock apart, shattering it into a thousand deadly shards. It was trembling, quavering to the rhythm of that approaching light source. The horn blasted again. It was close. Ear-piercingly close.

Jackie's chain was level and taut. It ran from a metal loop jutting out of the boulder, connecting directly to her manacles.

I lunged for the key, falling short by a good arm and a half. The bridge of my nose slammed against one of the tracks that ran along the tunnel floor.

There was a deafening crash. The boulder shattered down the middle, each half careening forward. One of the halves slammed into Jackie, crushing her into the ground, while the other kept going. Oscar threw himself to the ground, barely ducking the flipping projectile. He was screaming his sister's name.

Where Jackie's body had once been, bits of dirt, rock, concrete, and metal debris were crashing forward like a wave, propelled by the unalterable motion of the derailed train. The horn rang. My vision went dark.

When it came back, I was lying on my back, staring at the sky. It was like a giant blue marble, with little, slowly traveling wisps of white.

I wobbled to my feet. It was hard to keep my balance, because I was standing on a precarious heap of debris and rubble. Like crushed, scattered cinder blocks, toppled and piled together. Strewn.

I was at the top of a hill that surveyed a wide, massive valley, filled with knee deep grass that flowed and danced to the beat of the wind, like waves on the surface of an ocean. A river ran from one high point in the valley, flowing down, disappearing distantly between slopes that were difficult to see clearly with the naked eye.

Two mountain slopes bulged at the end of the valley. In front of these, a tower. It was jagged and metal and rusted, it's length dotted with jutting guns and turrets and machinations.

Closer than the tower, high in the middle of the valley, a creature flew. Its shadow traveled across the surface of the green valley, like the dark of a fish underneath a running current of water. It was crimson red, and reptilian in shape. It's long tail furled behind it, whipping and winding. Its wingspan was tremendous. As the wings flapped and flexed, sunlight glinted powerfully off of its shiny scales.

Its jaw unhinged, and a low, penetrating call echoed, bouncing back and forth off of the surrounding hills. Flame issued from its mouth, a thick, voluminous plume, like a wracked, red cloud.

I stumbled forward, out of the rubble and onto the grassy slope of the hill. I fell to my knees.

Rithium.

CHAPTER 6

I AWOKE TO THE sound of sirens. My dreaming and waking consciousness merged together, faintly registering the clang of frantic, high-pitched bells, overlaid with a harsh whooping sound. It sounded like a fire alarm, only...angrier. It sounded wrong. Dangerous.

A pair of smooth, cold hands gripped me, like icicles pressed against my skin, pulling me upright off the bed by one shoulder and the opposite wrist. By the time my eyes were open, I was practically standing.

It was Tanya. She was wearing a hoodie and a pair of pajama pants with little pink, cartoon kittens on them. Her hair was pulled back into a swirled bun behind her head, with what looked like a chopstick poking out of it. She was yelling something at me, but I couldn't hear it.

I shook my head at her, blinking. My eyes felt like they'd been rusted shut in the night.

Tanya clenched her jaw. Her small, alabaster hand slipped into mine, and she pulled me toward the slightly open door.

As the door swung wide, the alarm became louder, more immediate. The house was mostly shrouded in dark, but I could see flashing, multi-colored lights downstairs, through the railing. I covered one ear as Tanya dragged me down the flight of stairs and into the living room.

It was a comfy space with one long beige couch, two loveseats, and a brick fireplace. However, there was a tall, wheeled desk that had been scooted into the room, in front of the fireplace. Black cords ran along the carpet and over the fireplace brick. There was a desktop PC on the desk, with glass siding and flashing LED lights that cast rainbow-life images onto the walls.

My eyes were on the two monitors. One showed a livestream website. There was a webcam attached to the top of the monitor frame, with a conference mic set on the surface of the desk in front.

The other monitor appeared to be showing sixteen different security camera feeds all at once, broken up by black lines, like little boxes on the screen. They were tinted in green night vision, with lots of dark shadows, and some objects that shone a bright white, imposing themselves on the otherwise bland visuals like a floodlight, or a sun. The feeds covered various angles of the outside of the house. A circular gravel car lot, with a flowery garden mound in the middle. Another bit of cement driveway leading up to the garage. A pathway leading downhill on the other side of the house, winding between two garden beds.

Some of the footage looked like it was coming from remote areas of the estate, which I was starting to realize was a big place. One showed a naked tree branch bobbing, extending into the night like a petitioning hand. Others showed slopes of hills with small trees and clumps of grass and brush swaying in the breeze.

But the box that grabbed my attention and held it wasn't of trees, or wildlife, or anything else I would have expected to see on the property. It was one box out of sixteen, and it showed three black vans. At the exact moment that I noticed this, one of the vans' side doors slid open, and a dozen or so armored men with rifles started filtering out. They looked like a swat team. A side door on each of the other vans opened, with even more armored men stepping out in single file.

I sat up on the couch, my body tensing up. I suddenly felt very wide awake. Though, part of me debated whether I actually was. Maybe this was another surreal action sequence my subconscious had cooked up, like back in the tunnel.

But no, I was awake. This was all happening in the real. I wasn't an expert in much of anything, but I knew what it felt like to be in a simulated environment.

Tanya was at the desk. With a tap of her finger at the keyboard, the alarms stopped.

"There you are, you motherfuckers." Tanya said. She looked over her shoulder at me. "Ready to go live?"

"Live?" I said.

Leftie hopped over and into an adjacent couch. He was wearing his same outfit, only his tie was removed, with the top couple buttons of his white dress shirt undone. His hair was a little ruffled, he was sporting some five o-clock shadow along his cheeks and jawline, and he had dark circles under his eyes, but he appeared to be in obnoxiously good spirits. He winked at me and settled back on the couch.

"Okay," Tanya said, as she clicked something. "Here we go. Three, two, one—Hey, everybody!" She stepped back, waving to the webcam. Leftie waved as well.

"Go on, Kit," Tanya said. "Wave."

I wasn't looking at her. I was glancing at the front door at the far side of the living room.

"Oookay," she said, turning back toward the webcam. "My name is Tanya Bedford. But I also go by another name. I'm the current defacto leader of the Bannerets guild, Tara Vellis. To one side of me is someone you'll know as Sater, also a member of the Bannerets."

Leftie—rather, Sater—waved amiably.

"To my other side," Tanya said, "Is someone with whom you should be very familiar. In the real, his name is Kit. In Rithium, he's Winter Wolf."

The chat bar exploded, blurbs of text scrolling across the screen like they were in a race, like they were trying to get somewhere.

I barely noticed. I was thinking about the three or four steps it would take to get to that door.

The SWAT team was still making their way toward the house, navigating in a spread out, routine fashion across the grounds. They popped up here and there on the camera feeds, wearing hefty-looking nightvision goggles, like binoculars hanging off of their helmets, their rifles level and ready to fire.

What is the plan here? The four of us—if Rightie is the only other one— against a whole army? Like a shootout in an old western? High stakes 'Home Alone'?

Then again, what was the plan if I left the house and ran out there? Would the intruders shoot me? Would they detain me and send me back to Aberdale? Did I even know who they were?

I was startled by a shift in the couch's fabric as Leftie/Sater plopped down next to me. He put his arm behind me and leaned over to whisper in my ear, like you would a date in a restaurant booth. *"You won't get far."*

I smirked. I was off my meds, and I had recovered from being drugged. Now that I was fully awake, my mind was clear in a way it hadn't been for months, maybe even years, and I could feel this sense of calm certainty steeling over me. Or perhaps it was just resolve. Either way, I leaned over and whispered back: *"Neither will you."*

Just because I was a stupid junkie didn't mean I couldn't get even. I'd find a way.

Sater grinned, amused for some reason. He tossed a stick of gum in his mouth.

Tanya was still talking. "This house belongs to Sater's family estate. It is located on four-five-nine-five Ryder Avenue, Seattle, WA, zip code nine-eight-one-zero-nine. I'm telling you this because we're currently being SWATed."

She tapped a button on the keyboard, and the livestream transitioned from the webcam to the contents of the other monitor, where the approaching "SWAT teams" were clearly visible.

The chat was in a frenzy.

"Allow me to explain," Tanya said. "This is happening because my colleagues and I recently freed Winter here from a rehab facility. Winter had this object planted in his forearm." She held up the chip that had been removed from my arm not all that long ago.

Oh shit.

I winced and looked down at my forearm. In the excitement up until now, I hadn't even thought of my injury. I had felt it, but in a distant sort of way, deemed less immediately important by my subconscious.

Black stitches ran along the length of the closed gash, like spindly spider legs. It was red and swollen, and there was a faint yet consistent ebb of pain coming from it, like waves crashing down the length of my arm.

Lovely.

"Take a good look." Tanya said, rotating the chip in front of the camera. "It's authentic. As you can see, there's an encryption code on the side, here. For geeks like me, you already know what this is and how it works. This was a tracking device used to keep tabs on Winter, without his consent. And that's not all."

She reached into her hoodie pocket and pulled out something else. It was a dark, square object. A box, really, the width of her palm.

"This," Tanya said, "Is a Black Dart."

I found myself frowning, shaking my head. And not just because it looked like a box more than anything else. *Shouldn't they have called it...Black Box?*

I'd heard of "Black Dart". It wasn't real. It was a story started by hardcore criminals in the Rithium circuit. A story about the undercover cops infiltrating the game. Some people can't comprehend that a cop could be better at the game than they are. Or admit to themselves what really happens when you're in the system too long, or playing too hard. You die.

Rithium kills. Eventually, anyway. I knew that if I ever went back to it, it's what would eventually happen to me. But not everyone can face the facts like I can. People tend to look for other explanations. Other places to pit the blame.

"It was the police. They hacked the game. They killed my friend."

No. The police may have been involved. But nobody hacks Rithium; it can't be done. And I hate to break it to you, but your friend killed himself.

Oscar's face flashed in my head, like a mirage. This immediately precipitated a spike of pain that shot down the side of my head. It pulled on my eyeball, pushed against the inside of my skull. I keeled forward, pressed the palm of my hand against my eye.

I knew this feeling. It was Rithium withdrawal. The very thing that the drugs at Aberdale were designed to hold off, or at least control, the way day-drinking puts off the symptoms of an impending hangover.

Ah, memories.

The only thing worse than the persistent feeling of emptiness caused by hollow, unstimulated dopamine pathways in the brain was the headaches. That was when it really hit you, every time. That was when you knew you had to go back.

After a few moments, the pain began to subside, a bright sun smothered by passing clouds.

"As some of you may know," Tanya said, putting away the Black Dart, "The Bannerets have been in a longstanding rivalry with the Rifters guild. What you may *not* know is that the Rifters have been infiltrated by undercover police. Under the guise..." She paused. Her back was to me. For some reason, she seemed to be having trouble getting the words out. "Under the guise of a Rifter guild member, one of these undercover agents used a Black Dart against the leader of our guild, and took him out."

No. He overdid it. His brain couldn't keep up with his activity within the simulation.

But Tanya seemed to really believe what she was saying. She paused for a moment, long enough to be awkward. Then, her posture straightened. She seemed to be getting a hold of herself.

"Our plan is simple. We know the location of a piece of evidence that will incriminate the police and these corrupt institutions. With Winter's help, we will sync in, find the evidence, and catalog it using the Black Dart. We will prove the existence of these Black Dart operations. We will go public with said proof. And you, my followers, will know I'm telling the truth. Thank you all, we'll check back in with you later. For the time being, I'll leave up the security footage so you can follow what's happening. Peace."

Tanya turned off the webcam. She turned to Sater. "How was that, you think?"

Sater gave a thumbs up.

"I thought it was kinda infodump-y." Tanya said.

"You were succinct." Sater said. "You got the point across. Should give us the time we need."

I stared at the chip, still in Tanya's hand. For some reason, it bothered me that they had had their way with me. They had performed surgery on me without my consent. Not so that they could destroy the tracking chip, or help me, but in order to further embroil me in their schemes.

I raised my hand.

Tanya's eyes fell on me. There was a detached look to them, as if her mind was just coming back from somewhere else. I could see emotion behind those eyes, but it was churning far below the surface, being held at bay.

"Any chance I could get the chip back? "

Tanya tilted her head at me, eyelids scrunching together. "May I ask why?"

I shrugged. "When I got my wisdom teeth pulled, the dentist let me take them home."

Tanya folded her arms. "I'm not your dentist."

"Hey," I said. "The thing came out of me. If anyone should be holding onto it, it should be me, right?"

Tanya sighed. "I can't believe I'm having this conversation right now." She used her thumb to flick the chip in my direction. It went wide, but I reached out and caught it.

"You realize that thing is still active, right?" Tanya said. "Anyone could track it. I showed the code during the stream."

"I'll cross that bridge when I come to it." I said. *Assuming I survive this at all...*

"Course you will."

I started to say something, then stopped. Then started again. "Do—do we know each other?"

"Do we?" Tanya said, enigmatically.

No. The answer was no.

CHAPTER 7

"SO, WHAT HAPPENS NEXT, here?" I said, moving on. Perhaps it was the adrenaline, but I was starting to feel antsy. "Or was your plan to just sit here until we get surrounded by...whoever these people are?"

"Anybody want some coffee?" Rightie's voice called from the kitchen, footfalls ringing off the linoleum. He stepped into the living room. He looked exactly like the last time I'd seen him, minus the jacket. "I just made a fresh pot."

Sater put up a hand. "I'll take some."

"Are you people *insane*!?" I blurted out. I jumped to my feet.

"Easy, killer." Sater said. His gun was out in a flash.

"You're not gonna shoot me." I said. I was beginning to put that together. "Whatever any of this actually is, it involves me. How, I don't know. Why you guys seem to hate me so much, I also don't know. But I do know this: you people need me. You're desperate."

"You can still Sync In with a bullet in your knee." Sater said, lowering his aim. "No skin off my nose."

"I'm *not* syncing in." I said. "Get it? I've been in rehab for too long. If I go back now, all my progress goes away. I'll have to start over. The—"

Pain. White-hot pain.

I cried out, grabbed the side of my face.

—withdrawals will come back?

I gasped, panted. I took a step backward, putting some distance between myself and my captors. "Something's not right. This doesn't make sense."

Sater looked over at Tanya, uneasy.

Tanya took a slow, tentative step toward me. "Winter...Winter, I need you to calm down."

The headaches had been the first phase of my withdrawal symptoms. The first symptom to be eliminated, with time, during my treatment. There were a number of aches, pains and issues involved with rehab, but none of it so sharp and painful as those headaches in the first couple months. The same headaches that had acted like a ticking clock in my head during my time as a User, telling me it has time to go back for more. To Sync In.

"Or what?" I said. "Why should I calm down?" I took another step backward, toward the front door.

"What exactly do you think is going to happen when the government catches us?" Tanya said.

"Hands in the air? You have the right to remain silent? You have the right to an attorney? Oh, by the way, here's your free phone call?" Tanya gave a slow head shake. "Don't think so. The three of us—my two colleagues and I —know way too much. Dead on sight. Guarantee it."

"Don't take this the wrong way," I said, "But I'm not sure I care."

"Okay, fair," Tanya said, holding up her hands. "Makes sense. But what do you think is going to happen to you? How are they supposed to know just how involved you are with us? Do you really think it's just going to be a slap on the wrist?"

"I think I'll be saved from three crazy assholes."

"Okay," Tanya said. "Yeah, we're assholes. But you know there are facilities with higher security than Aberdale, right? Better safe than sorry, as far as the government is concerned. I mean, that would be your best case scenario, right? Relocation. Maybe to that place down in Santa Fe."

That gave me pause. And not just because she was starting to make sense.

I'd witnessed several patient transfers from the Santa Fe center, and there was one word I'd use to describe two out of three of them: catatonic. Aberdale staff brought those people in on stretchers, with an extra nurse to wipe up the drool.

Apparently, they used different drugs, down there. Experimental ones. It's enough to make you wonder where exactly we've decided the cure becomes worse than the disease—if I hadn't wondered every day of being inside Aberdale, already. Though to normal, everyday people, it probably doesn't matter.

"So," I said. "I should just trust you. The people who drugged me.

"Winter," Sater said, talking slow. "That...wasn't us."

I blinked. "What?"

"It's true." Rightie said. He was standing cautiously on the outer edge of the room. "We weren't the ones who had you put under for transport. All we did was intercept."

"That...that doesn't make sense. Why would..."

"We'll tell you everything." Tanya said. "In fact, you'll see it for yourself, soon enough. You're right. We do...need you." Those last two words seemed bitter in her mouth. "But you need us, too."

"What I need to do," I said, edging another half-step toward the door, "is get out of here before this place turns into a Michael Bay movie."

"Before you do," Tanya said, her hands still raised, as if I was the one holding a gun, "take a look at the monitor." She nudged her head in the direction of the desk.

I tilted my head, trying to keep every one of them in my line of sight. Soon though, my attention was completely absorbed by what I saw in the camera feeds.

Something strange was happening. The approaching SWAT teams had come to an eerie stand still. They were stuck in place, like mannequins, or toy soldiers, or a frozen game of Call of Duty that had pulled off the server and was about to crash.

Then, the squad leaders raised a hand, gesturing with two hands in the direction of the vans. They lowered their guns and began to march quickly and efficiently toward the edge of the property.

The throbbing pound of my heart against my ribs began to slow. Normalize. I swallowed.

"What was that?"

Tanya lowered her hands. Her body was loose, relaxed.

"They're not gone." Tanya said. "Not completely. They'll keep an eye on us. But for now, they'll let us be."

I took a step toward the couch. It felt like my breath was coming back. Like my body was remembering, *"Hey, maybe I don't need to go full tilt, all the time. I should take it easy. Pull up a chair. Recoup some of this adrenaline."* Something like that.

"They took the bait," I said slowly, working through it. "You convinced them you have incriminating evidence. And they'll have to track you in order to get it. Whereas if you all get shot now, in this house, it's a loose end. The data is still out there."

Tanya shrugged. She didn't seem all that pleased or surprised that I was keeping up. Now that I wasn't bolting out the door, she wasn't in much of a hurry to explain it to me.

"But," I said, sinking into the couch. "Why tell them? Why not just get the evidence?"

"Because—" Sater paused to take a steaming mug of coffee from Rightie. He blew on it. "It's not enough. We have proof the Dart was used, but no concrete ties to the Feds. Not that they know that." He blew on his coffee again, took a sip. It was straight black. "That's why we have to catch them in the act. It's a trap."

"Wait-wait-wait," I said, leaning forward. "These Rithium-hackers, people who have a way to kill you inside the game—these are the people you're 'trapping'?"

"We have our own ace in the hole," Tanya said, pulling the "Black Dart" out of her pocket and holding it out in front of me. "Or did you forget that, already?"

"Do you know how many hackers the Feds have?"

Tanya didn't answer.

"Could be one." Rightie said. He had one hand in his pocket and held a coffee mug with the other. "Could be two or three. Could be a dozen."

"Helpful." I said.

"They don't exactly walk around with neon signs above their heads," Sater said. "They try to keep a low profile. Most of what we know is from observing the aftermath. That, and what happened to..." He broke off, seeming distracted for a second. "Point is, there's a lot we don't know."

"Perfect." I said. "I suppose I should thank you for making me a part of this."

Tanya plopped into the couch across from me. "You're welcome, *Kit*." She hissed my name, spitting it, making sure there wasn't any left on her teeth. "Anything for you."

"Seriously," I said. "Have we met?"

A snarl formed on Tanya's face. She opened her mouth to say something, but Sater cut her off.

"Look," Sater said, turning to me. "Just how difficult are you going to make this?"

That made me pause. I could feel the tension in the room, all of them watching me. But that was nothing compared to what I felt inside. My insides were pulling, going taut, like a rope with a two ton weight at the end.

I'd like to tell you that I wanted to get away. That I was still considering dashing out that door, willing to face the risk of possibly getting shot, even if it meant being forced to Synchronize anyway, bleeding out from a gunshot wound in the process. I'd like to say that I wasn't willing to give in to these people's demands. That I didn't want to get pulled back into this lifestyle. But that wasn't true.

I doubted that it would be possible for the four of us to take down this government project, whatever it was. I also wasn't sure I even believed that this Black Dart stuff was real. But there was one thing I did know, even if it was something stirring deep down in the lower levels of my consciousness.

I *wanted* to go back. In every sense of what that meant. Once you've Synchronized, everything else in life pales in comparison. It somehow feels less...real. Despite the circumstances, and despite what it might do to me, I wanted to have that experience again, even if it was for one final time.

If you find that disappointing, I have to ask—what exactly were you expecting?

Still, as I sat on that couch, I couldn't help but think of this stuffy old greek myth—that I probably only know because of those stupid Aberdale classes anyway—where this guy convinces Hades, the mother flipping god of the underworld, to let him have his dead girlfriend back.

Hades, who seemed like a pretty cool guy in my book, says, *"Okay."* There's only one catch. All he has to do—like seriously, *ALL* this guy has to do—is walk back up the tunnel to the overworld. Hades will walk his girlfriend back up the tunnel behind him. But if this guy, Orphelus or whatever his name is, turns around to look at his girl during any point in the journey, the deal's off.

So what happens? Right at the end of the trip, when he can literally see the light at the end of the tunnel, he turns around.

Only...that little story doesn't really apply, now does it? Not to me.

There's no light at the end for someone like you. There never was.

I rubbed the side of my temple and rotated my gaze between the three of my captors. "What's happening to me?"

Tanya leaned forward, elbows on her knees, fingers clasped in front of her. "Let me ask you this. What do you think is a better motivator: the carrot, or the stick?" She let that sit for a moment, watching me.

That's not ominous.

I swallowed. "Oh, you want me to actually answer. Well then, I guess I would have to say Carrot. I'm an addict, after all."

Tanya stood. "Carrot, it is." She held out her hand, though she had a look of distaste as she did so. "Get us that evidence, and we'll tell you everything."

I stood, took her hand. "Don't think I won't hold you to it."

CHAPTER 8

RIGHTIE—I STILL DIDN'T KNOW his name—slid a steaming plate of scrambled eggs across the table toward me. I nodded to him.

The dining room chairs had that antique, carved, wooden feel to them. You know what I'm talking about. It looks like a fancy piece of architecture but it feels like a torture device.

Or maybe that's just me. I'm skinny. I've always been skinny. I was blessed with the ability to eat as much junk food as I wanted and never gain a single pound. It's something of a perk, but there are drawbacks. The worst one being: bony butts. My butt was pretty bony.

Luckily, my chair did have a seat cushion, tied to the back of the chair by little strings that wrapped around the cylindrical wooden spires. But because of the way I was slouching in my chair, the cushion kept sliding around. Straightening my back just caused it to move again.

Both Tanya and Sater were completely focused on their breakfast already, sipping between bites. Rightie brought his own plate of eggs to the table and started digging in himself.

I glanced around at the kitchen, which was right next to the dining room area. There was a small window just above the sink. It was dark out still, with a faint hint of blue light beginning to emerge. A clock above the window said it was about four-ten in the morning. Twenty minutes until they'd decided it was time to synchronize.

It made me tense, nervous, apprehensive. But also excited. It was all jumbled together, like a hot, bubbling stew of emotions. It was enough to make me feel sick. Though, maybe that was just the hunger talking. I'm never quite myself when I'm hungry.

What about when you've been kidnapped and forced to participate in...whatever the hell this is?

I forced myself to take a bite. The eggs had that puffy, fluffy texture you get if you mix in the right amount of milk or cream before cooking.

I swallowed, and held in a groan. I hadn't realized how hungry I was. A low rumbling echoed in my stomach. My next several bites came quicker.

Sater flicked open a switch-comb and started slicking back his hair, like a school bully in an eighties flick. He was looking at his reflection in the screen of his phone, which he'd propped up against his empty plate. There was a tie laid out neatly on the table next to him. A dark suit jacket hung on the chair next to his.

"Seriously?" Tanya said, turning toward him.

"Forgive me," Sater said, still combing intensely, "If I don't want to die in Hello Kitty pajamas."

Tanya gave him the middle finger while she took another bite. Then, after a few seconds: "I'm giving you the finger."

"I know." Sater said. He put the comb away and was carefully adjusting his hair with his hands, eyes still on his phone. "I have great peripheral vision."

A few moments of silent eating passed. I glanced at the clock. *Fifteen minutes.*

I had that feeling of unease, again. Or was it impatience? And not just to get back into Rithium, though that was a factor. Time was ticking down, now. Everything was coming to a point.

"I just had a thought." I said.

Nobody responded to that, except Tanya, who just gave me a dismissive, derogatory glance between mouthfuls.

"You doxxed us." I said to her. "Told people what you believe to be the truth. Won't somebody come for us? Do something?"

Tanya smirked. "Who? Politicians? Journalists? Perhaps the general public will band together to help us?" She leaned forward in her seat. "Does that seem like something that's likely to happen, to you?"

I frowned. "No." I admitted. "But I was thinking more like your internet audience."

Tanya laughed. It was a high, girly laugh, but there was disdain in it. "Those nerds on the stream?" She shook her head. "They wouldn't get far. Though I do get some satisfaction out of the fact that it's going to take some serious manpower to keep this under wraps, between leashing the media and setting up a perimeter around this place. No one's getting in or out of here. And that's exactly how we want it."

"What about Rithium?" I said.

Tanya shook her head, again. "Even the stream viewers with Rithium access don't know where or when it's going to go down." She pointed her fork at me. "This plan requires timing and precision. Besides, I can't risk any more people getting involved in this."

"Anyone besides me." I said. "You don't care if I die."

I said it matter-of-factly, and she didn't argue the point. She just gave me that same penetrating look I'd become so familiar with.

"Is it my face?" I said. "A lot of people say it's the face."

Tanya straightened. "Eat your eggs, Winter."

She turned to here as well. Oh, is it intentional and I'm just dumb? Rightie. "Everything ready to go?"

Rightienodded, set his fork down on his empty plate. "Cloudbox is upstairs. I'll go grab it."

Cloudboxes are integration kits for Rithium access. It's not quite accurate to say that a Cloudbox runs the simworld. It's more like a key that opens the door.

Or is the Cloudbox the door that opens to the simworld, and your mind is the key?

Whatever. All metaphors break down eventually.

The point is, you need a Cloudbox. And they're not easy to find. They were hard enough to get a hold of in the early days, before they became illegal, and the common enemy of well-meaning busybodies everywhere. You'd have an easier time smuggling heroin across the border. Supposedly, they even have dogs trained to sniff them out. Though what exactly a Cloudbox smells like, I have no idea.

I took my last bite and pushed my dish toward the center of the table.

Scrambled eggs: not exactly my first pick for a last meal. But it hit the spot.

Tanya walked around the table, picking up all the dirty dishes. She set them in the sink, turned on the faucet, and began washing and rinsing. For that poignant moment in time, she actually seemed domestic. Her back was to me, her shoulders hunched, arms moving slowly, methodically.

Evelyn hadn't had a dishwashing machine at the farm, and for most of my childhood I was the designated dishwasher, on top of all the other chores I'd been assigned. Which meant me spending a lot of time bent over in front of the sink, scrubbing frantically.

Tanya wasn't that kind of dishwasher. She enjoyed the process. She was scanning the surface of each plate, gently running her sponge over it, wiping away grime in an easy, satisfying way that reminded me of dish soap commercials. She held each washed and rinsed plate up to the kitchen light, admiring it, before setting it in the dish rack to dry.

When she was done, she shook her hands twice, spraying water droplets into the sink. She shut off the light above the sink. She turned to leave, but stopped at the edge of the kitchen and spun back around. Her head rotated slowly, studying the space, taking it in. She was looking at the room as if there were memories there, in every nook and corner. She was savoring those memories, as if for the last time.

She must have had some long-term connection to Sater. That much was obvious. She knew this place. Had a relationship with it, in the same way I had a relationship of sorts with Evelyn's farmhouse. Perhaps Tanya was a longtime friend of Sater's family.

"Don't take too long, boys." She said, before disappearing into the parlor.

Ten minutes.

It was so close. The feeling of immediacy was tangible. It was going to happen. It was coming, and whatever it was, it would be irreversible.

Sater seemed to feel it, as well. He was staring off into space, like a man on a hangman's platform, looking at the world through a noose. His eyes drifted and, in a moment of frantic awkwardness neither of us had predicted or could seem to break, met mine.

It was that feeling of being left alone at a wedding with someone you don't know but feel obligated to talk to, because he's *"a friend of the bride"*, or an estranged *"uncle who traveled twelve-hundred miles to be here"*, and wouldn't her father *"have loved to see her on this day, so beautiful."*

"Alone at last." I said through dry lips, breaking the silence.

Sater didn't answer, instead returning to his hangman's brood. He stood, whipping his tie off of the table. He turned up his collar and put his tie together in a half windsor with practiced efficiency. He wasn't someone who had to dress up with a tucked in, button-down shirt and tie every Sunday morning. He did this every damn day.

What a freak.

Sater slipped into his suit jacket. He pulled it tight, running a hand here and there over the cloth, looking for wrinkles, making sure it was smooth as silk.

Seeming satisfied, he left the room, without another word or look.

Five minutes.

I rapped my knuckles on the table. For luck, maybe? I wasn't sure. Probably just nerves.

Am I breathing? The thought echoed suddenly in my head, like a text notification. *How long since I last took a breath?*

I exhaled, long and heavy, expelling carbon so I could breathe in again. *Shouldn't this be automatic? Shouldn't this—*

I was in a loop. Like the first time I went in for my driver's test. Even though I wanted to pass, so badly, I wasn't thinking about driving while I sat in one of those DMV chairs, waiting to be called up. I was thinking about Steven Seagal, trying to figure out what the hell people saw in that guy. I was thinking about how when I got home, I'd have to move the hay bales in the barn again, to make room for the new barrels of feed. I was even thinking about a misplaced tile on the floor, and how much a person got paid to do something like that, and how every tile floor always seemed to have something just a little bit off about it. I was thinking about everything except the act of driving, my thoughts moving in erratic circles, avoiding the present moment.

And Rithium. This thought was clearer than the others, and an intrusion. It was the prattle of a know-it-all.

You thought about it every day and night.

Rithium had just started to make waves. It was new, prototypical. People didn't understand what it was; not yet. Perhaps they never would. Few had access to it. And lucky me, I was one of those people. It was my secret, and one I was damn well sure to keep to myself.

With one exception, of course. Oscar.

Oz knew. He understood Rithium. But that was because he was there alongside me, almost every time I synchronized. I wanted to share my experiences with other people. I needed a way to vent.

Instead, the thoughts, the excitement, just kept building. It swirled, revolving, mounting in pressure, like an engine without an exhaust valve.

I couldn't help but wonder if perhaps this was how serial killers felt. Secrecy is the key to a killer's success, especially if they want to keep doing it. But how lonely it must be. To such a person, it seems as if they have just begun to discover who they actually are. When they kill, and/or commit other taboo acts associated with killing, to them it must feel like these brief moments when they are truly themselves. Even though there is no one else around to see it. To *know* them.

This wasn't a prophetical sense of foreshadowing. I really had no idea of what my new hobby would become to the world, beyond the fact that Evelyn would be against it. She didn't understand video games, after all. She called them "escapism", and she always seemed to mean it in a bad way. To her, entertainment needed to have some kind of intrinsic value. Escapism is a sin; it requires redemption. I would describe something I liked, and she would say, *"But what is the* redeeming *value?"* Art isn't something merely to be enjoyed; surely not. It's not a way to escape into someone else's head, to experience life from a different angle. It's a transaction. Any sense of pure fun or excitement must be met with an equal, opposite, reactive force. In other words, there needed to be a *point* to the thing. If there were explosions, gunfights, or—God-forbid—sex scenes throughout, there had better be a good, long *'What have we learned, kids?'* moment at the end.

It wasn't hard to imagine what she'd make of experimental, neural-interfacing simulation technology. Not to mention a fact that would be even harder for her to understand, which was that the new interactive genre of "Simworld" wasn't just an escape, for me. It was becoming life itself.

Still, beyond the feeling that Evelyn would be disappointed if she knew, there was no guilt, no real sense of foreboding. Only the thrill. Only the constant counting down of moments until I could go back.

And now you can. After all this time. After all this...bullshit. So what are you waiting for?

I didn't know, and the fact that I didn't know made me nervous all over again, because it meant I would be in another loop, circling, looking for an answer that, thanks to my own distracting, procrastinative thought process, would remain just out of reach.

I pushed my chair back from the table and stood. Chair was uncomfortable, anyway. *Just keep moving. Stop thinking. Just move.*

Three minutes.

It suddenly occurred to me, standing in the now dimly lit dining area next to the table, that I was alone and unguarded for the first time in...shit, *six years*. Sure, I could join the others in the living room and do as I promised. But I didn't have to. I could leave. They weren't forcing me, not anymore. I'd given them my word. Meant it, at the time. And to them, that had been enough. But if I left now, who could blame me? You say what you need to when your life's on the line. *You'd think they would have known that much.*

How big was the estate, anyway? A couple miles in diameter? That's a lot of ground to block off. Full of tall pines and knee-height undergrowth, from the looks of those cameras. How hard would it be to disappear? It was possible that the property would be blocked off by now, but it was also possible that I could at least try to escape. That decision was open to me. I wasn't bound to anything.

That's where you're dead wrong.

It was derisive now, disappointed.

For the same reason Tanya knew she didn't need to keep an eye on you, anymore. You've always been bound. You always will. It's who you are.

The room suddenly felt cold, inhospitable. I turned, making my way toward the living room.

That's why, the voice continued, *you screwed over Oscar. Jackie, too. You're a pig. You can't fucking help yourself. And you'll screw over these people, too. You're disgusting. I hate you. You're—*

I closed my eyes. My teeth locked together, making a loud tapping sound.

When I opened them, it was two minutes to go.

CHAPTER 9

L EFTIE SET THE CLOUDBOX on a coffee table in the middle of the
room. This one was a blocky, aluminium-looking thing. Less like a game
console and more like something would go inside the engine of a car, like a
carburetor.

"Seems...legit." I said, stopping in front of the coffee table and looking
down at it.

"Government issued." Rightie said. "It integrates with the Black Dart."

"Weird." I said. "Why not just have that functionality baked in?"

Leftie shrugged. "An extra layer of security, perhaps." He flipped a clunky-
looking switch on the Cloudbox. There was a *click*, and a blue, circular light
came on.

The box was connected to an orange extension cord that ran into another
room, where a gas powered generator was revving noisily. I guessed this was
in case the Feds tried to mess with the power line. *Smart cookies.*

Sater had already laid flat on one of the couches and was making sure his
suit was tidy, laid out straight. He looked like he was in an open casket.
There was something kind of morbid about it.

Tanya was smoking a cigarette. Spirals of smoke traveled slowly across the
parlor, like bouts of fog. She held out an open pack of American Spirits.
"Want one?" she said, her lit cigarette bobbing on her lip.

I half-shrugged, half shook my head. "Don't smoke."

"Not ever?" She said, shaking the pack so a single cigarette poked out,
offering it to me.

I breathed out, trying to will some of the tension out of my body. "A'ight.
Why not."

I took the cigarette and propped it between my lips. Filter first—I knew
that much.

Tanya snapped open a shiny metal lighter and lit the end for me. I
breathed in. Not straight into my lungs, not right away; I also knew that.

It was warm and dark, kind of bitter. But it felt alright. It was distracting, at least.

"Thanks." I said.

Tanya gave me a tiny headcock. It was almost imperceptible. Some unknown factor seemed to have mellowed her out, a little. Perhaps the severity of the situation, though that would be bizarre. Perhaps the act of smoking itself. Her eyes traveled over my face, like she was trying to figure me out.

I sat down on the free couch, getting ready to settle in and lay back. I leaned forward and flicked a cylindrical section of ash off of my cigarette and into the ashtray on the coffee table, feeling a little like Humphrey Bogart in one of those forties flicks.

That's right. Circle. Don't think about it.

I grimaced, examining the cigarette like a newly discovered mosquito bite. Truly and honestly, did I really need a new addiction?

I gave another puff for good luck, then dropped the cigarette into the ashtray. I leaned back, arms resting on the back of the chair, and blew a wispy cloud of smoke into the air above me.

Leftie started handing out Transmitters—ear-piece-looking sensors that rest on either side of the temple, hanging on by the ears. They connect wirelessly to the Cloudbox, and facilitate the Synchronization.

I don't claim to know how it works, any more than I know how cell phones work. But I get the basic idea. I think.

You know how dreams start weird and vague? It's more like you're floating in a feeling, if there's even anything tangible enough to hold onto and remember at all. But over time, as you fall into a deeper sleep, things become more rigid. They start to take on a structure, a sense of internal reality. Near the tipping point of this deep sleep—REM sleep, I believe it's called—your brain is simulating reality so effectively that, at times, you would be hard pressed to tell the difference.

This part of your brain is key to the way that Rithium works.

Perhaps that was part of why Rithium access was damaging to a user's brain. Like a rubber band pulled too tight and too hard, getting used up before it's time.

I hooked the Transmitters over my ears. They were already on. I could feel the steady, electronic hum coming off of them. It was almost like a vibration.

I was starting to feel unnaturally drowsy. This was, of course, because of the radio waves coming off of the Transmitters. My mind was being prepped for transmission, ready to step over into the other place.

"Everyone ready?" Rightie said. He was standing next to the coffee table, looking around at us.

For some reason, it wasn't until that moment that I put together the fact Rightie wasn't going to be joining us. Though, it made sense that one of us should stick around and keep an eye on things. Rightie had gone to get the Cloudbox, and had handed out three pairs of Transmitters.

"Wait." I said. After a wobbly moment of hesitation, I held out my hand. "It would be a shame if I never got your name."

Wrinkled bumps sprouted on Rightie's forehead as his brows came together. His sarcasm-detector was at work, reading my face. Then, seeming satisfied, he clasped my hand. "Mason." He said. "Mason Alexander."

I nodded to him. "See you on the other side, Mason."

"Good luck," He said. "Keep them safe, in there, alright?"

Before I could respond to that, Tanya jumped out of her chair. Her arms slung around Mason from the back, tilting his large frame backward toward her. Her eyes were shiny, reflecting the yellow glow of the ceiling fan light above them.

"Whoa, easy," Mason said. He spun, hugged her.

There was a sigh from Sater, as if he'd just realized he had a similar obligation. As Tanya broke off the hug, Sater went in for the ol' Bro Hug with Mason. It was brief, with three pats on each other's backs before breaking away and nodding to each other.

"C'mere," Sater said, pulling Tanya in toward him. "It's gonna be okay, alright?"

She was nodding.

Curled against Sater, Tanya's eyes flashed, perhaps accidentally, in my direction. I decided that now was a good time to step away from the situation. I laid back on the couch, stared at the ceiling.

Tanya and Sater clearly had some kind of close relationship. I didn't think they were an item. There was something else tying them together. Something more than just being close, longtime friends. What exactly, I couldn't say. Not that I could also see how that bit of info was supposed to help me, though, except for the material that allowed me to keep circling.

What are you so worried about? You've done this a hundred times before.

That didn't stop my heart from hammering away. The more I told myself I needed to relax, the louder it got. The sound seemed to vibrate in my skull.

It took a second to notice Mason was standing over me, leaning in close. He smelled like eggs, and garlic, and Speed Stick. The Holy Trinity of Mason.

Bless me Father, for I have sinned.

"Listen," He said. "The others didn't want to lay this out explicitly for you. They seem to think we shook you up enough, already. They don't want to go too far and rock the boat. But I think you should know."

"If you don't cooperate in there, or if things go bad, and I decide it's your fault...well, I won't be able to let you wake up. You get it?"

"Can't wait to see you again too, buddy." I said, staring grimly at the ceiling.

I'd guessed as much. I knew I should be grateful he was being upfront and open about it. Mostly it was just kindling for the swelling, self-righteous anger I had for this entire situation.

He stood there for a moment longer, as if waiting for some other response.

"*I'm sorry.*" He said it so soft and quiet that I was almost sure I'd imagined it.

Then, louder: "Everyone ready?"

I raised a hand. "No."

"Okay, then." He said, putting a hand on the Cloudbox. "Three..."

The countdown almost made it worse. I took a deep breath, but it felt like my air was coming in through a straw.

C'mon, just relax. There's nothing for it, now. You chose this. It's two birds with one stone. You get to help these people, and you get to go back to Rithium, even if this is the last time.

"Two..."

My eyes were still open. I was laying flat, with my legs locked together, but my neck was at an angle, leaning against the armrest.

Someone was standing next to the opposite armrest, across from me. He was staring down at me, with an intense, perhaps even angry look. And it wasn't Mason.

It was Oscar.

"One."

WAIT!

The words were just behind my lips, a fraction of a second from bursting through. There wasn't any one intelligible reason why. Confusion. Terror—though I wasn't quite sure of what. It was impossible, within that tiny sliver to time, to internally articulate why, if I otherwise could.

My eyes were locked on Oscar's face, but it, along with everything else, was quickly sucked away, like debris in a whirlpool.

Of course, that wasn't quite right. *I* was what was being pulled away. I was in the current. My consciousness was yanked, without ceremony, into that unknowable place between waking and dreaming.

The place between reality and Rithium.

CHAPTER 10

HAZY ORANGE SUNLIGHT GLANCED through finger-width gaps in the barn wall, illuminating shiny particulates that hovered lazily in the air, like pixie dust.

My breathing had been raspy, interspersed with some grunts and coughs. Dust always seemed to have a bad effect on my lungs and sinuses, particularly in closed spaces.

Everything was so thick and trapped, here. Cloying. Dust stuck to every sweaty, exposed surface of skin, creating a waxy film that only a hot shower could clear away. If I so much as looked at the barn, though, it would be back.

I had tied a bandana around my neck, but that was beginning to feel like a symbolic gesture more than anything. Covering my mouth with it just made it harder to *breathe*, which was really my entire issue in the first place. Breathing.

Luckily, I was almost finished.

A brown and white mottled cow yelled at me from inside her pen. It was a long, fitful yell, rising in exclamation before tapering off dramatically, going quiet. Then she just looked at me expectantly with those giant cow eyes.

Cows didn't *"moo"*. There wasn't a single thing alive in the world that *"moo-ed"*. That was the most made-up thing I'd ever heard. Cows *yelled*. Mostly they yelled at each other. But once they realized that you were the magic man that brought the food, they yelled at you, too. It was just about the only thing they seemed to know how to do.

"Easy, Paprika." I said. I liked to make up names for them on the spot. Usually, I forgot them and had to make up new ones, but that was part of the fun.

Paprika was packed in with twenty or so other cows that had wandered inside, none of them giving me quite the degree of attention as her. So she got the name. Paprika.

Flexing my fingers inside my work gloves, I grabbed the pair of bale hooks hanging off a nail on one of the support beams. I hooked them through the twine of the nearest bale of alfalfa hay. It was a janky-looking thing, with one of the rolls of twine edging its way off of one of the corners. I figured it would stay together for a couple seconds of movement.

It didn't. As soon as the twine pulled off of one of the corners, the whole thing flipped and came apart. Alfalfa dust plumed, kicking up into the air, joining the dust and junk that was already there in a thick constellation of respiratory issues.

I coughed until I hacked something dark and green onto the barn's cement flooring, like a bug's innards on a windshield.

I caved, pulling the bandana up over my nose and mouth. I tied it tight against the back of my neck. I got down on my knees. I lifted up bits and flakes of the hay bale, standing and dropping them along the length of the feeder.

Paprika's face was in there immediately, biting and chewing, breaking apart the chunks.

It took a few trips down on my knees and up again before I had the majority of it off the floor and into the feeder. I snatched up the bale hooks again to grab another bale. This one actually stayed together. I set it next to the feeder, snapped open my pocket knife, and cut each length of twine. They both made a loud *POP* sound as I slit them. The bale expanded lengthways, but stayed in order. I pulled it apart in thick flakes, neatly stuffing them into the feeder.

The glows of light bursting through slits in the side of the barn were getting low, darkening. Breathing heavy through my bandana, I wrenched off one of my work gloves. My bare hand glistened with lukewarm sweat. I wiped it on my jeans, pasting muddy dirt against my palm. Immediate regret.

I sighed, scraped my palm against a support beam, and reached into my jean pocket, pulled out my phone. I clicked the button on the side. The screen lit up the immediate area and glared my eyes. It was stark against the shadowy interior of the barn, and even the gleam of the rapidly descending sun.

The digital clock in the center of the screen read: *6:49 PM*.

Underneath the clock was a notification of a text from Oscar. *"Where you at?"*

Crap. I was supposed to be on the road a half hour ago.

I stepped outside, into the cold April evening. My work boots crunched on the gravel path just outside the barn, leading past the garden and toward the house. I passed tomato plants, twisty grape vines, and the cool, slanted shade of some raspberry and blackberry bushes. The blackberries were nice to look at, but they were kind of a pain in the ass. They liked to get around, like weeds. Every year I had to help prune them back, keep them contained.

We usually didn't sell what we grew in the garden. It was just some odds and ends to pick and use. It gave the space something to do. And Evelyn liked to look out the kitchen window and see stuff growing in the field.

The real money-maker was the milk. The milking shed was on the other side of the garden, connected to the same field as the barn. It was smaller than the barn, but every inch of it was put to use. It was industrial and efficient, packed with stalls, milking equipment, machines for filtering and processing the milk. I would be out there with Evelyn at four AM the next morning, just like I was every morning. Every morning since I'd arrived there, and probably every morning until the end of time. I would be out there before the sun was up, helping my aunt set up for the milking, and while she was putting the cows away I would be using a pressure washer to hose down the grates as quickly as possible so I could get on with my other chores.

The period in between my morning and evening chores was for homework. This freed up the evening so I could spend time with Oscar, who got to go to an actual school. Lucky dog.

As much as I would have preferred a normal life and a normal school— something like my old life anyway, before the collision on Interstate 90–it hadn't been much of a choice. My dad's side of the family were the type of people that believed kids needed to earn their keep. Evelyn was no different.

There had been that brief, intermittent, impossibly long period of physical therapy. My body had gone through serious trauma.

I never completely understood it. The more doctors tried to explain it, the more confusing it became. My body was broken, and wracked with pain, but in a way, so was my mind. They didn't just need healing. They needed to be fused back together.

I'd never had to fight so hard for anything. At the time, I wasn't consciously aware how I was even doing it. How do you push yourself, make your body do what's necessary, when it doesn't function like it used to? When it takes all your strength and willpower to cross the street, and even then it's with crutches, and a caretaker walking you through it?

I say 'caretaker'. At times, it was a professional at a physical therapy clinic. At times, it was Evelyn.

I got better. I got worse. I got better again. All the while, Evelyn was there, patient with me.

I just had to be patient with myself, living life in a sort of frantic tunnel vision. All I knew, every day, was that I had to get better.

The romantic in me wishes I could say there wasn't a day that went by I didn't think about what happened on the Interstate. But sometimes—often, really—I would forget. It just didn't feel like it was a part of my life. The same way that any current stage of life—the *now*—feels like it's the only version of you that's ever existed.

Of course, inevitably, it would come to me, like a door cracking open in a dark corner of the house, leading to a room full of objects I used to own. And I would be like, *Oh...yeah.*

When that happened, the memories would seize me

(all or nothing, baby)

and my mind was helpless but to replay those last few moments before the crash, right up to the milliseconds, when my mom was laughing and teasing my dad, and he was insisting that if they were going to listen to James Taylor, they needed to listen to all the hits, because it was *"All or nothing, baby."*

All or nothing

All or

Nothing

All—

My hand was frozen on the knob connected to the back door of the house. The door was red. I helped paint it last summer. There was a small section of paint that had been chipped, somehow, and was barely connected anymore, falling away. I could see the white material underneath. I turned the knob.

I began taking off my boots and gloves in the mudroom. I couldn't see the kitchen, but there was water running in the sink. The pungent garlic-and-tomato smell of homemade marinara wafted down the hall.

By the time I got to the kitchen, Evelyn was lifting a strainer full of pasta out of the sink. Her biceps flexed. Membranous muscles corded her sinewy arms.

She had that tired smirk as she looked sidelong at me, the one she got at the end of the day, when the work was finally done. A brief section of time where she would finally start to relax, winding down for bed. Even without the smile, I could always see it in her posture. At the beginning of the day, she was always straight-backed, tight and focused. Over the course of the day, that tension slowly receded, and she started to hunch, almost like she was curling in on herself.

She set the strainer down and leaned against the counter. "Your jeans are filthy. Change them before dinner." She turned her back to me as she started dumping the strained noodles back into the hot, empty pot. "I've got some blackberry cobbler in the oven. Should be done any minute, now."

"I'm meeting Oscar, tonight." I unwound the bandana from around my neck. At some point I had hacked up a nice chunk of phlegm into it. I grimaced as I folded it up, balling it in my fist. "I'm already late, actually."

Evelyn turned back around, appraising me. "Again?"

I nodded.

"Try not to be gone so late. You know I need you fresh for work in the morning."

I nodded.

I started to step out of the kitchen, then stopped. "I was wondering if I could get another fifty bucks."

Evelyn set down a ladle she'd been using to stir the pasta. "We already agreed on your allowance. You get paid again next week."

"I know." I said. "This would be an advance."

It seemed like she was considering it, but that tension was slowly creeping back in her face. Wrinkles formed, making her a good ten years older than she actually was.

Money was always tight. If I wanted to know how bad it was on any given week, I just had to count those wrinkles.

Truthfully, I did feel guilty. It was my fault, after all. Years of treatment and physical therapy don't pay for themselves. Working on the farm ten hours a day, every day, was the least I could do. Because of Evelyn, I had at least some semblance of a life.

Still, for me, it just wasn't enough.

"What do you need extra money for, anyway?" She said. Alarmingly, one of her hands had moved down to her hip. Not a good sign. Not with her.

Take it easy, man. She's just probing. Just trying to be a part of your life. She doesn't know.

"Sometimes Oscar and I like to go out to the arcade." I said.

It was a lie. We *always* went to the arcade. We hadn't stayed in to hang out at Oscar's house in months.

"We buy some sodas. Play Pac-Man. Visit with some of the kids in town." *Socializing. She'll like that. It's perfectly normal to want to get off the farm.*

And yet, also a lie. They never got sodas. Never played Pac-Man. And they certainly didn't visit with people in town.

"Besides, you know how the truck is. It's a gas guzzler. Going in and out of town adds up."

This was true. But not so true that I would need a hundred dollars in one week.

Still, Evelyn seemed to be considering it. Her face softened. Some of the wrinkles disappeared.

"Are you sure you didn't...meet someone? You can tell me, you know."

"I...have not." I said, suddenly uncomfortable for this entirely new set of reasons. "But I will keep you posted...on...that." *Is it ever not weird when an adult asks a teen about their dating life?*

Why does it have to be so awkward?

A smile broke out on Evelyn's face. A wide, real smile. "It's more than normal for someone your age. Just be sure to let me know if you do. And make sure you're safe." She wagged a sauce-covered spoon at me.

I nodded. I decided not to ask her what she meant by *"safe"*.

Maybe I should *start going on dates. Maybe that would make my outings less suspicious.*

But I knew I wasn't going to do it. I needed money for completely separate reasons, and I wasn't willing to start dividing my already limited time and resources. Not quite yet.

Not that there weren't cute girls in town. And not that I hadn't thought about it. But they usually weren't the type of people who wandered into the arcade. And honestly it just seemed like a lot of effort.

Evelyn set down the spoon and folded her arms. "Next week." She said. "I wish I could give it to you now, but we need that money for groceries. The budget just won't stretch that way. Okay?"

"Got it." I said. I gave a little, half-hearted thumbs up. "I'll just have to make due."

In a moment of surprising warmth and empathy—with Evelyn, you could never predict when one of those was going to strike—she grabbed me and planted a kiss on my forehead.

She frowned. "You're still dirty."

"That I am."

Evelyn spat into the sink. "You better clean up. They might not let you into that arcade."

"That I will."

I hopped up the stairs.

I passed Evelyn's room. The door was cracked open. Her wallet was on the mantelpiece. She never used a purse, just a black leather wallet, fat with gift and membership cards, a square lump in the tight fabric of her woman's jeans pocket.

I froze in the hallway. Evelyn was still in the kitchen. I could hear the springy squeak of the oven door opening, then slamming closed.

I slid into her room and flipped open the wallet.

There were three fifties in there. I leafed through them, stalling. A month's worth of grocery money, if we were careful.

Just grab it. You're already this far. You need this money.

No I didn't. I *wanted* it.

I hesitated, a fifty dollar bill in my hand.

"Kit?" Evelyn called from downstairs. I heard the floor creak at the bottom of the stairs.

My heart jumped up into my throat. I lurched out into the hallway, the fifty crumpled in my balled fist. "Yeah?"

Evelyn's head poked around the corner. "You tracked some dirt in here. Be sure to clean it up, tonight."

I nodded. "I will."

Her head disappeared, and I was alone at the top of the stairs, still holding the fifty dollars.

My heart rate fell back down to a semi-normal cadence. The feeling of panic faded, but it was quickly replaced by something worse; a growing sense of guilt and dread. And a new revelation. It had taken this very act to see the situation in it's full context.

I didn't just *want* to synchronize. I *needed* to.

You're being dramatic. Rithium isn't mainstream, yet, but anyone who realized how special it is would understand why you need that fifty dollars. Even Evelyn.

It was a flimsy thought, but there was a spark of truth, to it. Rithium *was* special.

I decided to push those feelings aside. For now.

I would put it off. That was a normal, human thing to do, right? To put off problems? Even for "functioning adults". Maxing out credit cards with no feasible plan to pay them off. Staying in a toxic relationship when they know full well they need to move out, or get divorced. It was the way of the world. *Why not get used to it?*

But the feeling lingered. Even after I'd showered, and changed. After I walked past Evelyn's room on the way downstairs.

One last chance to be good, take it or leave it.

I left it.

After giving Evelyn a goodbye peck on the cheek while she watched Jeopardy on the tube TV.

After stepping outside under a pale violet sky and zipping up my jacket.

After slamming the pickup door and starting the engine, which thrummed loudly and made the seat vibrate, I put my palm on the gear shift, and a thought came to me. It was an insane, disjointed thought, but it was as clear in my head as if someone had said it out loud in the passenger seat next to me.

"It's all or nothing, baby."

CHAPTER 11

THERE WAS SOMETHING ABSURD—ALMOST comical—about the way the manifestation of my worst fear materialized, like a cartoon wrecking ball falling out of the sky and smashing a brand new car.

It stared at it, and it seemed to stare back; a pale apparition standing behind a brown, faded picket fence. It was just barely visible in the beam of the truck's headlights.

Most of it was obscured by the shadows cast by the fence, but the important parts were bright and clear.

The sign said in bold, red letters: *"FOR SALE"*. Below that was a real estate agent listing, a bit harder to make out.

My first thought was, *Huh.*

For a while, possibly several minutes, I sat frozen in the driver's seat, letting the engine idle.

You don't know. You don't know what it means.

But I did, though. I could feel the cold, numbing certainty of it. The reality. The only other time I'd felt this—though to a lesser degree—had been in the backseat behind my parents, just before the collision. The same *"Huh."* The same *"I wonder."* All the while, actually knowing.

Oscar's parents are moving.

The front porchlight zapped on, flickered. Oscar was standing on the front step.

I shut off the engine and got out of the car.

Oscar walked down the steps toward the front gate. I looked for some expression on his face, something to go off of, but it was just shrouded enough by shadows that I couldn't make it out. I was watching a clockwork mannequin, a moving statue in the night.

Usually, he moved with the type of comfortable, straight-backed confidence that never ceased to make me feel at least a little jealous. I always had terrible posture.

Honestly, I didn't even know how the straight-backed thing was even achieved. *Is it surgical? Are rods injected at the base of the shoulder and into the spine? I bet they are.*

But that night, he didn't have that comfortable-in-his-own-skin energy I was used to. He made slow steps across the grass, shoulders hunched, hands in his jean pockets.

It was hard to imagine I'd still been in a wheelchair the day we met. I had been trying to reach a comic on the top shelf of a display. The comic's cover said, in bold print: *"RITHIUM".* Volume number seven.

I still thought that volume had the best cover art in the entire series. It had this grassy, sprawling vista, with bits of grass being blown up into the air. A hunched figure stood in the foreground, at the edge of the vista, his back to the reader, his dark hair and trench coat tails flapping in the wind. He had a revolver slung at each hip, and a sheathed katana strapped to his back. High in the sky, a red-scaled dragon spread its wings, spewing flames into the blue.

Oscar, who'd come into the shop looking for the same volume, had reached over and handed it to me, letting me take the last copy.

It turned out he owned a limited edition figure of the character on the front of that volume. In my opinion, the best character in the whole series: The Drifting Gunman.

Rithium had been a world we both loved back then, but not in the same way it was now. Back then, it hadn't been a Simworld, a real actual place we could visit and see. Just a fantasy world. A fiction.

I suppose, in a way, both versions are just as real. As real and tangible a part of your life any fantasy world can become.

"Waylaid by bandits?" Oscar said. I still couldn't quite make out his face, even with the porchlight on, backlighting him.

"Worse. Chores. Also," I said, pointing in the direction of the sign, "I think someone's trying to sell your house."

"Did you get my texts?"

"No?" I said. I pulled my phone out of my pocket and started flipping through the notifications. "I haven't looked at my phone since I finished up. I showered, changed, and came straight here."

"I was going to talk to you about it, tonight." He came to a stop next to the waist-high gate. "And then, I wasn't sure if you were coming, so I texted you..." There was the shrill scrape of metal as Oscar opened the gate, stepped through it.

I glanced up from the phone. "Why wouldn't I be coming?"

I could see his face, now. It was wired with these uncharacteristically tense lines. He was bracing, on edge.

He thinks I'm going to flip out at him.

And maybe I was. I had a tendency to do that. I wasn't great at making friends, despite how desperate I could be for a relationship. I was so scared of being alone, especially now. But as soon as I got close with someone, there was always that sense of vulnerability, of needing another person. And that terrified me too. So something would happen, and I would lash out. Most of my memories with Oscar—especially my earlier ones—involved me hanging with Oscar at his place, sometimes talking about stuff we liked, sometimes playing RPGs and MMOs together. Being able to be his friend gave me this feeling of community and belonging that was unlike anything I'd felt before. But it also brought out the worst in me, marring the best memories with some of my worst. A heartfelt photo album tarnished by black, oily handprints and scuffs.

Oscar shrugged. "You said you might be short. Wasn't sure if you'd worked something out."

"Yeah, well, I did. I worked something out." *Stealing. I'm a thief, now, Oscar. Isn't that swell.* "I was just late with chores, that's all."

Oscar checked his watch, angling it at the light of my phone. "Hopefully, we won't be too late."

"He won't care. Not as long as he gets his money. *'We should talk'?*" I lowered the phone. "Way to be ominous. That's some girlfriend crap, right there."

"How would you know?" Oscar said.

"Ouch."

After a moment of hesitation, both of us standing there, neither of us knowing what to say, we both started to amble toward the pickup truck, and climbed in.

We slammed the side doors in unison. I started the engine.

I was looking into the rearview mirror, avoiding eye contact.

"I didn't know." Oscar said. "Not until just a few days ago. But you know they were always talking about it. My parents...they've never been crazy about his place. They don't like the schools. And dad always thought he'd be able to find better work somewhere else. Last week he got a job offer, and I guess he's taking it."

I had no idea what Mr. Wilson did for a living. He must have explained it to me four different times, and I still didn't understand. To be honest, I could never bring myself to care. Every time he opened his mouth about it I could feel my eyes going glassy. I would do that thing where I imagine the speaker's head being magically removed from their body and bounced around the room, knocking into various objects. This kept me stimulated and aware of my surroundings, appearing attentive. A trick normally reserved for hour-long sermons at church.

"Where at?" I said.

"Missoula." He answered quickly, all one syllable. Like ripping off a bandaid.

"Huh."

Honestly, it could have been worse. Missoula wasn't Paris. It wasn't Baghdad. It wasn't freaking Narnia. It was just a city on the other side of the state.

All the way on the other side of the freaking state. That's an eight hour drive, pal. When's the next time Evelyn's going to let you off of work for an entire day? And that would just be getting there. It's a whole other day to get back.

I decided to ignore those thoughts, for now. Nothing productive would come of it. Why ruin what could be one of the last times that Oscar and I got to hang out like this?

"You could always stay with me and Evelyn." I said, forcing myself to smirk. "Work on the farm. It would be a blast."

Oscar grinned. He knew how I felt about the farmwork. All I wanted was a life closer to what he had. Farmers don't get a day off, and the homeschool on top of that was making me feel increasingly claustrophobic, smothered.

"My parents think I can get into a decent college." Oscar said, looking over at me.

I frowned. "They've got those here, don't they?"

"Not according to them. Not like what they want. They really want the best for me."

And that involves getting away from me.

It was nothing Oscar had said, or even insinuated. Just my own personal suspicion. I could imagine them peeking through the blinds late at night, wondering where we were, wondering what I was doing with their sweet, precious boy. Time spent playing arcades and goofing around in town(even though that wasn't really what we were doing) was time that could be spent on productive, character-building things, like studies, and maybe a part-time job.

"So you're definitely not going to run away?" I said. "You could fake your own death. Or a kidnapping. There's a crawl space behind the wall in my room I'm pretty sure Evelyn doesn't know about."

"You know," Oscar said, "I know you're joking. But I also know you're kinda not."

"That settles it." I said. "Kidnapping. We'll leave a note at your dad's work."

"Not that we're *not* joking," Oscar said, "But you know my parents would tear your aunt's place apart looking for me. They'd find that crawl space."

"...well, yeah..." I said, eyes on the road. "Probably."

Then, it came to me. It was a silver-lining, of sorts. Or just the bargaining phase of my grief.

"Maybe there's a cloudbox somewhere in Missoula." I said. "Maybe—"

"Maybe..."

I felt my brows knit together. "What?"

Oscar shrugged. "I—I dunno."

"No, tell me."

He sighed, drummed his fingers on the dashboard, then seemed to freeze, head tilted at an angle.

"You remember that spring break when all we did was play Final Fantasy XIV?"

I couldn't help but grin. All that week I'd managed to cop out of a decent amount of my chores so I could leave early and head straight to Oscar's every day. We'd holed up inside Oscar's room with Doritos and Mountain Dew, with a chair braced against the doorknob to keep Jackie out.

"You're asking if I remember one of the best weeks of my sorry life?"

"It wasn't bad." Oscar said, looking wistful. "Sometimes it's good to just shut out the world, to get lost in something. And I think it was good for you, too, back then. I think it was one of the things that helped you get back on your feet. Literally."

"Yeah right." I said. "Look at me. I'm useless. I don't even know what the next step is."

"When I first met you, you had all those muscle problems. You couldn't walk. You kept getting those hand tremors. Couldn't even unscrew a bottle cap."

"Couldn't play Street Fighter, either." I said. "Talk about a disability."

"Now look at you. You've completely recovered. You earn your keep, doing honest work every day. You're driving. You haven't totaled the truck yet."

"Give it another month or so." I said.

"You're gonna be okay." Oscar said, looking over at me. "I believe that. But you've got to stop running."

"You know I don't like running," I said. "It's high impact. Hell on the joints—are you going somewhere with this?"

I could feel my jaw clenching up. I didn't like it when Oscar got like this. He was my friend, not my mentor. Certainly not my psychoanalyst.

Maybe sometimes that's what being a good friend calls for, though.

Yeah, no. Shut up.

"Look at it this way," Oscar said, adjusting in his seat. He seemed almost uncomfortable with what he was about to say. Nervous. "If you're moving at the speed of light—"

"A sensation I'm sure we're all familiar with."

"You're always going to be faster than sound. Sound is fast, too. But it's never going to catch up to the speed of light. The question is, how long can something maintain the speed of light? What happens when the speed runs out?"

"Wow, Oscar." I said. "Your existential crisis metaphor is blowing my mind right now, but what does—"

Just then, we went over a bump at the top of a hill on Ash Creek Road, and there was a loud thump in the backseat.

Oscar and I exchanged glances. I tilted the rearview mirror.

There was a thick, brown blanket draped across the backseat. Evelyn liked to keep there in case—I mean, I don't know. I got stuck somewhere and started to get cold, I guess. So it was normal that when I looked back there, the blanket was there.

What wasn't normal was that there was what appeared to be a human-shaped lump underneath the blanket.

CHAPTER 12

I PUMPED THE BRAKES, slowing at the bottom of the hill and pulling over onto the shoulder.

I put the truck in park and turned to Oscar. We were both braced, ready for anything. Even though we already knew what it was.

I held up three fingers. Then two. Then one.

We both reached into the backseat and whipped the blanket off the seat.

Jackie jerked upright, dark hair flying. The back of her head was messy and chaotic, with frayed, frizzy hairs pointing in every direction.

"Must have, uh, dozed off." Jackie said.

"In the back of my truck?" I said.

"Yeah, honest mistake."

I glanced past her, at the little window above the backseat. I knew from experience that it could be jimmied open from the outside. Not that it had ever worried me. Only someone with a frame like Jackie's—as well as her adventurous, indomitable spirit, if you wanted to call it that—could squeeze through that thing.

Mystery solved.

Oscar had completely turned and was leaning over into the backseat. "Don't change the subject. Jackie, we talked about this. You can't just insert yourself."

"But you guys are always doing fun stuff!" Jackie said. "C'mon. We're moving any day, now. And I barely ever get to hang out with you guys."

"Good idea," Oscar said, though his tone didn't seem to say so. "We should do that soon. But not tonight."

Jackie crossed her arms. "Why not?"

"Because." Oscar said. "You *snuck* into *Kit's truck*." Then, in a more playful tone. "You're a sneaker."

"Man's got a point," I said. "We do have a policy against stowaways."

Jackie took a deep, long breath. She was recuperating, assessing her options.

Oh, shit. As cocky as Oscar and I were with her, it was easy to forget how resourceful she could be. We only ever seemed to remember when it was already too late.

I gave Oscar an uneasy look. The same kind of look he was already giving me.

"Fine, then." Jackie said. "Just turn around and take me back. Although, I did hear you guys say you were already late. What was it you were going to do?"

"We don't have to tell you." Oscar said, but his face said he could already see the tower beginning to fall. He didn't even know how yet—neither did I —but he could see it coming. Jackie was like a little demolitions expert. Sometimes it seemed like she enjoyed finding our sources of fun and blasting them into tiny, pixelated bits.

In the early days, she got us banned from playing Resident Evil because she walked in on us and the game freaked her out. This all despite the fact that Oscar *had* locked his door. Jackie had worked it open with the help of a Youtube tutorial and one of her bobby pins. How fair is that supposed to be.

"Whatever." Jackie said. "Take me back. One other question, though: what exactly *is* a 'cloudbox'?"

This was a thinly veiled threat. As soon as she got home, she would go to her parents. *"What's a cloudbox? Oh, well, that's what Oscar and Kit are using whenever they go into town. They won't explain what it is, I just overheard them talking about it—"*

Crap on toast, I thought. *They'll think we're doing drugs.*

Any attempt to explain cover it up would fall on deaf ears. Oscar and I could lie, we could deflect, we could photoshop an arcade game with the logo Cloudbox, and none of it would matter. They would sniff the whole story. If not that, they would ground Oscar. The last few weeks of his time here(if that) would be spent under constant parental surveillance.

"Jackie," Oscar said, "I say this as your thoughtful, caring brother. You are an awful human being."

Jackie's eyes lit up with an afterburn of defiance. "What's the cloudbox, Oscar? What is it you guys are actually doing when you run off together almost every night?" She looked Oscar to me, then back again. "Anyone? Bueller?"

I put a hand on Oscar's shoulder. "Can we talk for a sec?"

I pointed a finger at Jackie. "Stay right here, please."

There was a brisk breeze out, rattling the yellow leaves in the aspens overhead. The truck doors *thunked* loudly in the night.

I waved Oscar over and across the ditch, putting some distance between us and the truck. Jackie had ears like a fox, when she wanted to.

Our boots crunched on sticks and fallen leaves. I spun and faced Oscar, who was folding his arms in the chill.

"When do your parents go to bed?"

"Usually early. They might be in bed, right now."

"Well, they haven't called you yet, so that's a pretty good indication that they haven't noticed she's gone, at the very least, right?"

"Yeah," Oscar said. "So?"

I breathed in. "I think we should take her with us."

"What?" Oscar said. "No! Kit—"

"What." I said. "Why not? He'll let her try it out. He doesn't charge for the first time."

"Yeah, because 'first one's always free' is never a bad sign." Oscar said. "You think this thing is regulated or approved? With all the secrecy, and the forms?"

"It's a prototype." I said. "They need people to test it. Jackie," I gestured toward the truck. "Could be one of those people. I don't get it. What's the problem?"

"We don't know what it is." Oscar said. "We'd be exposing my sister to something we don't even understand."

"So it was fine when it was just me getting involved?" I said.

Oscar ran a hand through his hair. "I mean, it's a little different, isn't it? We didn't even know what it was, before. And now that we do...I mean, think about it. There's always a trade-off. Look at cigarettes. Look at alcohol."

I stepped toward him, the soles of my boots scraping on rocks and dirt. "Why?" I said. "Have you been experiencing anything? Any...side effects?"

Oscar shook his head. "No. I mean, not yet. Have you?"

"No." I lied. It was probably nothing, anyway. Just, you know, migraines. Everyone gets migraines.

Migraines that go away once you synchronize, and don't come back until you've been away from Rithium for a few days?

Shut up.

"So what are you worried about?" I said. "She'll love it. She's a gamer just as much as we are. And this...this is the best game that's ever existed. Think about how we would have killed for something like this. But if we take Jackie back, she spills everything. And we'll lose out on...an entire world."

"It's just a game."

"Are you kidding me!?" I said, offended. "We have a life in there!"

"It's talk like that," Oscar said, waving a finger at me, "That's got you scaring me."

Suddenly, Oscar's weird speech during the drive was starting to make sense. Even though it didn't actually make sense. It was like the last piece of a puzzle clicking into place, giving context to the image it portrayed. The image of Oscar and I's relationship with Rithium.

"How long have you felt like this?" I said.

"Like this Simworld thing has become an obsession for you?" Oscar said. "Like it's become unhealthy? A long time, Kit. I mean, where did you even get the money for tonight?"

"Why didn't you say anything?" I said, waving off the change of subject. "Why keep going along?"

Light from the headlights of a passing car flickered amongst the trees.

Oscar, who'd been shifting his weight from foot to foot, suddenly froze. His eyes glistened.

"So I could be there for you. Like I always wish I could be."

Oh.

There's this cliche that guys (men, whatever) don't know how to communicate their emotions. I don't think that's true. We do communicate, but it's in a sort of code. We layer our feelings in a veneer of generic comradery. It's safer that way. Not to mention considerate.

Oscar wasn't doing any of that. Especially now. It was all out in the open. A pulsing heart on the outside of his chest. He was vulnerable and exposed.

"Oscar." I said, pleading. "We're running out of time."

"If you're counting in Rithium time." Oscar said. He rubbed his eyes with the back of his hand.

"Okay," I said. "How about this. We ask Jackie what she thinks."

"We already know what she would think. You know how she is. If *we* did it, she'll want to do it, too."

"Exactly. And she's gonna find out. Whether it's tonight or two years from now. It's going to market eventually. And she'll want to try it."

Oscar seemed doubtful.

"Look." I reached out, grabbing Oscar by the shoulders. "Nothing bad is going to happen. To me, or anyone."

Oscar held his gaze with mine. "Promise?"

I nodded. "I do."

Just then—as if on cue—a flash of pain streaked the inside of my skull.

I winced, running a hand into my hair, pulling.

"What's wrong?" Oscar said, leaning close. He seemed scared, alarmed.

"Nothing." I said. The bulk of the pain began to subside, ebbing in the background. "It's-it's nothing."

CHAPTER 13

M Y EYES ARE CLAMPED shut, lids clenched tightly. If I open them, I will see Oscar. It won't make sense, just as it hadn't before. But it *had* happened. I had seen him standing next to the couch, looking down at me, assessing me.

What would Oscar have been thinking?

"Look, it's Kit; my best friend in the world.

"Look, it's Kit; the asshole who snapped off the arm of my limited edition figure while reenacting a scene from the Rithium comic.

"Look, it's Kit; the guy—I feel my hands balling into fists—*the guy who sold out his only friends."*

I had seen Oscar—it was both undeniable and impossible. *Either the world is broken, or I'm going crazy. Can't say I like either option.*

Still, I can feel these dark thoughts beginning to ebb, solidifying in a corner of my mind, likely to haunt me in some way for the rest of my waking life. Another part of my mind, for now, is being tagged in. Because, even with my eyes closed, I can tell I'm *in*.

There's this feeling of being synchronized. It's a chemical thing. I've never taken recreational drugs, but I imagine it's similar. The closest parallel I can make using my own personal experience is what it's like to drink a great cup of coffee. That feeling of, *"Hey! I'm alive!"* Only more so. It's a vibratory thrum tingling throughout my body—or what I perceive to be my body. It slowly teases my eyes open with promises of excitement and sensation.

I'm surrounded by four walls. They are gray and sterile, without crack or texture or blemish. The room glows with a warm blue light that emanates from the floor.

A woman stands in front of me, wearing a formal pantsuit. Her complexion is a pale white, the lower part of her face perfectly reflecting the blue light from the floor. Her hair is just as pale a gray, bound up behind her head with two hairpins sticking through.

"Welcome back, Winter."

She says this with immaculate professionalism, without a hint of human peculiarity. Then, as if to counteract—or perhaps accentuate—this she adjusts her oval shaped glasses.

As the lenses shift I can see my own reflection in them. I look much like, well, myself; with some distinct differences. I am most similar to the 'me' from several years ago, the version of myself without as many dirty, pocked pores and dark circles under my eyes. Not to mention a few more wrinkles.

But it is also a more athletic version of me. My cheeks are tighter, my chin more pronounced. I'm wearing a gray, form-fitting onesie that accents all of my muscles and curves and joints.

This is the version of me that could give Spiderman a run for his money. This is the version of me that could take on the best sword fighter in the world and survive.

On the surface of the lens, my face lifts, lips stretching into a grin. The name comes to me, like deja vu in a dream. "It's good to *be* back, Janice."

"Ghost Oscar" has disappeared from my list of immediate concerns. An aberration in the Matrix, one I don't have the tools to deal with right now. A job for *"Future Kit"*. Right now, I'm here. I'm in. I'm *back*.

"Where's my Party?" I say.

"The Users who logged in with you have spawned in the southeastern quadrant." Janice says. A tablet suddenly appears in her hand and she makes a few tapping and swiping motions.

The floor and two walls of the room turn into a cohesive screen, giving us a three-dimensional view of the southern Rithium landscape. A camera—if you want to call it that—follows a dunebuggy rumbling across the rocky, dusty landscape. In the distance I can see mounds of green, marked with towering firs, like the blades of black swords.

No dragons, yet. But they're out there.

"They've made accommodations for you to join them in the buggy." Janice says.

"Sounds good to me." I say, remembering Mason's words to me before the synchronization.

"Would you like to get suited up, first?"

I can feel myself grinning again, grinning like an idiot. "That would be a wonder, Janice."

She smiles back, a tic based on computer code, designed to react to the user.

A door appears on one wall. I snap my fingers, sliding, dancing across the floor. I grip the knob, flourishing as I step through the door.

The second I'm in the room, hundreds of items snap into existence, clicking and clacking, coat racks and gun racks and sword displays.

I continue to slide, Michael Jackson-style, snapping my fingers, until I'm standing in front of a long, black, two-tailed trench coat.

Everyone knows cool people wear trench coats. It's a law of the universe.

"Incoming voice chat," Janice's voice echoes omnisciently.

I perk up, one hand reaching toward the trench coat.

"Where the hell are you, asshat?" Tanya's voice comes through clear as a mirror, reverberating softly in the space. What isn't so soft is the grinding sound of some kind of engine, punctuated by the grating of rubber tires over rocks and dirt and gravel.

"Literally just finished synchronizing...about sixty seconds ago?" I say.

"Well, we got company, princess. Get a move on. Just—what's taking you so long!?"

"Better question: how'd you guys hit a snag so quickly?"

"Not a snag." Tanya says. *"Rifters. You should come down and say hello. You would really hit it off. SHIT—"*

The voice chat cuts off, leaving me in stark silence.

I throw on a tight, gray shirt, and a pair of dark jeans. I wrench the trench coat off the hanger and whip it behind my back, sliding my arms through the sleeves in one smooth motion. Arms outstretched, I snap my fingers, feeling like a superhero suiting up for a mission. Or perhaps a supervillain in his laboratory.

I grab a gun belt. It has two holsters and a bandolier. I pull two shiny, silver revolvers off the gun rack. I spin them deftly in my hands, laughing, until I decide to go ahead and holster them.

I grab one of my own creations, strapping it against my back. It's both a sword sheath and a rifle holster, strapped together. The rifle is short, about the length of my arm. It's a lever-action, and accurate at a decent enough distance that I've yet to feel the need for anything fancier.

The sword is something the game classifies as a machete, though to me it looks like a cross between a machete and a katana. A kachete, as I've come to think of it. It's lightweight, with a wide, black blade and a circular hilt. The sharp edge is a silverish grey, the color of steel.

Once that's together, I equip a wrist-shield, strapped to my forearm. For now, it just looks like a black brace on the sleeve of my coat.

"I think I'm ready, Janice." I say. "Good to go."

"Affirmative." Janice says, a disembodied voice in the gray room. "Good luck, Winter."

Don't need it. Haven't you heard? I'm Winter Wolf. But I nod anyway. I stand tall, giving a stiff salute. "Ma'am."

Then, the floor opens out from under me.

CHAPTER 14

I'M FALLING.

Wind whistles in my ears, a fluting, high-pitched monotone, backed by a heavy whooshing of air pressure. It grabs at my coat, pulling and flapping, the tails snapping like flags behind me.

Below is the world of Rithium, laid out like a map. I'm a satellite that's fallen off its orbit, on a collision course with the planet. I holler into the wind, whooping and yelling.

At first the expanse between me and the surface is so vast that progress seems miniscule. I pass through wet clouds and turbulent air currents, flipping and toppling. I'm pulled, carried inexorably.

At the farthest point of visibility, near the curvature of the planet, I can see a dark shape, surfing on the west horizon. Whether a dragon, or a great bird, or some kind of player-designed airship, I can't tell.

Below, the world is a mesh of mingling colors and shapes, like an atlas. Streams squiggle across the landscape, spindly fingers connecting to hands that are lakes, connecting to arms that are great rivers that cut through hundreds of miles of land.

Far to the north, arcing up into the clouds like the hilt of a giant's dagger, is a tall black tower, the centerpiece of the city of Opus.

My descent starts to pick up in speed, as if there's a giant hand above me, pushing me downward.

I can start to make out individual details on the ground. It's possible to count the trees. The jagged points of rock on the cliff faces and plateaus. Dustdevils swirl, mad ballerinas on the stage that is the Redstone Desert.

Redstone—named after the patches and crags of red rock throughout—is one of my least favorite areas in Rithium. There's a lot to see and explore, but you have to be patient. Because of the storms and the shifting nature of the landscape, it can take a while to maneuver the inner sanctum of the desert and find what you're looking for.

The buggy, though, isn't heading toward the middle of the desert. It's heading north, toward the Red Cliffs, and the Andante Mountains.

And it's not alone.

Trailing behind is a serpentine formation of five dune buggies, kicking up a cacophony of dust and smoke like a herd of restless cows.

Below me is the dune buggy. My body hovers over it, tracking it, like GPS. Until it's closer, and closer, and closer, and then—

There's a flash of black, and suddenly I'm sitting in the back. My butt bounces uncomfortably on the seat, which appears to be a layer of rough, hard brown leather stretched over a metal chair thing.

Sater, in the passenger seat up front, turns and winks at me. "Thought you were gonna miss the fun!" He yells over the engines. He's wearing a puffy white shirt and a gray vest. His hair is slicked over, obnoxiously, the frayed ends flopping in the wind.

Not three seconds after he winks at me, a bullet sparks off of the metal frame just next to him.

"Crap!" Sater ducks down in his seat.

Tanya doesn't react. She's completely focused on driving, leg extended against the gas pedal, swerving around hunks of rock and over dune bumps, surfing desert waves.

I crouch down in my seat, making myself a smaller target. The pursuers are gaining on us, and I can't help but notice that they're breaking their long, serpentine formation, stretching out into battle lines. The kind of formation that would allow them to open fire without hitting each other.

I lean forward in my seat. "Tanya, now would be a good time to have a plan!"

Tanya's head snaps sideways as she glances behind. Her eyes are wide, bloodshot. "I didn't want to have to do this yet!" She yells.

I blink. "Do what?"

With one hand on the wheel, she holds up the Black Dart. "I'm gonna use it." She turns to Sater. "Ditch the buggy!"

"D—how!?" Sater yells.

She grabs Sater's hand and puts it on the wheel. Her eyes glint, a flash of light, like a lens flare. And then, she disappears.

It happens in a microsecond. It's as if the material making up her avatar curls in on itself, disappearing with a *whoosh* sound and a puff of air.

The buggy skids, spraying sand. Sater has one hand on the wheel, but apparently wasn't prepared to jump into Tanya's seat, or even steer from his own position.

Just then, the sounds of gunfire break out from behind. Volleys of bullets kick up rock and sand to the front and sides of the buggy. Another bullet pings loudly as it bounces off the frame. Sater winces, whole body jerking, pulling sideways on the wheel.

The world flips. Not the buggy(or so it feels), just everything else, like a snow globe tilting on its axis.

I put my head between my knees, tightly gripping the seat, praying the frame of the dune buggy will protect me from the landing.

The buggy spins, airborne, then lands on its side, impact slamming me sideways, bonking my shoulder into the frame bar.

Ow. Owowowowowow.

It's amazing how well the simworld can approximate pain, sometimes. Nothing too extreme. People don't feel brutal stabbings, or their arms getting chopped off. But the smaller bumps and bruises are weirdly annoying in their authenticity.

A continued barrage of bullets cuts through the sand just above my head, loud *FFFFFTT* sounds in my ears.

I pull myself out of the buggy and slide over to the nose side just as three of the pursuing dune buggies, engines whining, blast past on the opposite side. They keep going, engine sounds doppler-effecting in their intensity. They're already starting to make a circle so they can head back for round two.

Sater's eyes are shut. He's slumped sideways in his seat. There's a small spot of blood on his forehead. There's a layer of dust on his face and bits of sand in his hair.

"Hey!" I grab him by the shoulder, shake him. "Please don't be out, already."

His eyelids flutter for a second, then snap open violently. He wriggles out of the seat, pulling himself upright with one of the frame bars. "What-what's happening?"

I can't help but crouch there and glare at him, even under the circumstances. I shake my head. "You are all talk, Mr. Cool Guy."

Now he's glaring. The engines are getting louder again, more distinct. "How—how was I supposed to know—"

"Sit tight there, buddy, I gotcha."

Rolling my eyes, I heft myself upright from the crouch, and turn to face the dune buggies. The riders have already started to open fire again, puffs of sand shooting up here and there in the vicinity.

The rifle slides easily out of the holster on my back. I flip up the sight. My vision flashes as I activate my Action Skill.

Time slows. So do I, but this still allows me to be more accurate with the few crucial seconds I have.

Three drivers. Three pairs of hands gripping their wheels. Three heads with goggles reflecting simworld sunlight.

I zero in on the nearest one to my rifle's sight. The dunes make the movements of the vehicles erratic, unpredictable, until the one I have my sights on goes over a jump, trapped in a predictable, mid-air moment.

My finger clenches in the trigger well. There's a loud thump, a cracking gunshot. The soundwave is sluggish, stretched out, distended. The butt slams backward into my shoulder. For a second, I can just make out the bullet itself as it hurtles forward, a black, diminishing dot in my vision. Then the goggled head jolts backward, spouting red.

Gripping the reload lever, I spin the rifle. The motion is painfully lethargic, a windmill slowed down to one-tenth it's normal speed. There's an echoing *clack*. A black shell casing with white lines exits the chamber, flipping, hovering just next to my face as it courses through the air.

I raise the sight.

The vehicle with blood spurting from the driver's seat drifts sideways, nose heading into the broadside of the buggy just next to it.

Time speeds back up, jarring me, like a record player scratching.

The two buggies slam together, both lifted off the ground by the momentum, hitting the dunes, splashing sand like whales on a desert sea.

I take aim at the remaining dune buggy's driver, fire.

Nothing.

Suddenly Sater is standing next to me, a chrome-colored longbow in his hand. He loads an explosive-tipped arrow and pulls it back. I can't help but wonder why he didn't use it before, but it can't be easy to aim something like that while riding a jostling dune buggy. Same reason I didn't just open fire while I was sitting in the back—waste of bullets. Only in Sater's case, one mess-up could have led to their own vehicle going up in flames.

Sater tenses, one eye clamped shut.

"Wait!" I yell, almost without thinking.

Sater growls, carefully releases the pull without letting the arrow loose. "What!?"

I don't know what part of my brain worked it out. Maybe it was a subconscious deduction. Intuition of some kind. In all the immediate chaos after the dune buggy flipped, we hadn't looked at or thought of Tanya or the two other vehicles behind us.

Just as Sater yells *"What!?"*, Tanya's material poofs into existence in the backseat of the vehicle roaring toward us. It's like seeing something unravel in reverse, the way all her parts furl together out of nothing. She's holding a dagger, the blade slick with blood, shining in the sun. It glints as she flicks it around, nicking one of the passengers across the throat, impaling the other in the side of the neck.

The driver turns toward her, pistol in hand. A mere second before he lets off a shot, muzzle flashing, Tanya unfurls again, re-furling a dozen feet in the air above the car, the muzzle of her own pistol flaring, pointing downward.

The driver's head slams forward, into the wheel, sounding the blare of the car horn.

Reeling in the air, Tanya unfurls again. She furls back on the ground, legs in a wide stance, leaning forward, one arm low as the momentum from falling pushes her across the sand.

Her back is to us, bent forward, and I can't help but be reminded of Trinity in the opening scene of The Matrix.

Heaving, she pulls herself upright and turns toward us, huffing a curl of hair out of her face.

"Well," I say, "I can totally see why you wouldn't want to use *that*."

Tanya is still panting as she walks back toward us. "It gives off a signal. They'll be able to pinpoint this location."

Passing the halted dune buggy that's still blaring it's horn, she puts away her knife and gun so that she can gently lift and move the head of the driver. The horn stops immediately.

"*Thank* you." Sater says, folding his longbow and sliding it into a holster on his hip.

"Didn't they already know?" I say. "These Rifter guys; they were already scouting for us, weren't they? And they found us."

Tanya nods, shifting weight onto her other hip. She's wearing jeans, a white button-down shirt, and a brown, long tailed coat. She holds up a hand, shielding her eyes from the sun. "I'm not talking about the Rifters. I'm talking about the feds. Can't say I want them on our asses, just yet."

"Ah." I say. "Wait, if they know what we're up to, why are the Rifters in the way? Shouldn't they be trying to help us? Doesn't it bother them that there's undercover cops in the mix?"

Tanya shakes her head. "Think about it. The Rifters, criminal simworld groups—they're like the Cartel, running cocaine. What they do is illegal, but that's why people need them. If coke is legalized, what happens?" She wipes her dusty hands on her jeans. "They may hate the cops, but in a weird way, they kind of need them."

"Not to mention that Rifters actually *do* run coke, among other things." Sater says. "Safely, without being traced. Except for the cops that are now in the system, obviously, but it's still more secure than the internet, or meeting in person."

"Sounds like I bowed out just when things were starting to get...interesting." I say.

Back then, after wide circulation, Rithium *had* been made illegal. And people had kept synchronizing, anyway. But at the time, it had always been about the game. Now, it sounds like things are a bit more complicated than that.

"'Interesting' isn't quite the word I would use." Sater says. "Rithium used to be an escape. There wasn't always the risk of having to deal with pieces of scum like the Rifters or the Wolves. You might think you're playing a game, but to them, it's life or death. They'll track you down in the real, if they think you're messing with them. They'll cut you."

As if people in the mainstream needed any more reason to be afraid of Rithium.

Jesus.

"Wait," I say, "What about the Black Darts? Doesn't that change things? Is the risk even worth it, at this point?"

"Look," Tanya says, "As much as I'd love to sit here and debate the finer points of illegal substance economics..." She turns toward the dune buggy with the noisy car horn. "You think this thing is still running?"

CHAPTER 15

"SO WHERE ARE WE headed, exactly?" I say, lounging in the backseat.

"Just beyond this stretch of mountains." Tanya says. She's sitting in the passenger seat, this time. Sater has the wheel.

"And we're getting some kind of...evidence?"

Tanya nods. "The weapon..." She cuts off, looks past me. After a couple seconds, her eyes come back to me. "The weapon that was used in the assassination."

"I was gonna say...not that I could really think about it at the time, but I was pretty sure you didn't straight up kill those Rifters, back there."

"No," Tanya says. "There's a specific weapon you have to use in order to do the deed. That's what we're on our way to pick up. It's connected to the Black Dart. We're the only ones that know the exact location."

Makes enough sense, I suppose. I'll go along with it.

We've been moving north at a steady pace, at our fastest when we were crossing the desert. We slipped through a canyon in the cliff's face at the edge of the desert, coming out into a yellow valley on the other side. Now the jutting red rocks are becoming increasingly sparse, hidden by the sprawling fields of tall, hazel-colored grass.

We've been sticking to a winding trail, one that's dusty and gravelly, and yet to be overrun by the grass. The engine emits a constant, low growl. The going is bumpy and jerky, but I'm too distracted by the view to be bothered by it.

None of it is real. It's just a collection of information being transmitted into my consciousness. The real me is laying on a couch, eyes probably flitting back and forth under the lids.

But it *feels* real. I can reach out my hand as we pass an intruding blade of grass, its scratchy texture scraping my palm.

I'm pulled back in my seat as the buggy dips up, moving at an incline, pulling up a wide, mostly barren hill.

The whole situation is a bit beyond me. Less than an hour ago, I didn't even know that Black Darts were real. Now, I'm involved in upending a conspiracy surrounding them. I'm a blind man, being led by...well, people that I sure hope aren't also blind. That would sure be a pickle.

What if it's the opposite of that? What if they know even more than they're letting on?

It's true that this could be a setup. For a while now, I haven't been able to shake the idea that some vital snippets of information have been kept from me. And not just the part about the pair in my head. Slivers of the truth— the fact that the Black Dart is real, the involvement of the feds, etc—could be used to distort reality. If all that was even true. Heck, how hard is it to stage a SWAT team raid?

"You seem to know your way around the Dart." I say to Tanya.

She shrugs. "Not as well as I'd like, considering the situation. Unfortunately, the thing doesn't exactly come with an instruction manual."

"Sure." I say. Honestly, I'm not completely sure what I was fishing for. "Say, did you notice anything odd back at the house, right before we synchronized?"

"Odd." Tanya says. "Like how?"

"Like, uh..." I freeze. "Nevermind."

"Okay, weirdo."

"You know," I say, "It's not too late to sound the horn. Get a hundred or so geeks on our side. Feds wouldn't stand a chance. I could even wave a flag."

Tanya's expression goes dark. "You haven't seen what these guys can do, yet."

"Can they do the Fandango?"

Tanya's jaw clenches. She adjusts in her seat, facing me. "Don't face these guys head on, Kit. We need to lure the feds to collect the data, but that's it. After that, we're out."

She watches me, as if trying to make sure I understand. Honestly, it's kind of unnerving.

"What's with the concern, all of a sudden?" I say.

She points a finger. "Don't fuck this up, Winter." Then, she swivels back around, arms folded.

CHAPTER 16

THE SUN IS JUST past it's apex when I see the dark shape in the sky. For all I know, it's the same one I saw when I spawned in.

I can't quite make it out. It's just a black blob, with occasional undulations around the edges, like the shadow of a manta ray.

At first, I don't think much of it. It's of passing interest, an oddity in the corner of my eye. Something to glance at, occasionally.

But recently it's been getting closer, more defined. At an alarming speed.

I lean forward. "Hey. Hey, guys?"

"For the last time," Sater says, "You do *not* have to use the bathroom. That got old like a half hour ago."

Tanya's already rolling her eyes.

"No, not that." I say. "There's something in the sky. I think it might be a dragon."

Tanya perks up at that. "And?"

"Couldn't it be, like, I dunno...a Black Dart thing?"

Tanya suddenly seems tense, alert. "Maybe. Could be. Where is it?"

I point.

She holds up a hand, shielding her eyes from the sun. "I see it." She rummages in the inner breast pocket of her coat, pulls out a spyglass. She extends it, holds it up to her eye. "Easy. Slow down a little bit."

Sater lets up on the gas, engine throbbing dully.

I'm suddenly more aware if the omnipresent heat. Thankfully, there's a slight wind to combat it, causing it to wax and wane. It drags across the valley, pulling on the limbs of trees, rustling tall, dry grass against the rocks.

Tanya's spyglass snaps loudly as she closes it. Her face is pale. "Get us off the trail."

"Where?" Sater says, already turning the buggy.

"That tree." Tanya says. "In the bushy area."

It is indeed a bushy area. Some of the bushes are taller than me. The tree's long branches extend outward over a ring of them, a mother hen covering chicks with its wings.

The nose of the buggy parts the tangled arms of two thick bushes, wheels crunching and cracking as they slowly roll over sticks and rocks and dry leaves. The vehicle dips sideways from the bulging roots as Sater pulls up next to the trunk.

"Kill it." Tanya says.

Grimacing, Sater pulls a lever, shutting off the engine.

I don't like it, either. Even though we're almost completely shrouded here, that just makes me feel all the more exposed, like we could be routed at any moment without even seeing it coming.

Tanya's head is tilted at angle, gaze rotating between the skylit gaps overhead. If she were a hound, her ears would be perked up, twitching.

All I can hear is the scraping and scratching of the leaves. There's a slight ringing in my ears, as if my brain is trying to fill the sensory hole the sound of the engine has left behind.

But then there's something else. A gentle, white-noise pressure. A low, constant *whoosh* feeling. And it's growing, like a dim rumble coming out of theater speakers, building in intensity until it feels like the seats themselves are shaking.

I find myself thinking of a blind man at a crosswalk, listening for an approaching car. *"Is that...is it coming this way? Is it—yeah, yeah, I think it is. Yeah, definitely is."*

Shadow casts over the skylights in the tree, turning everything cold and dark.

THWUMP.

The sound echoes overheard. The entire tree shakes with the vibration of it, branches clattering. Surrounding bushes bristle, like living things. Dry leaves lift off of the ground, swirling.

The darkness lasts for a split-second. It feels like several minutes. A tense, suspenseful pocket of time without relent or escape.

The spinning leaves dissipate. Light returns, bursting down through the canopy. Tanya and Sater's frozen faces are smattered with mingled pockets of sunlight and shade.

The rumble fades

(*"Yep, there it goes, it's passed, now..."*)

Leaving only that faint white-noise behind, until even that seems to pass.

"Okay," I say. "Now I really do have to go to the bathroom."

Sater's eyelids narrow down to slits. "What the hell did I tell you about that?"

"SHHH!!" Tanya says. "Both of you, keep it down. I'm trying to think."

Sater seems about as uncomfortable with that as I am. Stopping to think means dwelling on the mounting facets of uncertainty.

"We'll have to continue on foot." She says, finally. "It's only another couple of miles."

"Yeah," Sater says, "Up and over two or three ranges of mountains. No problem."

"We'll stay low," Tanya says, ignoring him. "Using whatever cover we can."

"Wait a minute, what's the problem, here? Why can't we just..." I gesture like I'm throwing a harpoon. "Kill the dragon. Keep moving."

"You don't get it, do you?" He leans low, suddenly aware of how loud his voice is getting. "The dragons were killed off a long time ago."

"What, do you think I'm slow?" I say. "I literally just felt one pass over us."

Tanya bites her lip. Her hair is messier than ever, a cascade of frizzy curls in every direction. "It's a dragon, alright." She says. "Someone's riding it."

CHAPTER 17

WE DECIDE—RATHER, TANYA COMMANDS us—to stay in the shadow of the bushes for a few more minutes, to make sure the dragon doesn't double back.

Sater folds his arms and leans back against the tree, staring up through gaps in the leaves, listening.

Tanya is standing on the outer edge of the tree's shade, watching and waiting. Her hand absentmindedly reaches for her jacket's breast pocket, feeling for a pack of cigarettes that isn't there.

I find myself sizing her up all over again every time I see her. She's short and petite, and in this world, somehow muscular at the same time. A fun-sized ball of intense energy. Like a goblin, or a harpy.

She's the one leading me blindfolded into this thing. The same way she led me down those stairs by the hand, steering confidently, without fear of retaliation or rebellion. She's one step ahead of me, controlling me, this entire time.

She knows about Aberdale. About that chip in my arm. How much, I'm not sure, but at this rate it'll be more than I ever know.

"Listen," I say.

"Shhh!" Tanya's eyes flick throwing knives at me, before going back to surveying the sky.

"*Listen,*" I say, quieter. "The longer I'm part of this, the more I feel like I deserve to know what's happening."

Tanya sighs. "I should probably tell you."

My breath catches. Tanya is still watching the sky.

"Our destination, where we're going to pick up the weapon...it's in the Rifters' headquarters."

My breath ejects in a hollow gasp, which I cover with a cough. "What?" Not what I was fishing for, but it's shiny and distracting. "And where's that, exactly?"

She folds her arms. "Opus."

Opus is the one of the most visible, iconic landmarks on the map. The tall, black spire identifiable from orbit is the Tower of Opus, sprouting out of the center of the walled city.

"What part?"

Tanya heaves her shoulders, something like a shrug. "All of it."

That makes me smirk. "What do you mean? Opus is the most populated common area in the whole game."

"Used to be. It's just a hidey hole for the Rifter gang, at this point."

"Hidey hole." I say, flatly, mulling it over.

It's a difficult thing to reconcile with my own memories. In my head, Opus is a packed, bustling city. A place to socialize, sell cool items, and show off. A place where people express themselves artistically through the craftsmanship of their wares and the designs of player-owned housing.

"People mostly go there to set up IRL drug deals, anymore." Tanya says. It's like she can read my mind and is deliberately trying to bum me out. "Among other things."

"What kinds of things?"

"I don't know." Tanya says. "Illicit things, I guess. Do I look like a Rifter, to you?"

"You're telling me one gang took over an entire city?"

"The *most populated* gang." Sater calls from his leaning post. "Do we really need to play Twenty Questions like this?" He takes a step toward me. "We know the facts, you don't. Shut up, listen to us, and follow our lead. How about that?"

Sater's hand brushes the hilt of the knife holstered at his belt.

There's an involuntary twitch at the corner of my mouth. I hope it's an obnoxious smirk.

"Yeah," I say. "That's not gonna work."

My hand eases down toward one of my revolvers.

Suddenly, there's hard metal pressing against the side of my neck, denting my skin. I hear the *click-snap* of a hammer being pulled back.

"What are you doing, Winter." It's not a question. It's a warning. Tanya's voice is dangerously soft and breathy. I've never heard her speak like this.

"I'm not dying out here without knowing what those assholes did to me."

"Really?" Tanya says, cocking her head in my peripheral. "Because that's where you're headed. We made a deal with you. Lord knows why, since we're holding all the cards. Are you going to hold up your end?"

"Guess you'll have to find out."

Mercifully, Tanya pulls the barrel of her pistol away from my neck. I rub at the spot, feeling a fresh bruise beginning to sprout there.

Then, she grabs my shoulder, jerking me toward her. Her head comes up to my pecs. Her face is turned up, glaring at me. Her brows are scrunched together, eyes bright pinions of intensity. The barrel of her gun rests just below my left nipple.

"Don't." She prods my ribs with a finger, emphasizing the word. "Screw with me."

That one's a Freudian. A joking thought I decide to keep to myself.

I cock my head. "Question: did you mean for it to come out that way?"

Yeah, or not.

Tanya takes in a slow, deep breath through her nostrils, eyes never leaving mine. "There's more riding on this than just you and me."

"Are you willing to risk all of it just to slight me?" I pause. "Or is there more to it? I wonder, would I still be cooperating if I actually knew the truth?"

It's weird how cute Tanya still is, even with her face taut and snarling like this. "What truth?"

I shrug. "You tell me."

I risk a glance over at Sater. His arms are folded, legs spread apart. His attention is rapt, his expression tense.

I'm onto something. I know I am.

Tanya widens her stance, rolls her shoulders. "If you're gonna do something, Bigshot, now's the time. If you have a card, play it. Cuz now's the only time I'm gonna tell you."

"That's not how cards work." I say.

"It is when you're playing with me." Tanya says. "What's it gonna be?"

Her body is practically pressing up against mine, pistol jamming into my ribs. I can smell the sweat in her hair.

Such a weird detail to have in a sim. There's no sex, drugs, or cigarettes, but sweaty people still reek. Seems a bit tilted, to me.

Though, it makes sense, I guess. Immersion is about details. Specificity. It's the vivid, lifelike things that make it real. Like the slick shine that skin has in the heat—the kind I could see on Tanya's face now—or the way a slight breeze pushed through a person's hair.

Tanya's lips part. "Winter. I swear to God."

Then, it happens.

Hey.

It's like there's this door opening in my mind, revealing things previously unseen.

Hey, wait a minute.

There's a gleam, a previously unidentifiable glint in her eyes. I couldn't see it before. Or at least not so clearly. But now, I can.

It's like a switch flipping, a light going from *completely off* to *completely on*. Like turning the valve on a fire hose. The truth—stark, violent, and unrelenting.

She knows *me*.

CHAPTER 18

IT HITS ME ALL at once. There, under the tree, Tanya leering up at me, sunlit face speckled with the wavering shadows of leaves.

No. I realize.

It had started hitting me the moment I first locked eyes with her. Perhaps it really has taken this long for the idea to form fully, like a fuzzy moth excising itself from its cocoon.

That look. That flash of....knowing.

Mason and Sater, too. All of them. There's something going on here, just underneath the surface. Not all is as it seems.

It's shocking. It's chilling. It's like that moment in a good thriller when you can just about see the twist coming.

Which, of course, is different for everybody. Some people put the pieces together right away. They're not stuck in the story, immersed in the same way as other readers or viewers. There's a certain distance, a critical voice talking in their ear. I always wished those people, when they *do* get the twist, would keep it to themselves, so I don't have to overhear them whispering in the theater seat in front of me, predicting the ending.

Thanks a lot, geeks. Trying to enjoy the movie, here.

I'm not a viewer, or a reader. I don't have the luxury of distance. I'm *in* the story, in the sense that it's the story of my life.

Maybe that's part of the problem.

I'm Jimmy Stewart.

Okay, that was a weird thought. I need to work backward, figure that out.

"C'mon, Winter." Sater says. There's a nervous edge to his voice. "Spit it out."

My eyes are still in a deathlock with Tanya's. It's a moment frozen in time, like an exhibit in a wax museum.

If I look away, if I relax even a little, she'll know. My face will change. I'll

Oh, yeah. Jimmy Stewart.

There's this Alfred Hitchcock movie my aunt always liked, where these two guys strangle someone with a length of rope—the movie's called *Rope*—and stash his body in this big chest. They throw a blanket over the chest, disguising it as a dining table, and invite a couple friends(one of whom is good old Jimmy Stewart) over for dinner.

For the most part, them and Jimmy are hanging out, laughing, having a good time. But at some point, Jimmy realizes, hey, wait a second, there's something underneath this tablecloth!

I'm Jimmy Stewart. I know there's something underneath the cloth.

I just don't know what it is.

More immediately, I don't know what will happen if *they* know that *I* know.

"I fold."

Tanya doesn't react right away. There's a loosening in the tightness around her eyes. What exactly she thinks she sees, I have no idea.

She puts a hand on my chest, pushes me.

I take a step back.

She jams her pistol back into her belt. "We done fooling around?"

I snicker. "You just can't help yourself, can you?"

She shoots me another glare as she walks past, stepping through the bushes.

Sater is still watching me. It's an uncertain look, like maybe he thinks I know something, and he doesn't know what to do about it.

Don't worry. I'm still just as confused as ever.

I bow, waving him ahead of me. "After you."

Sater shakes his head, arms falling back down to his sides. "You are so freakin' weird." He says, as he walks past.

CHAPTER 19

IT DOESN'T TAKE LONG for the zigging and zagging between the bases of hills to get old, crouching among the trees and underbrush. Supposedly, our destination isn't all that far away, as the crow flies. The problem is that we have now taken it upon ourselves to get there as invisibly(and inconveniently) as possible.

When I imagined one last trip into Rithium, I can't say this is exactly what I had in mind.

Don't get me wrong, there's a lot to see and explore if you go hiking in the simworld, if that's what you're about. The vast amount of incredibly lush and impossibly detailed space is part of what makes the world feel real. There's something both lonely and thrilling about getting lost in it.

But Rithium isn't just about that. It's about the stuff *between* all the space. The towns. The player-built cities. The discovery of ancient ruins or artifacts that lead players to debate finer aspects of the lore, or change the way that you play the game—if said artifacts have any in-game usefulness.

There's monsters to kill; sometimes tucked away in deadly, dangerous areas that most players avoid. Some of these areas are in the form of cave-like dungeons to explore, with secrets waiting to be uncovered: treasure, rare equipment, or Skill Crystals.

Perhaps most of all, it's about screwing around with other players, whether it's an exciting feud between guilds, or showing a bunch of bullying posers just how good at the game you are, by taking them out and grabbing their stuff.

Sorry, losers.

It's about taking on bosses singlehanded, or with the help of only one or two friends.

It's about making memories.

Oh, I'm making memories, all right.

Ahead of me, Tanya throws up a hand, signaling us to freeze, halting our uphill climb through the brush. There's enough twigs and dry leaves caught in her hair to start a campfire.

Maybe they should have waited until Rithium's night-cycle to do this, I think.

Not that they really had a choice. The arrival of the SWAT team had been necessary for the plan to work. Now that the process was in motion, we needed to follow it through to the end. All eyes have to be on us. The story can't just be real and corroborated. It has to be airtight and irresistible.

I'm crouched low, listening.

This isn't a game, to them. Maybe it never was. It's not like it was for you. Not to them.

Especially not now.

Tanya is still frozen, hand in the air, like a monument. The Tanya Bedford Memorial.

That's a bit grim, don't you think?

Sater crawls past me with painstaking slowness, careful not to make a sound.

"Tanya," he whispers. *"What—"*

There's a threatening jerk from Tanya's hand, silencing him. The whole stretch of her forearm is taut, unflinching. Her body is still.

Something about that actually kind of scares me. The wordless intensity of it.

I turn, scanning the darkness. Sunlight is muted here, cut off by the twisting, crisscrossing brambles, overlaying, shrouding everything in shadows. My vision blurs as layers of growth come and out of focus. I'm suddenly and keenly aware of all the surrounding pockets of darkness, a many-layered abyss full of unknown things.

Something flashes. An adjustment from light to dark, then light again. Not light itself, but a color. The color white.

Something climbs out of the blackness. Not literally, but figuratively, like a picture with an ominous, creepy thing in the background you don't notice right away, Or those social media posts with a picture that has *Something that doesn't belong; only geniuses will see it!*

At first, as far as your brain is concerned, nothing is there. And then, with horrific suddenness, something *is.*

Only, it's not a something. It's a someone.

INTERLUDE

I PUT THE TRUCK'S gear in park. I could see the red cones of light from the brakelights extinguish like torches in the rearview mirror. I turned the key, shutting off the engine and all of the truck lights, bathing us in shadow.

Somewhere, perhaps a couple blocks away, a dog decided to start barking.

Oscar hadn't spoken in six hours. He seemed to be in a sort of catatonic state, slumped in his seat, staring sightlessly.

I gripped the steering wheel tight with one hand, wrenching, the bumpy textures digging into my palm.

"Tank's almost empty." I said it just to say something.

Oscar gave no discernible response. If he was breathing, it was low and quiet. Occasionally, he blinked.

I envied that state. That unawareness of himself. Perhaps of everything else around him.

I'd spent the last six hours in a sort of manic fervor, mind looping endlessly as I drove.

So much so that, for a long time now, I hadn't looked in the backseat.

Neither had Oscar. Sometimes, even in his dreamlike stupor, he would begin to turn in his seat, glancing over his shoulder. But then, it was as if something would catch him, turning him back, his eyes glassy and refractive.

I started, seeing some slight movement from Oscar in my peripheral.

Oscar still faced forward, but his Adam's Apple bobbed as he swallowed.

"You said she would be okay." Oscar wasn't looking at me. As far as I could tell, he wasn't looking at anything.

There was a momentary catch in my throat, but I managed to speak. "She's...she's gonna be fine."

Oscar swallowed again. This time, his throat made a loud click.

"She's...she's just sleeping." I said.

"Really." Oscar's head pivoted toward me, his face lax and placid. His eyes were no longer glassy. Red veins pulsed in the whites. "Then why don't you lift the blanket?"

My fingers wound tighter against the steering wheel. "Oscar..."

Something thin, hot and wet was winding its way down the side of my face, underneath my eye.

"She's dead." Oscar said. It didn't sound like an accusation, or an indictment. It was just a fact. Like a comment on the weather.

He turned away from me, nodding to himself. "She's dead." This time with a downward inflection, a tone of finality.

"We don't know that," I said. "She—"

Oscar's eyes flashed, turning on me. His arm lashed out.

I cringed.

Instead, he reached behind, pulling the blanket off of the backseat.

Jackie was sprawled on her back, eyes closed, hair in disarray, muscles limp.

"If you think she's alive," Oscar said, not even looking at her, eyes still on me. "Why have you been driving us in circles? Why didn't you drive us to the hospital?"

"They...they would ID us..." I said. "We'd all go to prison...or worse..."

"Un-fucking-believable." Oscar said. His face was twisting, becoming gnarled. "Guess there's no cloudboxes in prison, huh?"

I didn't have the energy to defend myself. I could see the pockets of moisture forming on my shirt from the tears sliding off my face.

"O-Oscar...D-don't..."

Something had gone wrong. I didn't know exactly what, and I probably never would.

Perhaps it was because Jackie had been registering to the system, synchronizing for the first time, just when the power had gone out.

We'd sat in darkness, until the backup lights had flickered on, revealing Jackie, lying on the floor, only the whites of her eyes visible in their sockets, her entire body trembling.

That was when Samuel(the owner of the old arcade) had pulled his gun.

It wasn't until afterward, during the long drive, that I had truly put the pieces together. And yet, even in that moment when Samuel had pulled his gun, I had known.

Oscar and I were accomplices. Part of something...illegal. Either altogether, or in the sense that Samuel had obtained the technology illegally, to use for his own gain. It was his golden goose.

Our names were all over the paperwork he gave to his superiors, his records. There was plenty of video footage to implicate us as regulars, even though all we ever did was head into the backroom with Samuel. Plenty of eyewitness accounts to substantiate this, besides.

We needed to get out of there.

Bizarrely, though the gun was in his hand, watching us carry Jackie out of the backroom, it didn't seem like he was going to use it. He had followed us, running a hand through his greying hair, telling us, *Oh god, they're going to kill me, oh god, wait, you can't do this—*.

It wasn't until we were almost to the front door that something snapped, and he started shooting—loud cracks that echoed inside the arcade, drowning out the throbs and beeps from the machines.

He had missed every shot. I have to wonder how hard he was actually trying not to. Not that there was time to contemplate that in the moment.

Glass had shattered. Chunks of sidewalk had splattered up into the air. Sirens had sounded.

For a while, Oscar had held Jackie in the backseat. She'd wriggled in his grasp, convulsing. Then, at some point, she'd laid still.

Oscar had run his hands over her, shaking her. He'd held his palm a few inches over her nose and mouth, feeling for her breath. Then, he'd pulled his hand away, his whole body sagging.

After a time—I'd been unable to look, instead keeping my eyes on the road—Oscar had pulled himself away, dragging himself up into the passenger seat. And there he had stayed.

Until then, parked in front of the hotel.

Oscar popped open the passenger door. The cool, night air intruded. I hadn't bothered to turn up the heat in the truck, but there was still a slight discrepancy in temperature, a crisp clearness. Through the open door, the night had a blue, dusklight cast to it, unfiltered by the tinted windows.

I turned, hand still tight on the wheel, as if stuck there. "Oscar, wait—"

The door slammed. The whole truck seemed to shake a little with the force of it.

I stared at my hand. It seemed to have a mind of its own, wrapped tight against the wheel, cord-like muscles rising up through the skin. It ignored my signals, my authority over it.

C'mon...let...GO.

I gasped as I felt the muscles in my arm yielding. My fingers unclenched. I reached for the door lever, popped it, and stepped through the widening gap, out onto the gravel lot.

I could still hear the dog, barking frantically a few blocks off. It seemed I wasn't the only one, as lights started to flick on from behind the motel curtains.

Oscar was making a slow walk toward the edge of the lot, as if in a daze.

I ran, boots kicking up gravel. In seconds, I caught up to him, reached out, grabbed the sleeve of his jacket.

Oscar yanked, pulling me off balance. The next thing I felt was a sharp pressure in and behind the bridge of my nose. Warmth gushed, oozing down the lower part of my face, running between my lips, tasting the way old coins smell.

I fell to the gravel, scraping my palms. Scraping my legs, even through my jeans.

"*Hey!*" called some woman's voice, somewhere in the direction of the motel. "*Hey, stop that!*"

I tried to turn and look, but instead I saw Oscar's boot coming directly for my face.

I held up my hands, catching the boot and pushing my own knuckles back into my face.

I keeled back, spitting blood, shaking. I put my arm out, trying to get my balance so I could get back to my feet, knees wobbling.

Oscar was standing over me, rubbing knuckles that were bloody and bruised, the skin broken from punching me. His face had gone back to that placid look, like he was unfeeling—though that was far from the truth. Whatever was going on inside his head, it was beyond words. We were both beyond words.

Suddenly, he was on top of me, hitting me in the cheek, pounding the back of my head into the gravel.

Distantly, I could hear screaming.

I wriggled, legs kicking, trying to scrabble out from underneath him. With every consecutive hit I could feel the skin over my cheekbone splitting, tearing.

My teeth locked together in a clenched grimace. I brought up my right fist, slamming it into the side of Oscar's face with a loud *smack*, stunning him, body going rigid for a couple seconds as he fell sideways.

I rolled over on top of him, heart thumping in my head.

Distantly, over the scratch and clatter of gravel as we kicked and rolled in the lot, I could hear the sound of police sirens growing louder. People were yelling. Lights flashed up and down the street, tinting Oscar's gritted face with hues of blue, white, and red.

There were three loud *whoop*'s from the approaching cop cars, tires crunching as they slowed to a stop at odd angles in the lot.

Car doors swung wide. Flashlights beamed at us, bobbing and weaving as boots stomped on the gravel. Orders were barked, but I couldn't make them out. I mostly just saw Oscar's face, eyes so red the vessels would surely pop. And then I realized his hands were on my neck. And then I realized I couldn't breathe.

A pair of hands seemed to appear out of nowhere, grabbing Oscar by the shoulders and pulling him off of me.

The throttling pressure disappeared from my neck. I coughed, feeling hoarse and sick.

"Stay on the ground. Keep your hands where I can see them."

I squinted, unable to look directly up at the cop due to the way he was shining his light down at me.

"Can I see some ID?"

I blinked, squatting, holding my hands off to either side of my torso. "Do —do you want my hands where you can see them, or do you want my ID?"

There was a tense pause after that. I couldn't see the cop's face. "Which pocket?"

He didn't sound mad.

"My right." I said.

The dark silhouette of his head nodded. "Slow." His arm flexed as he unsnapped his holster.

I did move slow, slipping only two of my fingers into my jean pocket, carefully gripping and sliding my wallet up and out. I could hear the other cop talking to Oscar just ten paces away.

I handed over my ID. The cop held onto it.

He moved the beam of the flashlight away from me and over to the pickup. The driver door was wide open.

"Is that your vehicle?"

I looked away, suddenly fascinated with all the bystanders standing out in front of the motel, their doors ajar.

No matter how long I stared, it seemed I couldn't quite block out the image in my head of Jackie lying limply in the back seat, lifeless and doll-like.

"Sir?" The cop said.

Just lying there on the floor, eyes rolling, lights flickering—

There was a crackle as the cop grabbed his radio. "Yeah, can you run those plates? And the ID? Yeah, here it is..."

The cop went on to read off my license number.

She peed herself. That vivid detail, withheld by the same part of my brain that had kept me driving thoughtlessly for hours, came whooshing back. The dark, warm, growing stain on her sweats as Oscar and I had lifted her up.

"Stay right here," The cop said, suddenly. "Don't move."

He walked away from me, past Oscar and the other cop, toward the pickup.

Oscar was prostrate on the ground, hands spread, while the second cop stood over him.

I felt an insane urge to call out to him, say something. Instead, I coughed and spat, hacking up blood onto the rocks. I could feel the blood from my broken nose trickling down the back of my throat.

"Hey!" Someone yelled. It took me a second to realize it was Oscar. He was still flat on the ground, head cocked at an awkward angle, looking at the cop approaching the pickup.

"Hey!" He yelled. "Stay away from her!"

The cop slowed, turning to glance at Oscar. Then, something about that seemed to worry him, because he sped up, jogging toward the car.

"HEY!"

Oscar pushed himself up onto his feet.

The cop standing next to him grabbed his shoulder, his other hand going to his gun. "I'm gonna need you to stay on the ground—"

Oscar spun, knocking the cop's hand aside. There was the sound of gunmetal rubbing leather as the cop pulled his gun.

The cop started yelling. It was so loud and aggressive, words running together. He was telling Oscar to step back, get way, to put his hands on the ground, "—RIGHT NOW!! RIGHT NOW!! RIGHT NOW!!"

Oscar didn't step back. He didn't get away. He didn't put his hands on the ground. Instead, his arm whipped out, reaching for the cop's gun.

There was a flash of light, a tiny prick of yellow lightning in the dusk.

I flinched, eyes clamped shut. I could feel a high-pitched ringing in my left ear. It was already gradually falling away, being replaced by a dull, painful throb in the ear.

When I opened my eyes, Oscar was on the ground. The cop was stepping backward, putting distance between them, handgun gripped tight in both hands and held at arm's length, levelled at Oscar.

I was already moving.

I heard multiple shouts. The cop who shot Oscar rushed forward, tried to put himself between us. I swerved, ducked under one of his arms. I slid to the ground, scraping my forearms.

He was already a shell. I remember thinking that.

He was on his back, one arm broken from the fall, twisting out at an angle. His face was turned sideways, facing me, eyes unblinking.

Something dark was leaking out the back of his head, seeping into the gravel, pooling like a thick resin.

I felt hands grab me, pulling me back. I thrashed, screaming, struggling, even after the handcuffs had clicked home, numbing cold metal encasing my wrists.

Chapter 20

I T'S THE EYES. THAT'S what the white color is. Two dark hazel dots surrounded by white globes. For a split second, they'd disappeared, lids closing over them. Then, they'd opened again. Looking directly at me.

It takes another moment of visual comprehension for the rest of him to come into focus—I say *him* because I know who it is. Somehow, I do.

He's crouched, hunched over, ghoul-like. Black mud and grime cakes his clothing; a look that he has seemingly embraced, slicking back his hair with it. The same black mud(unless it's paint) is smeared across his already dark-skinned face.

In one hand he's holding a pistol. It looks like a Beretta M9. It's odd, completely out of place in Rithium, a world of swords and Wild West guns and cobbled-together machines. There's nothing about the game's aesthetic style or a player's unique craftsmanship to it. It looks like something that was built in a factory; cold and utilitarian and inanimate.

Slowly, Oscar raises a mud-coated finger to his lips. *Shhhhh.*

Something seems to catch in my throat, making a *click* sound. Thoughtlessly, my eyes flit from Oscar to Sater and Tanya, up ahead of me, neither of whom seem to know what's going on. They're both frozen, both listening.

I look at Oscar. His neck flexes as he shakes his head, slow.

That's it. I think, resigned. *I belong in a loony bin.*

Oscar gives me a chin twitch, motioning me over.

I don't move.

He brings up two fingers, wags them, waving me over.

I don't move.

Because if I do, I will truly and finally discover just how crazy I really am.

Oscar cocks his head, eyes narrowing. He shakes his head at me, disappointed.

I shrug apologetically. Inside, my heart is jackhammering my ribs.

I'm miming with a ghost.

Unless he's not a ghost. Or even a projection of my drug-addled mind. There are alternatives.

The last time I saw Oscar, the back of his head had been leaking blood, or brains, or both. And before that, he'd been mental, in a rage. At the time, I'd been afraid he was going to kill me.

This Oscar isn't like that. He's watching me intently, but without any clear signs of malice. He just wants me to step away from Sater and Tanya, and over to him.

Could be a trap.

I suppose it could. Whether or not it's Oscar. But if it is—

Oscar holds up a finger, tracing it in the air. Silent, crackly letters manifest in front of him, bright and neon. Though it's perfectly legible, he traces the words quickly, like a hastily scratched note.

"JACKIE"

My breath catches. My racing heart trips over itself, reeling. There's a long, painful moment before it starts up again.

It's as if there's this brass chain that's been hanging from my neck for that last ten years. Etched into the length of each link is Jackie's name. *Jackie,* with a flourish at the top of the J and a heart shape at the top of the I. And someone just came along and yanked on it.

I shoot a look over at Tanya and Sater. Their backs are still to me.

The text has already dissipated. Oscar makes another waving motion at me, then holds up three fingers.

After a second, he lowers one of the fingers.

My heart starts hammering again. As if on it's own, my body is tensing up, getting ready to spring.

He lowers another finger.

Oscar lowers that last finger, making a fist.

Then, he unfurls.

Twigs and tree limbs snap and crack, pulled toward the sudden influx of air.

Someone yells out. It takes me a second to realize it's me. A startled yelp, if I'm honest with myself.

Oscar reappears directly in front of me, in a whirl of upset twigs and leaves. His shoulder crashes into my chest, ploughing me backward.

Some of the oxygen in my virtual lungs ejects with an *"Oof!"* My feet leave the ground. My body's practically horizontal in the air. I can feel Oscar's arms pulled tight in a vice around my torso.

I can see the blue sheen of the sky beyond a layer of twisted branches. Bizarrely, some of the branches seem to be twisting inward toward me, a vision punctuated by a sickening cacophony of crackles and sputters.

What follows appears to be some kind of gravitational anomaly. Ribbons of matter compress, taut guitar strings of wood and leaves and air circling me, wrapping, some of it flying hard and fast toward my face.

My eyes clench.

There's a whooshing pop of air.

I hit the ground. Only it's *not* the ground. It's flat and alien and cold. The sky is an unobstructed curtain of blue.

My hands immediately go to the holstered guns at my hips. I'm a quick draw. Always had a knack for it.

Of course, by the time my pistols are leveled at him, he's standing over me, his Beretta pointing directly at my face.

"Easy." Oscar says.

"I was just gonna say that to you. Whoever you are."

There's a surprised expression on Oscar's face. Followed by a hurt look. "You know who I am. Don't you?"

I stare at him. I can make out certain idiosyncrasies. The occasional, nervous twitch at the end of his eyebrow. The way he clenches his jaw, but in a way that's a little offset, like his bite is off.

"Yeah," I say, exhaling. "I know."

Oscar studies my face for a second, then grins. He puts his gun away. I put away mine.

Something swells in me. A series of deep, powerful emotions, rolling one after another, waves on the sand of my mind. So powerful that it's a wonder I'm not crying, not bawling my eyes out. Then I realize: there are no tear ducts in Rithium. It's all internalized, roiling inside me. Unless Oscar can see some—if any—of it on my face. The face is a portal into the soul, after all.

But it's not enough. That's one of the things I'm feeling; that I need to externalize. Whether he knows or not, whether he forgives me or not, I need to tell him that...that...

I'm sorry.

I sit up, running my hands over a smooth, obsidian, marble-like surface. There's a strange blemish the size of my hand running across it, a crack of white, as if struck by a god's hammer.

Oscar clasps his hand in mine, pulling me to my feet. "Careful." He says.

What I see next makes me dizzy.

I'm...I'm standing on the Opus tower.

Vast plains of the land of Rithium stretch out below. I can just barely make out the tall walls of Opus in the lower part of my vision. The rest is the valley and plains surrounding it, much of it wooded and sloping.

The forest seems to have been cut back quite a bit since the last time I was here, allowing for a wide range of visibility in every direction in a circle outside the walls.

I can't help but wonder how exactly Tanya was planning to infiltrate this place.

Perhaps the same way you just did? Somehow?

"You're working for the feds, aren't you?" I say, almost without fully understanding what it is I'm saying. I haven't had time to consider all the implications of that yet, but it's an isolated realization.

Tanya's words echo in my head. *"Don't face these guys head-on, Kit."*

"We'll talk," Oscar says. He steps toward the edge. "But first, I want to show you something.

On the distant horizon, adjacent to Oscar's silhouette, are the black peaks of mountains, tinged with silver snow, making him look like a giant. A torrid breeze rustles the hair on the back of his head.

I take a few careful steps, until I'm standing next to him. One more step, and I'd be tumbling down the side of the tower, like Saruman in Return of the King.

Oscar puts a hand on my shoulder and points toward a stretch of forest southwest of the city walls. There's a dark specter circling there, imposing itself on the panorama—a black dragon. The points of it's scales glint sharply in the sunlight. As it swoops low, it's massive maw opens, and a jet of flame erupts downward into the trees.

"I'm gonna guess that's yours." I say, a dark pit opening up in my stomach, though I'm not quite sure why.

Oscar claps my shoulders. "We're going to smoke them into a corner. The guy, anyway. Tara Vellis might require a bit more...finesse."

Just then, there's a loud pop behind us.

CHAPTER 21

I START TO TURN. I see a flash in the corner of my eye, and then my reflexes take over.

I push Oscar, shoving him off to the side. I duck sideways. My arm lashes out. Two of my fingers squeeze together, catching the hilt of a windmilling throwing knife where Oscar's head had been.

The momentum from the knife pushes my arm back, rotating me and putting me off balance. I lean into the spin, one foot off the ground for a half second until I right myself, my back to the dropoff.

Oscar rights himself.

Tanya is standing on the opposite side of the platform. Her legs are in a wide stance, her hand wrapping itself around the hilt of her gun. She draws.

Oscar unfurls, disappearing just as Tanya squeezes the trigger and the gunshot rings out.

Gunsmoke hovers for about a second before being carried away by a dry gust.

"Kit," Tanya says. Her face is strained, pleading. "You've got to listen to me—"

Oscar furls, just behind her. He grabs her, and they both disappear.

I drop the knife—it clatters, scratching the platform—and rush over to the edge.

A gunshot sounds, echoing from below.

I start circling the edge, scanning the streets below.

The city is dirty and unkempt. Not at all like what I remember it being back in the day. Clumps of dirt and dust cling to the surfaces of its buildings and walls like rust-colored barnacles.

There's a laziness to it, as well. There are wide open spaces where only five or so figures can be seen at a time, most of them lounging or meandering around. They all seem to be wearing armor and carrying some form of weaponry.

There are two explosive poofs as Oscar and Tanya reappear down in the market district. Old booths are knocked over, tables upended. Dust is kicked up, trailing in the plaza. There are several more gunshots, before they both disappear again.

Suddenly, the gang members throughout the city start to perk up, some of them scrambling in the direction of the noises, ants in an overturned hill.

There are more gunshots, some rattles and bangs. I can't see where they're coming from, perhaps because it's happening too close to the base of the tower.

I circle the edge again, this time looking for some kind of trap door or ladder.

No luck. Every inch of the platform is smooth and polished, without blemish, save for the white crack of marble running across it.

Same with the outer surface of the tower just below the platform. There are no ladders or poles or notches or anything I could use to safely climb down.

There's only one option open to me. There are these black spires that run up the length of the tower, curving outward toward the base, almost like a ski slope, or the world's deadliest waterslide.

I could slide down that, I think. I crouch, perched dangerously, the toes of my boots poking out past the platform. *I could use the roof of one of those buildings to dampen my fall.* They don't look well-maintained. The materials could be old, malleable.

The answer of why is simple, and one way or another I'm going to have to confront it. *If*—and it may be a big *if*—Tanya was telling the truth about what happened, then that *would* mean Oscar was the one who got in with the Rifters. He could be working for the feds. He could be...

A government assassin!?

It seems crazy. I can't make sense of it. But before whatever happens next, I need to know. I need to be sure.

Don't you know Oscar? Don't you trust him?

I did *know* him. I did *trust him. Ten years ago.*

I lower myself, butt on the platform, legs hanging over the edge. Below me, a dozen floors below, is one of the spires, arcing away from the tower at a steep angle.

I think *floors,* but really there are no floors. The tower is purely aesthetic in design. It's a landmark. A beacon. Something you can see from almost anywhere on the northern continent.

I close my eyes for a second. The wind picks up, causing my hair to whip around and tickle my face.

If my avatar dies from the fall, I'll be temporarily booted from the game. I'll wake up on that couch, Mason standing over me, a gun barrel pressed against my head; if he was telling the truth, though the severity of the situation seems to support that he was.

Perhaps worse, I can feel this sense of foreboding, like I might miss another chance to do...something. I'm not quite sure what, but that seems to almost make it worse.

When I open my eyes, I can see thick boughs of smoke rising from the woods, murky and black. A pair of dragon wings extend, flapping, obscured amidst the plumes.

I glance down at the spire again, starting to feel kind of stupid. *You'd die in the fall. The slope is too steep. The curve is too sharp.*

I pull myself up and start circling the platform, giving it another once-over.

That's when my eyes settle on Tanya's knife, lying in the middle of the platform. I reach down and pick it up. It's light, weighted, but still sharp-looking. There's a symbol etched into the center of the blade: the face and mane of a lion.

For a moment, I stare at the symbol. There's something almost sinister about the way it makes me feel, harboring a sense of deja vu that's both alien and familiar—as deja vu always is.

Slowly, as if of its own accord, I feel my hand moving up to the left sleeve of my jacket. The fabric is thin and loose. I slowly roll back the sleeve down the length of my arm, until my forearm is exposed. Perfectly revealing the black, minimal tattoo of a lion's head and mane.

CHAPTER 22

THAT. BITCH.

I shove the rolled sleeve back over my forearm, fabric scratching my skin. What feels like my skin.

The wind suddenly starts to roar. It pushes hard against me, cold and inhospitable and seeming like it's trying to propel off of the tower.

I crouch down, waiting for the gusts to pass. Everything's drowned out. I can no longer hear the gunshots, the crashes and explosions. The echoing sounds of whatever might be happening down there. Just ghostly, shrieking wind.

I stare at the knife, at the lion's mane symbol etched into the blade.

For most of my life, it feels like I've been pulled along, trapped in the maelstrom of events outside my control. The death of my parents. Working for my aunt. The accident with Jackie—though I did have blame in that. Prison. Aberdale.

And now, this. Whatever this even is. Whatever they had even been doing to me at that Aberdale place, between my drugged out dazes. Whatever lies Tanya was now using to get me to do what she needed. Because even if she isn't lying, she's withholding the truth. Too much of it.

"It's impossible." I say, running a palm over my forehead. "How...how could..."

Because. The thought is crystal clear. Clearest I've ever had. *You're a victim. You've always been a victim. And you always will be.*

Suddenly, the wind clears, just as there's a flash right in front of me.

I stand quickly, the knife's handle gripped tight in my hand.

Tanya stands directly in front of me. She's panting. She has multiple scratches and cuts on her legs, arms, torso. Her coat is torn, frayed fragments fluttering weakly.

She searches my face. Her eyes are frantic, pleading. Then, her arm shoots out, grabbing me, and we both disappear.

We reappear inside the upper floor of a dusty, dilapidated shed. Our bodies fall sideways, slamming into protestingly creaky floorboards, knocking up a fresh storm of dust.

Tanya rolls sideways, away from me. In a flash, we're both kneeling, guns drawn, peering at each other through thick, falling clouds of dust.

"You know," I say. "As with most things, this wasn't my choice. I'm just caught in the tide. I'm used to that."

"Kit..." Tanya starts.

I click back the hammers with my thumbs. "Too used to it. I gotta say, I'm at a point where whatever agency I have left, I've gotta take it. I have to make a choice, even if it's the wrong one. So you need to tell me about the tattoo. In fact, you need to tell me everything. And you need to do it right now."

Tanya swallows, closes her eyes, and lets out a slow sigh. She slowly eases her arm back. She holsters her gun. And then she opens her eyes again.

I hold my revolvers steady.

"There were three undercover agents to begin with." Tanya says. "There's more now, but they usually aren't all operating at once. It takes them a lot of time and effort to get each one up and running, anyway."

She pauses, as if waiting for me to ask her to expand on that. I don't.

"Three agents." She continues. "One for each of the top guilds. There used to be three. Now it's just the Rifters and the Bannerets, though the Bannerets have an expiration date at this rate, I can tell you.

"Anyway, each agent was assigned to infiltrate their respective guild, using the information to track down criminals in the real. Sometimes, in order to prevent violent crimes, they would use Black Darts to execute criminals. I've already told you about that.

"The reason we were even able to confirm that this was happening was because agents were starting to turn. One of the agents came clean to the guild. Another agent did the same. Us members of the guilds found a way to free them from their respective facilities.

"One of them," Tanya was saying, eyes locked on mine, "Was Aberdale."

My revolvers start to shake in my hands. It's like I already know what she's going to say. Even though I don't. Even though it's impossible. Downright impossible.

"At first, we were successful." Tanya says. "We went on the run with them, kept them safe. They were going to help us fight back. We were going to get documented proof of what the government was doing.

"Then..." She took a deep breath, as if collecting herself. "They tracked down where we were hiding the second agent, the member of the Bannerets. They took him away. They..." She swallows. "*Did* something to him. Something so that when he synchronized again, he lured the third agent into a trap, and....and killed him."

Tanya's face twisted up. I could only stare, uncomprehending.

"The third agent was my brother. My little brother; Liam. The first agent was your friend, Oscar. The second agent...was you."

The barrels of my revolvers droop. Tension is leaking out of me, terror flowing in.

Tanya crawls toward me. Her fingers pry the gaps between boards, pulling herself forward.

My body is frozen. My mind is stuck in a circular battle of incomprehension, particles slamming into and negating each other in the hadron collider of my mind.

Sensations make themselves known, like emerging shapes from a dense fog. Tanya's trembling fingers move along the front of my jacket, upward, toward my neck and cheeks. Her face is contorting, forming tearless, sob-like spasms.

My hands are empty. At some point the revolvers slipped free of my limp hands and were now cradled in the gaps between boards.

Our faces are inches apart. Her forearms are shaking, laid flat against my chest. Her fingers touch the sides of my face, feeling my skin. She leans forward. Our noses touch first, hers nestling against mine, rubbing as she moves closer. Her lips press on me, on mine. Even though I'm cold and unreciprocating, a statue in her arms, she continues to press in closer.

Something snaps. I push her.

She falls back, sprawling, smacking on the boards.

I snatch up my revolvers. "I don't know you." *Especially not this version of you.*

"Sorry." Tanya pulls herself up. "Please, I'm sorry."

Though there's no tears, I swear there's something glassy in there. I can practically see myself in her pupils.

"I don't understand." I say. "You wanted me to implicate myself...and my best friend?"

"I wanted to free you!" Tanya says. She's standing now, stepping back toward me. "They're using you, Kit!"

"No." I say. "You are. How do I know—"

"The weapon." Tanya says. Her posture is suddenly firm, upright. "Once you have the weapon, you'll see."

I nod slowly. I'm suddenly, somehow, starting to feel like there's a way out of this. A way through the maze. A destination.

"Where's the gun?" I say.

"Oscar has it." Tanya says. "He'll give it to you. You'll see."

"Why?" I say.

"Because," Tanya says. "You're the second agent. The one who killed my brother. The gun belongs to you."

I can only grit my teeth at that. There's no point in arguing anymore. Not until I can see the truth for myself.

"Oh," Tanya says, reaching inside her shirt collar and removing the Black Dart necklace. "You're gonna need this."

"Why?" I say. "Because I'm the 'second agent'?"

"Because you know how to use it."

I take the necklace, hold it up. "I've never seen this before in my life."

Tanya shakes her head. "You'll see."

Again, no point in arguing with her. I holster my revolvers. I put on the necklace, letting the cylinder slide down underneath my shirt, strangely hot against my chest, dangling from the leather loop.

There's no weird feeling coming over me, no sense that anything has changed. Just a necklace, it seems. At the moment.

"Once you take the weapon, it'll be tied back to your character, and cataloged on the Dart. We can extract the data later, use it as evidence."

"I suppose you have some plan to do that." I say. "I bet you're already cooking something up. Some way to trick me."

Tanya slides her handgun out of the holster. I tense up, beginning to draw, but then she just tosses the gun. It clatters on the boards.

"You're gonna turn me in." She says.

"Um. Okay?"

"It's the only way to see for yourself." Tanya says. "Once he gets Sater, he'll give you the gun. And then he'll tell you to kill the both of us."

"No he won't." I'm smiling. I'm actually smiling. It's ridiculous. "He would never do that."

Tanya's face falls. She looks sad. Miserable, really. "And you would never kill my brother."

CHAPTER 23

THERE'S A BAR ON the outside of the shed, locking the doors closed, which seems like a weird choice. Anyone wanting to break in would only have to lift the bar. Not to mention there's nothing of value here in the first place. There are remnants; tables and racks mottled with dust and specks of dirt. Likely used to store materials and personal equipment. All empty. Old reminders of the way things used to be.

One exception. A length of thin rope hanging limp off the surface of a workbench.

I use the rope to bind Tanya's wrists.

"Let me know when it's too tight." I say. "You're gonna need to be able to break free."

Tanya nods, avoiding eye contact. Her wrists are slim, pale, and cold, like porcelain bars.

"Ouch." She mutters, flinching.

I slacken the knot. "How's that?"

She rotates her wrists. There's some flexibility, but at a glance it looks secure, like she shouldn't be able to break free.

"That should do it." She says.

I take her throwing knife and slide the blade through the gap in the doors and yank upward. The board pulls free of the brackets and falls to the ground.

The doors immediately begin to creak open.

I grab Tanya and lead her out into the open.

Tiny little dust devils lift and spiral in the square. The cobblestone street is smothered in layers and spots of slippery dust.

I have one of my revolvers drawn and pressed against her back. I lean close, whispering in case anyone's around.

"I thought they'd be here by now. You know, because we...furled."

"...what?" Tanya whispers back, almost hissing.

"You know. Furl?"

Tanya peers up at me. " Is that...even a word?"

"Yeah." I say. "You know, because you...unfurled, right? And then...what?"

A little smile is starting to curl up at the corner of her lips. "Maybe there's just something wrong with me, but it seems like you never stop being cute."

I stare at her for a second. "Yeah, there's definitely something wrong with you." I grab her by the shoulder and push, putting a little distance between us.

Still, it's hard not to think about that first impression I had of her, when the garage door opened. She's a cute one. And definitely my type. And isn't it just what everyone wants, to have that person in your life who never stops fixating on you, on the qualities they find attractive in you?

Maybe. But I can't afford to focus on that, right now.

It's all too...confusing.

"Point is," I say, "Shouldn't he be here, by now? You said they can track the thing."

"Generally speaking, yes. He knows we're in the city. He might even know what part."

I glance up at the sun, then over at the tower. We were in the eastern side of the city. Probably quite a ways out from the market plaza south of the tower, where I'd seen the bulk of any activity earlier.

Seemed like a good place to start.

"C'mon." I say, pushing her. "Let's get moving."

*****

Time seems to compress. Every step on the cobblestone walk brings us closer to the inevitable.

Tanya walks a few paces ahead of me, hands bound in front of her. Dust rolls around our feet, like a river churning. Around us, doors and shutters bang and creak on their hinges. The hems of Tanya's coat riffle in the breeze, bullet holes whistling as air squeezes through them. Loose, torn tatters flap like little flags.

I find myself staring at the back of her neck, bare and pale. Tiny beads of sweat cling to the hairs of her lower scalp.

I could have been in love with this woman. She could have been telling the truth. I had told myself I couldn't afford to think about it, but here I was.

Because of course she hadn't been lying. No one can lie with their eyes, like that. With touches like that. If such a thing is possible, then the world is far more lonely and sinister a place than I had previously imagined. And I have quite the imagination.

I knew it was true. Of course I did. I just didn't know what to do about it.

That's not the only thing that's true, I think. *If she's telling the truth. The world in which you love this woman is the same world in which you kill her brother. But then, that's just the sort of thing you do, isn't it?*

Something in me recoils, protesting.

This person Tanya had been talking about, the "second agent". She claimed it was me. But it wasn't. If anything, it was some other version of me. Like a figment, or a spectre of some alternate reality.

I didn't have the second agent's memories. His thoughts and feelings. His experiences. Tanya could spend hundreds of hours explaining what had happened in that interim, and I could do my best to try and imagine them, but they would never truly be mine. It was a bizarre, surreal sort of tragedy, unfolding right in front of me. Nothing I could do to stop it.

Don't.

But I have to ask anyway.

"Are they my friends?"

Tanya cranes her neck, looking back at me. "Who?"

"Mason and Sater."

She nods. "You're very close. Though at the moment they do hate your guts. And who could blame them?" She faces forward. "There's something so strange about watching one of your best friends suddenly turn around to kill another. It's a difficult visual to reconcile, no matter how you try to explain it away."

A sense of unease creeps over me. It feels improper to be talking about this figment, this alternate reality. Like I'm butting in on business that isn't mine.

Don't.

"Do you hate me?"

Tanya makes a quick, surprised glance at me. "Like I said. It's...difficult to reconcile."

I should feel something from that, if I'm the agent. Sadness and disappointment and loss. Instead, I'm clinically turning this information over in my mind, a casual observer overhearing someone else's gossip. Any memories I might have of her, any feelings of love, are behind some unseen veil, inaccessible to me.

I'm startled by a pair of dark figures in the path ahead, backlit by the afternoon sun. Even from their shadowed, barely discernible body language, I can tell they're surprised and excited to see us.

One of the figures stands stock still, wary of us. The other jogs over.

As she draws close, her features come into focus. She's about my height. Curly hair. A fedora. A long dustcoat. She has a pistol at her hip and a double-barreled shotgun in one hand, its stock bouncing against her waist as she runs.

I grab Tanya by the shoulder and pull her closer.

"We've been looking everywhere for you, mate." She says, stopping in front of me. She's friendly and personable. No guard up at all. She recognizes me, and doesn't seem to have any doubts that I wouldn't recognize her.

They trust you completely. As far as they're concerned, you're on their side, now.

"I've been looking for you guys." I say. "Had to tussle with this one." I prod Tanya in the side with the barrel. I can't see her face.

Curly Hair nods and gives Tanya a hard look, looking her up and down. "Bitch was giving us trouble, but I knew we'd take care of her. I can take her off your hands for ya."

"I got it." I say.

Curly Hair gives Tanya another glare. She turns toward me, cocks her head a little, seeming to take that for a reasonable answer. Though somehow not completely happy about it.

"Where's Oscar?" I say.

Curly raises an eyebrow, giving me an otherwise blank look.

I get the hint after about a half second. "Peacelock." It's a username Oscar came up with back in the Final Fantasy XIV days. It managed to stick.

Curly points. At first I think it's in the direction of the market plaza, but her arm continues to angle upward, in the direction of the tip of the tower.

I gaze toward the sky, putting up a hand to shield my eyes from the sun.

There's something up there. A little pinprick of darkness poking out of the tower, stark against the sky's open blue, like the shadow of a fish in the ocean. The shadow undulates, and I can just barely make out Oscar's raised arm, waving to me.

I wait for a couple seconds. Oscar doesn't move, continues to wave. Here on the ground, Curly watches me, expectantly.

I'm hesitating. If I'm honest with myself, I'm worried about what's going to happen if I leave Tanya alone with these people. But if I don't move, things are going to start to happen without me. I'm going to get left behind.

I look over at Tanya. It's not a lingering look, but it's enough for her to look back. There's no overt signal. No nodding or tilting of the head. Just a look. But it's enough. It's okay to leave her.

She'll be okay. She will.

I push her toward Curly. "Take her to the plaza. Wait for us there."

"Rock on, then." Curly says. She puts up a fist. I fistbump her, which she seems to appreciate. She grabs Tanya by one of her bound wrists and begins to drag her away. As she does, Tanya tilts her head towards me, mouths three words.

"You got this."

And then, her back is to me, as she's carted away, into the enigmatic future.

I pull myself. I stare up at the tower. At Oscar. Then, I close my eyes. I imagine myself at the top of the tower, near that white crack in the center of the platform, breeze fanning—

CHAPTER 24

THROUGH MY HAIR, THE low whooshing of pressure against ——— and around the girth of the tower.

Reminds me of the time Oscar and I decided we were going to start a podcast. The first episode was useless. We did it outside on a windy day. The recording was completely ruined by the blustery wind. Playing it back, it sounded a lot like the top of this tower.

I open my eyes.

Once again, Oscar is standing with his back to me, at the edge.

"Where were we?" he says, "Oh yeah." He waves me over.

I take a few tentative steps over to the edge, next to him. The heels of my boots are slick with dust from the streets below.

"We took this city together, you know. The two of us." Oscar says. "It was really something. Like something out of a Marvel movie."

"Did we have to kill anyone?" I say. I can't help it. The question, and the hard, accusing edge it has to it. I need to know. No matter what, I need to know.

Oscar sighs, looking out over Opus. He's annoyed. I can tell.

"I should probably ask." He says. His irises are the color of wet leaves in the fall. "When was the last time you remember seeing me?"

I think back to that time out on the gravel lot, Oscar's blank face pressed against the rocks.

But that's not right. Not really.

"You're gonna think I'm crazy." I say. "Honestly, maybe I am."

"You're not crazy." He says. "After all you've been through, you have every right to be. But you're not."

"We'll see." I say. "Oscar, I—just before I synchronized. I saw you. In the Bedford house. I—" It hits me. Oscar's expression confirms it. "That was actually you, wasn't it?"

Oscar nods. "I'm in the room, right now."

For a second, I just stare at him. "Fuck."

"And a squad." He says, glossing over my outburst. "We disabled the stream hours ago. Blocked off the roads. No one's coming. No one's getting —"

"Mason?" I say. "What happened to him?"

"He's not going to be able to make due on his promise." Oscar says. "He can't hurt you."

A heavy stone drops in my gut, pulling me down.

There was a time when this information would have relieved me. But now I know that Mason didn't actually want me dead. He just wanted to motivate me. He wanted us all to get out of this.

I can't understand why they didn't just tell me.

Would you have believed?

Maybe at this point it doesn't matter.

"Hey." Oscar grabs my shoulders. "Before that, though? What do you remember?"

Something snaps. Everything that's been building in me for the past ten years.

I shove Oscar's hands off me. "What else? You. Dead on the ground. Because of me."

Oscar slinks a few steps away, eying me like a stranger.

"Don't you have anything to say about that?" I say. "What I did to you? What I did to your sister—"

"Everything we could say about it has already been said." Oscar says, face falling. "We've had this conversation before, okay? More than once. And it always ends up the same. Because Jackie isn't actually dead."

The wind picks up and rustles Oscar's hair, dangling tendrils against and around his face like reeds in a stream.

"What?" I say.

"Medically, in a way, she is. But her mind...she can still come here. When they allow it."

"What the hell are you talking about? Who's *'they'*?"

Oscar just looks at me. Then, "They really did take everything, didn't they? All of it."

"I was kinda hoping you'd tell me it wasn't true." I say.

Oscar swallows. "Come with me."

*****

We unfurl in the middle of the market plaza. Dust kicks up in tall, ragged plumes, briefly obscuring the sagging, decayed buildings surrounding the square.

It's difficult to determine what parts of the damage are from the gunfight minutes ago, or just the result of the steady, unhindered progress of time. It seems that even virtual worlds, sufficiently simulating real life, cannot escape the reality of entropy. Like a hurricane-ravaged shipyard.

The Rifters, dotted amongst the graveyard of buildings, are like bits of wreckage bobbing in the wake. They are young and old, male and female, short and tall. There's no one element unifying them as a group, except perhaps their penchant for survival and adaptation. There's more on the line than just the game for them. They need Rithium. It is a way for them to stay in good standing with criminal gangs in the real world. For some, it's the one thing keeping them out of prison, or the rehab facilities.

I know this, because I can see it on their faces. None of the wild-eyed excitement and enthusiasm that I associate with the early days of Rithium. Only a tense, focused expression. I feel like a sports player in the field, looking up into the stands, seeing a silent wall of expectant, anticipating faces. It's the one thing that is tying them all together, in this moment. That, and the name of Rifter.

They don't trust me. Not all of them, anyway. They want something from me. They're looking to Oscar, not me.

I can tell this as Oscar walks ahead of me. He whistles, loud and shrill, two fingers clamped between his lips.

Damn. Always wished I could do that.

A series of loud *thumps* echo in the air. Something long, black-scaled, and definitely a dragon swoops up over the Opus wall. It passes over the sun, casting a long, cold shadow across the square.

There's a person clutched in its claws, talons interlocked like the bars on a cage.

The dragon's wings grow louder, the force of its flaps causing dust to push off of the cobblestone street. The remnants of surrounding buildings creak and moan, wobbling on their support beams.

The talons spread wide, and Sater's limp body falls soundlessly against the stones.

Oscar marches over, Beretta in hand. He kicks Sater in the shoulder. "Come on. Up."

Sater jolts upright. He clambers to his feet, wiping the dust from his eyes.

Oscar's free hand moves quickly, snatching Sater's knife and bow and tossing them away. He snaps his fingers. Two of the closest Rifters bound forward, grabbing Sater and dragging him over to where—

Tanya.

She's on her knees in the outer edge of the square. There are several Rifters standing next to and behind her, weapons at the ready, watching her.

She's watching me. She's just barely far enough away that I can't read her face.

The two Rifters set Sater down next to her, before stepping off to the side, awaiting further instructions.

There's another loud flap as the dragon circles, veering to the other side of Oscar, facing me. It extends its legs, bracing for the landing. Then, it drops. Its talons puncture the street, sending out spiderleg cracks in the cobblestone. The ground tremors. To my left, a support beam finally gives out, and an entire structure snaps apart and crumbles, wood splintering.

Oscar turns to face me. Behind him, the dragon crouches, its eyes on me, waiting obediently.

"This must be so confusing for you." Oscar says.

"It was." I say. "I think I'm starting to catch up."

Oscar nods. "We'll talk. I promise we will. But first, unfinished business."

He walks toward me. Somehow, it feels like there's this massive gulf to be crossed between us. One he crosses in the space of twelve paces, in the middle of that square.

He stops in front of me, draws a tucked pistol from his belt, and puts it in my hand.

It's a glock. It's black and cold. The handle is dimpled and scratchy against my palm.

Something strange happens, as soon as it's in my hand. Something I've never seen happen in Rithium, before. The entire glock shimmers, turning see-through, white outlines making out the shape of it, before going back to normal, like some weird glitch in the matrix. There's a sudden warmth there, a pulse.

The data transfer.

The weapon's data has been restored to the Black Dart. If we get out of this, Tanya can upload the information, use it to prove what happened. That the weapon was used to—

For a moment, I just stare at it, like a dead fish from a stranger. Like I don't know what I'm supposed to do with it.

Do it.

I hold it up. I use my index finger and thumb to pull back the slide. I peer into the ejection port. A bullet rests snug, ready to be fired. The shell is pitch black, with intermittent white lines running across it.

"Lines have been crossed." Oscar says. His voice sounds far away. "Transgressions made. But I fought for you. I convinced them things could be different. All we had to do was turn back the clock. Things would be different, I told them. So I let them. I let them do it. Because—"

"Transgressions were made?" I say. I hold the glock limply in my hand, almost dropping it. "I was on the wrong side, so you had to sort me out?"

"Kit, you made a promise to me." Oscar says, firmly. "Like I said, we've already talked about Jackie. You know what you told me? You said that you would do anything to make it right. Are you telling me that's not true, anymore?"

I have no recollection of this, but I know it's true. I would have done anything for Oscar. Anything to try and make things the way they were between us. To make things better. Years of medicating myself with Rithium still hadn't changed that, or done anything to take away my guilt. Even though my memories of this are apparently just fragments anyway, and my brain's attempt to piece together some kind of cohesive whole. Yes, there was a period of time, before I was locked up in rehab, when I continued to associate with people like Samuel, so that I could stay away from the law, and put off the withdrawal. The rest is a blurry, drug-addled flash of images that could have been several years inside Aberdale. It could have been only the last month, or a week. It's a broken puzzle, so many pieces strewn and disconnected. Most have fallen off the table. I may never see them again.

"If I don't remember that conversation," I say, "Did it actually happen? Was that person even me?"

Oscar's jaw clenches. He's starting to look impatient. "Don't get abstract and philosophical on me. WE are the Black Darts. It's us. These," he holds up his Dart necklace. "These are just tools. We use them to get the job done. Because the government tells us to. Because the consequences of disobedience are worse than the actions themselves. We knew that. You can't just disavow that. You can't just walk away, pretend it never happened."

"You can always walk away." I realize that now. I don't know why now is the time that it comes to me, after so much of my life believing otherwise. Such a sweet, terrible lie extended out over so much time. Such a grand, horrible truth.

I always had a choice. I was never a victim. Perhaps no one ever is.

"You're right." I say. "It was always a flawed plan. There was always going to be one thing standing in the way. And it's you. You're what's stopping the Bannerets from putting an end to this.

"Stop it." Oscar says, face twisting into a snarl. "It's over. This operation was saved, today. Things will continue as they always have. The only question is, are you going to be a part of it?" He gestures toward Sater and Tanya, hands bound, on their knees against the stone.

I look at them. Sater with his messy, gel-infused hair, full of dust and dirt, bruises scoring his arms and face. Tanya, with messy curls of hair veiling her eyes. She jerks her head, waving enough of the hair away that she can look at me. She's panting, like a runner who's tripped and fallen, her mess of hair rising and falling to the beat of her lungs.

She trusts me.

I can tell, even from that wide-eyed look, as sure as if she'd spoken it aloud. She was shaken. Discouraged, even. But she still believed we were going to get out of this.

It's then that I notice Oscar has his back turned, putting some distance between us as he walks closer to the dragon. When he turns back around, there's a sad glint in his eyes, a sheen that could be mistaken for tears. He unclips his holster strap, fingers brushing the gunmetal, ready to draw.

"Do it, Winter. Or I will. First him. Then her. Then..." He breaks off. "C'mon, Kit. It's now or never. They're not gonna let me stretch this out."

Slowly, I lift the gun, gripped tight in my palm. I point it at Oscar.

There's a cacophony of gun clicks, cocks, and slide snaps as the hundred or so Rifters surrounding the square level their weapons at me.

Oscar just shakes his head. "You pull that trigger, you're gonna wake up dead."

I pause for a moment, then lower the glock. I could never do it. And there wouldn't be any point. It's a failed bluff.

I pull the glock back, sliding it in my belt, cold metal pressed against my lower back. My hands fall to my sides, hovering a few inches from my revolvers.

"No. I'm done. You're gonna have to do it yourself."

Oscar's brows furrow. "No remorse, huh? No guilt? Don't care what you did, anymore?" Lines draw. His face twists up with rage, teeth bared. "You knew it wasn't safe. You didn't care. You put yourself first. You *did* this."

I stare at Oscar, eyes dancing between his face and the fingers touching his Beretta. But in my mind's eye, I see his lifeless face, laid back against the cold gravel. For one long, interminable moment, it's all I can see.

I jerk my head forward. A curt nod. An admission. "You're right." I say. "I knew it wasn't safe. I didn't care. I put myself, and my problems, first. I *did* this."

I let out a long, low sigh. It's something I've known all along, though I could never quite admit it. So much energy to put into something so futile. Perpetuating the untruth. Defying gravity.

Because it wasn't that it was who I *was*. Calling myself worthless, and a piece of shit, was somehow easier.

It was something I *did*. An action I took. A choice I made. Not some nebulous sense of self. A vivid, definite reality.

It's not about me.

It's not. Still, I can feel the relief and catharsis pouring over me, filling me up. Even if Oscar never forgives me, maybe I can still face this. Maybe, there's hope.

"I'm sorry." I say it without thinking. No need to think. No need to filter, or obfuscate. To myself, or anyone else. Not anymore.

As my exhale tapers off, and I take a deep breath, even though I'm not in the real, it feels like the first real breath I've taken in ten years. I can finally breathe again.

I drop my hands further, slowly cupping the bone-white revolver handles with my palms. My legs are spread apart in a steady, ready stance.

"I hope one day you can forgive me."

"Then *do* it." Oscar says. His face falls, slackening. "*Please.*"

I slowly rotate my head, teeth clenched tight in my mouth. "I'm sorry." I say again.

For a second, it seems as if Oscar might break. The wind ebbs, winding its way through the market. Oscar is motionless, save for the tangles of hair dancing against the side of his face.

Then, as the gust wanes, his brows knit back together.

"Me too."

The joints in Oscar's wrist go taut as he clamps down on the Beretta, knuckles white.

I activate my Action Skill. At the same time, there's a hum coming from the Dart, throbbing against my skin. That's when I realize-

Tanya was right. I do know how to use this thing.

Something kicks in. Muscle memory. Intuition, perhaps. The Dart buzzes. I can use it in conjunction with my Action Skill. I can use it to draw it out, augment it-

Oscar draws his Beretta. It's happening slow. Painfully slow. And there's nothing I can do to stop it. All this time I'd been trying to provoke Oscar, to turn him on me. But it didn't work. Because he's pointing the Beretta at Tanya.

For a brief flash of motion, I can see the bullet itself. And then it's in her.

CHAPTER 25

BLOOD ARCS OUT OF Tanya. She keels backward, pulled by the force of it. Her body flashes see-through, then solid again, like the Glock did in my hand.

"Well, what are you waiting for?" He yells. "*Get him*. Before his Action charges back up."

Nononononononononono

Thoughts compress, jumbling together.

(*Not the gravel lot, not the gravel lot*)

I Unfurl(eyes open, this time), pulling in on myself, matter disappearing, like there's a black hole in the center of my chest. For one microscopic second all of Rithium seems to morph, becoming a grey void, every person, object, and thing replaced by scrolling walls of text, lines of frantic code.

No time to stop and wonder.

Everything morphs back to normal as I Furl next to Tanya's fallen body. Time still moves slow. Flashing lines of lucidity run across her like bolts of electricity. I'm already pulling my revolvers from the holsters, cocking back the hammers with my thumbs. To the other side of me, Sater is on one knee, pushing himself upright. His wide eyes pivot in their sockets, turning toward me with almost comical lethargy.

I point one of my revolvers at his face. *Sorry, bud.*

It's the only way to keep him safe, now.

I pull the trigger, initiating a loud *thump* that echoes loud and relentlessly, soundwaves overlaying, trapped by my slowed perception of time passing. A spark of red issues at the tip of the barrel. Recoil bounces the revolver in my hand, pushing back against my palm.

Sater's face caves in, a massive hole bored by the sheer force of the bullet. His neck snaps sideways, body pulled inexorably toward the street.

There's no flash, no see-through stuff. I would have had to use the Glock for that. I already told Oscar I wouldn't do it. Never would. But this way he might be safe in the real, at least for another few moments.

That's why I aim the other revolver at Tanya's head. Her eyes are pure white, irises rolled back as she writhes in slow-motion on the ground. Something strange is happening, but she might not be dead yet.

Please be okay.

I pull the trigger, turning away just as the bullet makes impact with her skull.

Then, I turn, leveling a revolver in Oscar's direction, while I try to raise the barrel of the other revolver up toward my head, so I can off myself. The movements of my arms and hands feel frustratingly sluggish, like wading in waist-high mud.

The revolver moving to point toward Oscar reaches its destination first. Oscar has his Beretta angled at me, one eye clamped shut as he looks down the sight. In my peripheral, I can see the clumps of Rifters behind and near me scrambling, pushing each other, trying to get out of the danger zone.

I pull the trigger, just as the tip of the Beretta flashes yellow. There's a spark of light as the two bullets collide, pinning together in an arcing bit of shrapnel. They spin, swerve, and hit a Rifter in the head just a couple paces to my side. His head blows apart, body flashing once before falling, lifeless. Dead.

I can feel my Action Skill starting to wind down, time speeding back up to its normal cadence. Too late, I notice the bits of air curving inward on Oscar as he prepares to Furl. He disappears, and I feel a blast of air from behind, jostling me, whipping at my coat. I feel one of Oscar's hands grab the revolver I'd been trying to point toward my head. His other hand is groping inside my coat, reaching for the Glock. I pivot, trying to shoot him, but his fingers find the Glock, and the motion allows him to easily pull it free from my belt. That feeling of the Dart's connection to the Glock goes away as soon it's off my person. Oscar releases my hand and sidesteps, ducking a shot from one of my revolvers and furling again.

Oscar refurls on top of a building on the opposite end of the plaza. He tucks the Glock away.

CHAPTER 26

THE RIFTERS ARE STOCK still, frozen with apprehension, despite Oscar's orders. They've gone from expecting(or hoping) to see me come back to their ranks, to watching me kill their hostages, to Oscar turning on me again, with one of his errant bullets taking out one of their comrades.

The Curly-haired woman from before looks to the fallen Rifter, then to Oscar, then to me. There's a metallic snap as she pulls back the hammers on her double-barreled shotgun.

Nope.

I unfurl, refurling on top of a support beam on the edge of the square, just in time to hear the shotgun blasts go off in the street below. Bits of the beam start to shred apart from gunfire as I set my eyes on an alley below, out of sight from the market square. I teleport, hitting the ground running. I alternate between capping off the ammo of both revolvers with fast, practiced motions.

My Action Skill is still charging, but they can't get me, not as long as I stay on the move. Oscar knows that. He's trying to distract and keep himself out of the line of fire. All I have to do is get the Glock back. That, or take his Dart away. Or just shoot him. That's an option for me, too. And he doesn't want that. He doesn't—

There's a rush of hot air behind me. I glance behind in time to see a stream of flame running down the alley in my direction. Turning down another alley, I unfurl. As I furl, boots skidding on alleyway dirt, I slam into something. It's Oscar.

He slams into my shoulder, knocking me backward. At the same time, his arm lashes out like a snake, fingers closing around my Black Dart, dangling from it's necklace as I fall backward.

He pulls. The string pulls tight against the back and sides of my neck, digging in. All at once, the threads snap.

I try to shoot him midfall, but his boots dig into the ground and he shoves forward into me, unfurling us, our surroundings disappearing.

When everything comes back, we're still hanging in the air, falling. Behind Oscar, all I can see is the sky, like a massive blue ball marbled with white.

He kicks me, somehow pushing me further down, accelerating my descent.

"WE'LL ALWAYS HAVE THE MEMORIES." He yells. "WELL, AT LEAST I WILL. GOODBYE, WINTER." He gives me a stern salute.

I bring up both revolvers, but he's already gone. It's just me, and the sky, and the whistle of the wind in my ears, the flap of my clothing, like flags on a pole.

I turn, revolving in the air so I can face downwards—

My right shoulder and side slams into a slanted roof, which immediately gives way underneath me. Below is an attic floor. I crash through that as well, boards snapping and splitting, beams creaking at the joints. I flip in the air, back crashing against the floor.

For a few horrible seconds, it feels like I can't breathe. I'm motionless on the floor, staring up at a hole in the ceiling looking more than a bit like a rip in a picture book. Dust falls like ashes around me.

Miraculously, I still have the revolvers, fingers wrapped so tight and taut around the handles that it feels like they've been fused to my body.

I jump to my feet, dust swirling around me. I'm on the bottom floor of an abandoned, ransacked house. The only thing that remains is an ugly, floral-print couch in the corner, sitting on a dusty, hardwood floor. I glance down and see my silhouette in the dust, like a snow angel, along with some spider leg cracks in the hardwood.

There's a loud bang from just outside the building. A gunshot. A Rifter signaling I'm here, in this building? I can hear dozens of pairs of boots clattering on the street, coming close.

He has the Gun. He has the Dart. That means it's over, doesn't it?

Maybe. Perhaps it's just the inevitable playing itself out, at this point.

Tanya. I can see her collapsing on the ground, writhing, blood welling on her chest, running down her neck and into the dirt.

My jaw clenches. It's gonna play out, all right. All the way.

I quickly snap open the cylinders on my revolvers, topping off one then the other with bullets from my ammo belt.

He doesn't want to face me. Wants his lackeys to dispose of me. Once I'm in the real, he'll do the same. He'll want to give me some speech, maybe even offer me some chance at redemption. But he won't want to pull the trigger. He'll leave the room. Maybe drive off, first, out of earshot.

I know it's true because if the roles were reversed, I wouldn't want to pull the trigger, either.

Perhaps a bit too much credit to give to Oscar—or this version of Oscar—at this point, but it does seem like one likely explanation.

I flick the revolvers, snapping the cylinders shut, just as the shots start.

CHAPTER 27

THE IMPACTS START AT one end of the house, blowing bits of wood and brick debris into the living room, little craters scissoring their way across the length of wall.

I dive to the floor in time to hear the volleys whistling over my head, cracking and crumbling the walls, baseboards, and hardwood all across the bottom floor of the house. Puffs of stuffing explode from the ugly couch like popcorn.

There's so many gunshots, so much noise, that it all seems to run together, morphing into some massive, ear-wrenching superbomb of sound.

Then, all at once, it stops, replaced by the *clicks* and *clinks* and *chik-chik*'s of a hundred people reloading their guns.

Amateurs.

I push myself up and begin dashing for the window I can see through the open bedroom door on the opposite end of the house. As I pass one of the windows by the front door, I let off four shots in the direction of the mob out front. I don't stop to see the damage.

I quickly cross the threshold of the bedroom and jump, diving for the window. As I break through the wood frame and glass I've turned my body to face the front of the house.

Sure enough, as I hit the ground—landing on my left shoulder—two excited Rifters appear around the corner. They haven't finished reloading yet, and are fumbling with their weapons.

I shoot one in the head, then the other.

I scrabble to my feet just as I've let off the second shot. A gaggle of extra Rifters have started to appear around the same corner. I dash to the other side of the alley, still firing as I crash sideways through another window.

Adrenaline is kicking back in. I'm in the zone, acting without thinking. Gaming. I've been doing this for years, and I'm just starting to get warmed back up.

My revolvers are empty. I put them away for now as I book it toward a staircase at the opposite side of the house.

They must be able to see or hear me, because the shots have started up again, cutting wood, shattering glass, whistling and pinging.

I grab the stairwell railing, whipping around the corner and up the stairs, just as a bullet zips just past my head, sending wood shrapnel flying from the far wall. My steps sound crazy loud as my boots thump on the stairs, even with all the gunfire. Bullet craters follow behind me as I run, one hand on the railing.

Two floors later, and I'm at a door leading to the roof. I slow, grabbing and wrenching the knob.

Locked.

I take a second to pull out the rifle strapped to my back, then kick the door, crashing it open and causing it to swing wide on its hinges.

I dive forward into a prone position on the roof, fully expecting that the doorway itself will quickly be blown apart by gunfire.

I'm right. Bits of wood spray across the roof like fresh flakes of snow. I turn left to see three figures standing on top of the building next door. I swivel in their direction, still prone, and begin firing, cocking the lever between shots, empty shell cases bouncing up and past my right eye. I start with the target on the left and keep firing until they're all on the ground, then I jump to my feet, turning toward the doorway leading up onto the roof, where I hear dozens of boot steps pounding up the stairs.

Without pausing to discern what's on the other side of that doorway, I start firing into the shadowy stairwell, muzzle flashing. As I continue cocking and firing I step toward the doorway. Between shots I can hear the crashing sounds of people being knocked through the railing, or backward and into their Rifter colleagues, leading to a fleshy, downhill domino effect.

As I step into the doorway I can clearly see the dozens of fallen Rifters all along the stairwell, struggling to untangle and get back to their feet.

I keep squeezing the trigger, arcs of blood streaming up out of fallen, trapped bodies, like sandbags filled with red dye. Those that aren't trapped are trying to maneuver back down the stairs, or over the railing. I aim for those, too.

Click. Click. Click.

Empty.

Immediately, an array of barrels poke up through the railing and out from underneath some of the bodies.

I dive backward, avoiding the hail of the gunfire as I land on my back on the roof. I roll off to the side and start running to the edge.

I jump. The buildings here are packed close together, each alley only a couple paces wide. I land on the rooftop next door. I can hear Rifters running and yelling on the street below.

Need to get off here. Soon these rooftops will be brimming with them, I'll be completely out in the open. As I run, I scan for some kind of ladder or fire escape. Gusts of wind start to pick up, rustling my clothes and pushing me, like a hand pushing me, each rush punctuated by a loud whump sound in the air—

Nope. Not the wind.

I turn just in time to see a thick, scaled, obsidian tail swinging toward me, striking me across the torso.

I'm thrown sideways, wind rushing in my ears, lungs seizing. As the world flips around me, I'm reminded of the first and only time I rode a rollercoaster in the real. I can almost hear the rumbling squeal of the rails.

Don't throw up. It's super uncool to throw up.

I'm on a horizontal trajectory toward the rooftop of a neighboring building. I'm upside down, my head lower than the rest of my body, watching the corner of the rooftop fly toward me. Too fast for me to move or adjust.

One side of my face hits the corner, and my body bounces, skidding across the rooftop, everything spinning. Roof, sky, roof, sky.

The roof runs out, just as my spin slows, and I'm looking at the roof of a market booth in the square. I crash through it, wood splitting, beams crashing down on top of me. One of them hits my upper back. Another one lands on my leg, pinning me.

I'm already wriggling underneath the beam on my upper body, trying to roll it off of me. No time to assess the damage quite yet. Not time to—

Wet warmth trickles down the left side of my face. I reach up to touch it, but as soon as my fingers make contact with my left cheek, I can't see that hand anymore. Because the left eye is gone.

I can hear the Rifters cheering, rushing toward the square.

I heave, lifting the beam and dropping it off to the side. I sit up, reaching for the one on my leg, pushing it, twisting my ankle. I manage to slough it off, pain registering in my ankle as I do so.

I push myself up onto my feet, in the middle of a tangle of dilapidated booths smack in the middle of the square. The nearest place I could even try to disappear is on one end of the plaza. Though the fronts of the buildings are all boarded up, there's a slim, dark alleyway in the gap that would at least limit their visibility of me.

I start limping, slipping through and climbing over the wreckage until I'm in the open, dragging my bad leg.

Behind me, the sounds of the mob's footsteps have petered out, replaced by laughing and cheering. One of the Rifters lets off a shot that ricochets off a chunk of cobblestone a few paces ahead of me. Not aiming for me. Not even a warning shot. A taunt.

I don't even look back. I just keep limping forward, my one good eye on the dark alleyway ahead.

Behind me, there's the loud snap of a double-barreled shotgun being reloaded.

"Give it up, Winter."

I recognize the voice. It's the curly-haired one from before.

I freeze, perhaps ten paces from the alleyway's opening. With effort, I turn around.

Curly is standing ahead of the rest of the group, shotgun leveled at me. The rest of the fifty or so Rifters, fanned out behind her, have their guns trained on me as well. The second I reached the alleyway they would have unloaded on me.

It's over.

CHAPTER 28

J AMES "SATER" GIFFORD SNAPPED awake.

He cocked the shotgun. "Get in the car, *boy.*"

He was on his belly, cheek pressed against the grainy carpet. A dull blue bar of light ran across the floor next to him, beaming down from the skylight, imposing itself on the shadowy room.

Somewhere in the room, he could hear an intermittent hissing sound, like pressurized air leaving a canister. It happened every two or three seconds, every gap as silent as the dead of the night in a giant house, or at least the moments when a house wasn't settling, creaking and moaning like a person alive.

It was like a ghost story. He was on the ground, vulnerable. There was something strange in the room, something he could only just barely perceive, but it was there.

Sater started to get up—a motion not unlike doing a push-up—and felt a sharp jab in his lower back, shoving him back down against the carpet.

"It's alright," a firm, male voice said. "Sit him up."

Gloved, scratchy hands grabbed Sater by the shoulders, pulling him. He considered struggling, but the earlier hit had taken the air out of his lungs, leaving him gasping. Besides, it seemed preferable to die sitting rather than pressed face down into a carpet that, by his estimation, hadn't been shampooed in seven years.

The hands belonged to a pair of outfitted SWAT Officers. They wore long camo sleeves and bullet-proof vests, and the lower halves of their faces were covered in dark cloth. They had rifles, hugged tight against the body by straps that looped over the shoulder. There were a dozen or so of them, most standing stiff and still, shadowed statues on the far side of the room, past the couches.

After sitting Sater up, the officers stepped back in the dark parts of the room.

Of the three couches, one was empty. Kit was still lying on one, apparently still synced in to Rithium. Sater wondered if Kit realized it was over, yet.

There was a man sitting on the third couch. He was leaning back, fingers interlocking behind his head. Sater couldn't see his face.

Sater glanced around the room, hoping to spot Mason. In the dark of the room, it took a moment to realize Tanya was lying on her back on the floor. Her eyes were clamped shut, but her jaw was trembling. It seemed like her entire body was shaking.

Sater leaned over to—

"Don't." It was the man on the couch.

Sater ignored him. He felt her, trying to tell if she was having a seizure.

"She'll be dead soon enough." The man on the couch said. "They always are."

Sater opened her mouth, checking to see if she'd bit her tongue. He pressed a hand against her neck, feeling for a pulse. Her heart was pounding. It was beating so fast.

Oh, T. Nonono....

"It's funny," The Man said. "Someone gets shot in a drug bust and there's paperwork, ballistics, forensic investigations. But if someone OD's on Rithium...well, it's just the way of the world, isn't it? Thousands of people die from Rithium every year."

"It's not Rithium." Sater said, distantly. What was he even doing? He wasn't a doctor. He had no idea how to help her. "There may be side effects, but it's the drugs that do it. The ones pharmacists peddle to the doctors. The ones they pump into people after you lock them up."

"You can't prove that." The Man said.

Sater turned toward him. "Not yet."

There was an awkward silence following that, occasionally interrupted by the hissing sound. What *was* that?

The Man leaned forward on the couch, half of his face cutting into the bar of light cast by the moon.

The Man was clean-shaven. He had a clean, short, tapered haircut, combed and styled. He wore a white, button-down shirt with the sleeves rolled up and a long, black tie.

"Do you know why you're still alive, James?"

Sater cringed at the use of his given name. To all his friends and associates, he was Sater. To his estranged parents, Police officers, and the DMV, he was James.

He didn't answer.

"I almost have to wonder, myself." The Man said. "After all, we can't exactly let you live. And, I mean, look at all this." He waved around at the room, indicating the officers. "For a bunch of gangly wimps like you. Kind of overkill, don't you think? I don't even know who half these guys are."

The Man gestured at one of the officers. "Son, what's your name?"

"Richard Davis, Sir." The Officer said.

"Huh." The Man said, smiling to himself. "See? Didn't know that. Anyway, we could paint this whole room with your insides, if we wanted to." He pointed a finger at Sater like a gun. "We're talking blood, guts, bits of bone flying everywhere. Brains blowing out the back of your—" He stopped, just as he was gesturing with his hands, articulating what such a brain explosion might look like. "Point is, we're not going to."

He watched Sater, clearly waiting for him to ask why not.

Sater said nothing.

"Because," The Man said, as if Sater had asked the question, "Down at the department, we like things clean. Ballistics are not clean. Forensics teams scouring this whole house and carrying out little plastic baggies with bullets in them is not clean. Four unfortunate criminals OD'ing on Rithium? Clean as a whistle. That's why," He checked his wristwatch, an analog with hands that glowed bright blue when he tapped the glass. "In about...seventeen minutes, we're gonna log you back in and finish the job."

"Fascinating." Sater said.

"Thanks." The Man said, leaning back on the couch. "I know that the circumstances aren't so favorable for you, but it's nice to be able to converse about my work. It's not exactly the kind of thing I can talk about over dinner."

"Why not?" Sater said. "You don't think people want to know you killed four innocents, today?"

The Man smiled and wagged his finger. "Don't you try that with me. I'm not the one breaking the law here. There are consequences. You broke into a rehab facility, drugged a patient—"

"Nobody broke into anything." Sater said. "You're the ones who drugged and moved him. All we did was intercept."

"You can't prove that." The Man said.

There was something disgusting about the dysphoria at work, here. Conflating the ethics of a thing by whether or not he would get caught doing it.

"Besides," The Man said, "Not to split hairs or anything, but I don't kill anybody. That's up to our rockstar, here. Have the two of you met? In real life, I mean." He turned toward one of the officers. "Why don't you push him forward, I don't think he can see him."

The officer stepped back into the dark, and suddenly, somehow, Sater knew. This was real life, not the movies. People are easily broken. When they are, they rarely come back whole. When they do, it's considered a miracle.

Sater heard wheels turning, grinding against the carpet. A silhouette of both the officer and the wheelchair he was pushing slowly came into focus, like a conjoined creature. There was another loud hiss of air, and Sater realized it was coming from whatever was in that wheelchair.

The officer stopped wheeling the chair once the entire front of the subject was easily visible, subtly painted by the blue light from above.

Dark skin. Matted patches of hair, as if most of it had fallen out long ago. Tubes running out of his nose, connected to canisters on the back of the chair. One eye that spun about the room, examining every corner, taking in every detail. The other eye was dull and grey, like a clear, glass marble. His neck and head were contorted, angled so that his dead eye was mostly turned away. It seemed like he couldn't move or speak. It seemed like the only thing he could control was that one, frantic eye.

Just as Sater was thinking this, the eye settled on him, fixated.

"Oscar, meet Sater." The Man said. "Sater, this is Oscar."

The eye didn't move. Didn't seem to even blink.

The Man watched Sater, studying his reaction. "Incredible, isn't it? This thing is the backbone of our operation." He turned, eying Oscar with some distaste. "It rather defies belief. I mean, so good at what he does. But...just look at him."

Sater's teeth clicked together. He glared at The Man. "It's enough to make you sick."

The Man balked. "Oh, don't look at me like that. We've given this kid a life. A purpose. Enforcing the law!" He reached over and patted Oscar on the shoulder, then drew his hand back, regret written on his face. Oscar's very presence seemed to gross him out.

"Did he ever have any choice in the matter?" Sater said. "Oh, who am I kidding. Who wouldn't want to throw in with the likes of you?"

"Now, don't try to butter me up." The Man said. "We've already discussed this down at the department. If the Bannerets can turn the Winter Wolf, they can turn anybody. Except for our rockstar, of course." He started to reach out and pat Oscar again, but he stopped himself halfway. "No, it's time to wipe the slate clean. Start fresh." His countenance suddenly became serious. Or self-serious, anyway. "No more kid gloves."

The Man's phone rang. "Yes?" He stood and began pacing the room. "Uh-huh. Yes. Of course."

He put away the phone, turned and looked down at Sater. "Slight change of plans. Sounds like some of your Banneret buddies have decided to brave the machine. We'll see about that."

The Man walked over to Oscar, knelt down in front of him. "Time to put down some Bannerets. You ready? Look at me, Rockstar."

Oscar's eye finally left Sater, turning on The Man.

"Good." The Man said. "Now, once you take care of the Bannerets, it's time to bring this chapter to a close, alright? You gave your friend a chance. He didn't take it. End of story." Without waiting for an acknowledgement, The Man stood. "Send him back in." He said this to the officer standing just behind the wheelchair. The officer leaned forward and pressed a couple buttons on the side of the chair.

Oscar's eye, which had turned back on Sater, started to flutter, until it finally clamped shut.

The Man dropped back onto the couch and clapped his hands together. "Everything's clicking. Feels good." He tapped the glass on his wristwatch again. "Making good time, considering. Seven more Bannerets. Easy money, my friends. Easy money."

Sater found himself reaching for his belt, where he'd kept his gun. Ridiculous, of course. They had removed it already. If only he could will one into existence. Hack real life, like using a Dart in Rithium.

He would have used the gun, too. Even if it meant dying immediately afterward. He was on his way out, anyway. At the very least, he could try and throw a wrench into the Feds' plans, possibly saving some of the Bannerets in the process. He could put a bullet right through The Man's smug, pristine face.

Only that wouldn't work, would it? The only way to ensure the success of the Bannerets' mission would be to eliminate the one threat standing in their way. It would mean killing Oscar.

Suddenly, for no real reason, Sater remembered.

"Where's Mason?"

The Man frowned. "Who?"

"The only other person who was here?"

The Man snapped his fingers. "Oh, yeah! Mr. Pudgy. This is actually kind of embarrassing, considering everything I said earlier. We were forced to...you know." He made a slicing motion across his throat. "Could've been handled a little better. Still, nothing a little shampooing won't take care of. Seems like this carpet could use it."

It took every ounce of willpower Sater had not to rush him. To jump up and over the coffee table, grab him by the throat. He'd be dead halfway there, but that almost seemed an insufficient reason to hold back.

"Now, don't get mad with me. The man was armed. Really, it was self-defense." But judging from his smirk, this was not a sincere sentiment. "Look, if it makes you feel any better—"

He stopped, put a finger on a little earpiece he had in his ear. At the same time, all of the officers were exchanging looks, seeming unsettled.

The Man stood suddenly. "Could you repeat that?" Then, "What fire?"

That was when Sater noticed the reddish, yellowish, flickering lights being cast outside the window. They seemed to be growing, carrying with them the increasingly obvious, acrid smell of smoke.

*****

They cuffed Sater, cool frames of metal clamping down over his wrists. They carried the unconscious forms of Kit and Tanya, heaving their limp bodies up and over the shoulder, like lumberjacks carrying blocks of wood.

One of them carried the cloudbox. Another tagged behind, carrying the mobile power generator the cloudbox was connected to.

Oscar's wheelchair seemed to have it's own battery-powered cloudbox built into it.

Two officers walked on either side of Sater, holding him by the arms. A third walked behind, and had made it clear his rifle was trained on Sater's back.

It was crisp and cold out, stars glimmering like frost under a moon. Except when the wind picked up, carrying with it gusts of warmth from the east edge of the property, and smoke.

Together, a strange and unlikely caravan, they walked half the length of the estate, crossing the long, thin, flickering shadows of trees.

There were two black vans on the outer edge of the property, just off the road. For almost the entire trek The Man had been on the phone. Once they reached the vans, he put it away.

The Man started pointing. "You, and you. Get over there and—"

He froze.

It took a moment before Sater heard it himself. The low growling of an engine, somewhere in the dark. Building in intensity, growing close.

"Get to the vans! Quick, move your asses!"

Headlights lit up the road. Tires screeched as the vehicle, whatever it was, started to slow.

Sater was practically picked up and carried, closing the gap to one of the vans within seconds.

Someone opened the side door, and The Man stepped in first, with Sater being pushed in behind him.

That's when Sater saw it, thanks to the ceiling lights inside the van. Sater's own gun, wedged inside The Man's belt.

Without much thinking about it, Sater dove forward and snatched the gun, pressing the barrel against The Man's lower back.

It took a split-second to realize just how light the pistol was, that the magazine was missing. And yet, The Man had stiffened up at the touch of the barrel, frozen. Which meant he either hadn't removed the round in the chamber, or couldn't remember whether he had done so.

"Where's the magazine?" Sater said.

"Bad idea." The Man, putting an upward inflection into the words, like admonishing a child. "Really bad idea."

"I'm a dead man with one round in the chamber." Sater said, loud enough that he hoped all the officers could hear, even over the rumbling engine of the unknown vehicle just outside. He resisted the urge to turn and look behind. "If you don't do as I say, it's going right into your spine."

"Right front pocket." The Man said.

Sater looped his free hand around, reaching into the pocket of The Man's jeans. He pulled out the magazine, heavy with rounds still, and fed it into the pistol. There was a resonant click as the slide snapped forward, loading a round into the previously empty chamber.

"Mother *fucker*!" The Man spat, clearly having heard it.

Sater grabbed him by the collar. "You're coming with me." He yanked, pulling The Man backward and out of the van.

When they turned around, the dozen or so officers were facing them, rifles in hand.

Sater curled himself behind The Man, jamming the pistol tight against his back. "Tell them to back the hell off. And leave behind my friends. And the cloudbox."

There was a moment of silent apprehension.

"Do as he says!" The Man barked.

The officers slowly stepped backward, leaving the cloudbox, Kit, and Tanya lying on the ground in front of them.

"Further!" Sater said. "Keep it moving."

The group took a few more reluctant steps backward.

Sater pulled The Man along, rounding the corner of one of the vans so he could get a look at the new vehicle. It was a dark—maybe even black—Humvee. The sides and tire treads were caked with mud and dirt.

The front passenger door popped, and someone stepped out of it. He was wearing loose, unbuttoned leather vest and a bandanna over the lower half of his face. He waved.

Sater blinked, bleary-eyed, trying to stay focused. "Who are you?" Sater said.

"Does it matter?" The masked figure said back. "It's not like we came up with a code phrase."

For a second, Sater studied the guy, trying to decide if he recognized him.

They had to be Bannerets...right?

And did it matter, anyway?

But the masked man didn't wait for confirmation. He slapped the hood of the Humvee twice. Two more doors popped open, introducing two more masked people. The three figures walked slowly. They picked up the cloudbox and generator, Kit, and Tanya, and headed back toward the car.

Sater started to follow them, then stopped. "Wait. The one in the wheelchair. Him, too."

But the SWAT team had already made a barrier in front of Oscar. The officer Sater was making eye contact with slowly shook his head.

"Huh," Sater said, leaning forward into The Man's ear. "Sounds like they have orders to protect him over you."

"*Shiiiiit.*" The Man said. "*Shitshitshitshit—*"

"Shut up." Sater said, pressing the pistol even harder into his back. "And try not to make any sudden movements. Wouldn't want my finger to slip."

Perhaps it was the adrenaline just as much as the hatred Sater felt for this man, but the fact that he hadn't pulled the trigger already seemed itself a testament of self-control.

He led The Man around to the back of the Humvee. One of the masked people opened the back hatch. Kit and Tanya were laid flat in one corner.

"Get in." Sater said, nudging The Man into the opposite corner of the hatch. "You don't want me to ask twice."

"What happens if you do?" The Man said over his shoulder, snarling.

Sater didn't hesitate. He slammed the butt of his gun into the bridge of The Man's nose, cracking it like a nut.

The Man yelped and gurgled, blood spurting through the nostrils of his flattened nose.

"Counting to three, asshole." Sater said. He was more than ready to hit him again. The rage building in him wasn't even close to being spent. Seeing The Man respond with this much shock and alarm to violence against himself, a man who committed murder without batting an eye, just sprayed gas onto the fire.

"You'll regret this!" The Man shrieked. But he crawled into the hatch, back pressed into the corner.

Sater hopped in after him, putting himself in the middle of the hatch, between The Man and where Kit and Tanya were laying.

Someone shut the door. It was still bright inside the hatch, with light beaming in from the front compartment.

Sater laid on his side, gun pointing at The Man, who had been disfigured into a mad, bloodied, petulant creature.

The engine revved, and they were moving.

Occasionally The Man's mouth moved, slurping up the flowing blood like soda from a can. He didn't move, barely even blinked.

"Know what you did?" The Man said, once they were out and speeding on the highway.

Sater gripped the pistol tight, didn't take his eyes off him.

"It's not gonna be clean." The Man said. "Not anymore. I can tell you that."

Sater didn't answer, but he was starting to get a sinking feeling somewhere in his chest. He angled the pistol, pointing it at The Man's face.

He should pull the trigger. It would be the only thing about this entire situation to come out right. To make sense.

But he could feel his grip on the pistol relaxing. A little.

"I gotta wonder, what's gonna happen to you once this goes public?" Sater said. "Once we prove what you did. Where will you go?"

The Man didn't scowl, or balk. Quite the opposite. His lips spread in a bloody, grotesque smile.

"You have no idea what you're messing with, do you?"

"Tell me."

"You're—"

Sater bashed the butt of his gun into The Man's nose. Again.

The Man howled, recoiled, slammed the back of his head against the side of the hatch, thrashed.

Sater thumped the roof of the hatch three times with his free hand. "I think it's time to drop off the trash."

"Couldn't agree more," someone said from up front.

The Humvee slowed. One of the side doors popped. One of the Bannerets came around back and opened the door.

"Out." Sater said, indicating with his pistol.

The Man scooted, flopping out of the hatch and onto the asphalt. He jumped to his feet, stepping backward away from the car.

Sater stepped out of the hatch and shut the door, still facing him.

Past The Man, in the distant dark, Sater could make out the headlights of two different vans heading steadily toward them.

They needed to move.

"This isn't over." The Man said, limping backward.

Sater turned and ran for one of the side doors.

"This isn't over!" The Man yelled.

But as soon as Sater grabbed the door, a gunshot went off. It was a shockwave of sound, crashing against the hill on the opposite side of the road, ringing like a bell.

The Man keeled backward. Blots of blood speckled the asphalt, illuminated by the neon red brake lights.

The Masked Man was holding a pump-action shotgun. There was a loud mechanical click as he loaded a new round, and the plastic *ping* of the red, empty casing bouncing on the road. He took a few steps toward the downed Fed, leveled the barrel down at him.

When he fired again, the sound was just as deafening. Sater shrank back—though he should have been ready for it—and pressed his body against the Humvee.

When the Masked Man pulled the trigger, the only part of his body that moved was his shoulder, absorbing the force of the shotgun blast.

Sater's eyes were locked on the Masked Man. He didn't look down, afraid that what he would see would be less like a person and more like a spilled pot of spaghetti in the road.

The Masked Man turned and slowly headed back to the car, seemingly unperturbed by the rapidly approaching van headlights.

For a stunned moment, Sater just watched him.

"Didn't catch your name." Sater said.

The Shotgun Wielder lowered the mask covering the lower half of his face, revealing a hooked nose and a stubby chin. Sweat glistened on his wrinkled pate.

Though Sater had never seen this man before in real life, he was unmistakable. Avatars in Rithium are projections of the consciousness of the player. While there are always differences, most of the physical features tend to be the same.

This man was Diren, leader of The Wolves.

"You've gotta be shitting me." Sater said.

Diren smiled, revealing a glinting, silver tooth at the corner of his mouth.

CHAPTER 29

THERE'S A THIN, DARK alleyway just a few steps behind me. But I'd never reach it in time. I'm facing down fifty gunmen, fanned out in the square.

Seems like I lost my rifle in the fall. My two revolvers are still intact, but they're both empty. Sword feels like it's still there, strapped to my back. For whatever help it could possibly be in this situation.

Dying in Rithium means waking up. It means having to wait twenty minutes before being able to log back in again. Which, I wouldn't be able to, anyway. It's over.

Only, it isn't. The others are waiting on Curly, and I don't think she's ready to send me on. It won't be enough. I can see it mapped out on her face, the way her brows are knit together and her jaw keeps clicking back and forth. One of her friends is dead, and in her mind, it's because of me. This brief moment where I'm in her power is almost over, and she doesn't want it to end.

But it will.

Curly clicks back the hammers on her shotgun. "One last thing before I send you on, yeah?"

"Incoming party request. Do you accept?" Janice's sudden announcement cuts through the awkward silence, making me flinch. Only I can hear it, but for some reason I look at Curly's face to see if she did, or if she can tell if something's off.

Well, she probably can now, genius.

No idea who the party request is from. But at this point I don't think it matters. No time to ask, anyway. Whatever buttons are left on the console, I'll push them.

"Yes?" I say.

"Confirmed." Janice says. Then, she goes quiet.

I have to stop myself from looking up, trying to spot my new party members. Whoever they are.

"Incoming voice chat." Janice says, once again startling me.

"Don't look up." A new, unfamiliar, female voice says. *"Stall."*

"Why don't we make this interesting." I say, eyes locked on Curly, interrupting whatever she was about to say. I've got an idea forming. It's not ideal, but it's something.

One of Curly's eyebrows lifts upward. "What, are we playing games, here?" But the barrels of her shotgun droop a little.

She wants more from this. She wants to defeat me completely. To humiliate me.

"One against fifty isn't much of a game." I say. "Hardly fair, anyway."

"It would only take me. The rest of them just got in my way."

"You a good draw?" I say.

"Better than you," she says. She turns to the nearest Rifter, scowling. "You. Give me your iron."

After seeing the look on her face, the Rifter doesn't hesitate. He unclasps his gunbelt and hands it over.

Curly hands the Rifter her shotgun. She straps on the belt at her waist, holster resting against her thigh. She draws the revolver and spins the cylinder, checking to make sure it's full. Satisfied, she sets it back down in the holster.

"Load up, little man."

I'm a fast reload. This comes from years of practice inside Rithium, as well as researching world-record techniques on YouTube. But right now, the game is to stall.

Every movement is a calculation. A test to see how slow I can move before being called on it. Each individual bullet carefully grasped by my finger and thumb, raised up to chest-height, hesitating for a couple seconds before being dropped into the next cylinder.

"What the hell is taking so long?" Curly yells, as soon as I've loaded my second bullet. She's shifting weight back and forth on the balls of her feet, practically bouncing.

"Just give me a second." I hope she thinks I'm nervous, shook up. She wouldn't be entirely wrong.

If she wasn't so worked up, she would probably be able to hear the sound of the party that's slowly spawning in, descending from the sky. I can hear it, but mostly because I've been waiting, listening for it. It's a faint whistle, echoing down from above. Barely discernible.

Yet.

As I go to load my third bullet, my hand 'slips', dropping the revolver onto the dirt, spewing the once-loaded bullets onto the ground.

"Seriously?" Curly says.

"One second," I say, leaning to pick it up.

"Nope." Curly says. "Stop. Kick it over. This is ridiculous. I'll load it myself."

I shrug. "Okay." I pull myself back up to full height. I kick the revolver. It skids, bounces and scrapes across the dusty, uneven cobblestones, coming to a stop when it hits Curly's boots.

She snatches it up. "Geez. It's like you've never played this game before." After opening the cylinder wheel, it takes her a little under six seconds to load it, deftly snapping up each individual bullet and clicking it into place, spinning the wheel as she goes.

Once she's finished, she closes the wheel with a sharp *clack*. "Here."

She tosses it.

I move to catch it, but instead I let it bounce off my hand and onto the ground.

At this point, Curly is scowling. "You're beginning to make me wonder if there's even any point to this. *Winter*." There's a mocking edge to the way she says my name. The name of someone she used to work with and look up to, but has now turned his back, and is going to pay the price.

The whistle coming from the sky is getting louder. I lean to pick up my gun. Out of the corner of my eye I see one of the Rifters tilting his head back. The person next to her follows suit, followed by several others. By the time I'm upright again, revolver in hand, dozens are now gazing up into the sky, toward the loud whooshes of air, growing closer every second.

Everyone except Curly. Her eyes are still on me.

"Forsythe!" Someone yells, which is apparently Curly's name because he reaches out and grabs her by the shoulder.

She shrugs him off. "Don't touch me—"

I angle the revolver at waist-height, aiming at Forsythe's face, and pull the trigger.

Her head snaps back, face concave, gore slingshotting out the back of her skull.

I squeeze the trigger again, aiming for the guy who grabbed Forsythe by the shoulder.

I hit him in the neck, causing him to choke, knocking him backward into the crowd of Rifters, just when the rush of air from above starts to sound like a speeding car, the Doppler Effect in action.

Then, the street explodes.

CHAPTER 30

BITS OF THE STONE plaza fly up like fireworks, materializing from the thick, newly-formed clouds of dust between me and the Rifters. There are no gunshots, no shouts, no running footsteps.

I myself have a vague feeling that I shouldn't move just yet, frozen in apprehension.

As the dust begins to clear, I can start to make out the backs of my six new party members.

One of them swivels toward me. She's wearing gray, metal pauldrons, with a black hood, and a black cape embossed in gold with a lion: the symbol of the Bannerets. She holds a lever-action rifle at the ready.

Her expression is anxious. "Go!" She hisses. "Fight!"

So few words. So much ambiguity. Or perhaps not.

Not that there's time to ask questions, anyway.

Bannerets have shown up to fight, or at least to buy me some time. Tanya didn't want to endanger them, but here they are, risking their lives.

Whether they've shown up for my sake or for the Bannerets is a moot question. I *AM* a Banneret.

And I'm not going to let them down.

I make an about-face and hurl myself into the dim slit of an alley, barely able to fit the width of my body inside, shoulders practically scraping the brick walls as I run. Have to put some distance between myself and the Rifters. I don't know what the next step is, but I doubt it's getting shot and ejected from Rithium. Not that.

Gunshots popcorn behind me in the plaza, crackling and pounding. The shots echo ominously in the walls, transmitting clearly along this thin length of alley that's three or four stories high and who knows how many blocks long. There's something strange and unnatural about it, suffocating.

I hit an intersection and keep running. The alley feels like a narrow trap, but as tempted as I am to loop out of it, it makes more sense to keep putting as much distance between me and the Rifters as I can.

Thankfully, the alley starts to widen, curving outward, and then I see something that makes me run faster. Then, once I'm sure it's what I think it is, I'm running as fast as I can, boots stamping over the mud and stones.

It's strangely damp here. Damp and cold. A shadowy crevasse in the city.

I slow to a stop, skidding on the mud. Oscar is just ahead of me. His back is to me. He's crouched, back and neck hunched forward, hands pressed over his head.

I don't know how to interpret this. What it means.

More than anything, a part of me wants Oscar to get out of this unscathed, get things back to the way they were. As unlikely as that might be.

"Oz?"

I shouldn't have said it. I should have rushed him, tried to take him by surprise. But the word is already spoken, hanging in the air.

Oscar's head tilts toward me. His eyes are wide and bloodshot, his expression strained. He jumps to his feet.

"Oscar, wait!"

But he's already running.

I chase after him. Twisting and turning through corridors and passages, him always just barely within my sight, barely out of reach.

He begins running up a steep, stone flight of stairs. I take after him. I try to outpace him, but no matter what, the distance between us stays the same, like there's an invisible force field keeping us apart.

He hits the top of the steps and disappears from sight.

"Oz!"

I race up the stairs. They level off onto a plaza not unlike the market square. Dust turns and travels lazily across the ground, carried by a slight breeze. Over uneven cobbled stones. Past disheveled buildings.

I recognize this place. It's at the center of the city, sitting just next to the Opus Tower itself.

Sure enough, on one end of the street there's a black, all-encompassing wall, like voidspace. As if the end of this street was in fact the end of the world.

Standing in front of that obsidian voidspace, facing me, was Oscar.

He no longer has that strained, panicked look. He looks calm. Focused. Intelligent. Like he has some kind of plan, and there's no question it's about to be carried out.

I walk over to face him. Slow, watching his body for any sudden movements.

I'm suddenly wary of him. Closer to the level of caution that I should have had before, if I had actually been thinking clearly. The problem with me and Oscar, is that things just aren't clear.

Oscar regards me, unhurried. Waiting.

In the distance, I can hear the gunshots. Yelling. The dragon roaring, the air pounding with the beat of its wings.

They got it. They're holding off the rest of the forces so that I can take this chance. However slim it might be.

Movement.

I can feel muscles throughout my entire body tensing. My fingers twitch, extending toward my holstered revolvers.

Oscar could draw his pistols at any moment. It would take one shot. One shot, and I would be dead. Really dead.

But instead, he reaches into the pocket of his cargo pants and pulls out a Black Dart. My Black Dart.

I reach out and catch it one-handed, my other hand brushing against the revolver at my hip.

Oscar smirks, seeming to take satisfaction from my tense reaction, thinking it's some kind of trap.

It might still be.

"Why?" I ask, eyes locked on him. My fingers are wrapped tight around the cord. The pendant dangles.

Oscar shrugs, face falling a little, out of the smirk. He looks sad. Solemn. "It's time to play. For real."

He wants to play with you. Like a cat with a mouse. But why?

But perhaps I know. Perhaps it's the only thing he has left. The only part of our relationship left. The last thing he can siphon away before it's gone.

Like always, we will play.

Still, I feel a plume of righteous anger building up in me, like a hot lance in my chest.

"This isn't a game." I say. "This isn't split screen Call of Duty." On a Saturday night. A minifridge in Oscar's room topped off with OJ and Mountain Dew. An open bag of chips on the floor between them. Both of us laughing with excitement over a crazy play.

Jackie politely knocking on the door, asking to play. Oscar and I exchanging glances, neither of us wanting to share the smaller screen on the tube TV.

"You're right." Oscar says. "It's better."

"You think Jackie would say that?"

He doesn't answer. But that in itself is an answer. He just looks at me. And I know. What I should have known. What I always did know.

Jackie really is dead. Jackie is dead. We killed her.

I killed her.

I feel the hot lance in my chest dissipating, falling. And falling.

"Why?" I don't have to elaborate on the question. *Why did you lie to me? Why did you give me a long-lost ember or hope, only to snuff it away?*

Oscar's hands move down to the black, holstered guns. "So that you would play."

My jaw clenches, teeth grinding together.

Screw it. Let's go.

I pull the hand off my revolver so I can put the Dart necklace over my head.

"Still not a fair fight though, is it it?" I say. "Your guns kill."

Of course, it's a silly and perhaps pointless ploy to try and get my gun back, get the data I need, end this right now.

Oscar shakes his head. "If I don't win this game, we're both dead."

I don't get what he means by this. But one thing at a time. One giant mountain to leap over at a time.

"I don't know how to use this thing." I say, gesturing to the Dart necklace. "Not as well as you."

"That's okay," Oscar says, patient. "You'll remember."

Then, he jumps, flipping backward. When he lands, he's standing firmly on the side of the tower, defying gravity.

He motions, beckoning.

"Come on," he says. "What are you waiting for?"

CHAPTER 31

SATER'S NOSE BROKE THE first time Diren's boot made contact with it. Diren followed this first stomp with a frenzy of kicks, a look of focused consternation on his face, like he'd discovered a rat on his kitchen floor and was trying to crush it completely.

He was sitting upright in the corner of the Humvee hatch, one elbow resting on the back of the backseat. His shotgun was gripped tight in both hands, propped on one leg, the end of the barrel pointing at Sater's face.

Sater found himself staring into the bore of the shotgun, the way one might be transfixed by a deep, gaping hole in the earth. Occasionally he would bring up his hands in an attempt to block or deflect the kicks, only to have his own knuckles shoved back into his face.

His nose no longer felt like a part of his body, something that belonged to him. It was an aching, throbbing piece of pulp, attached to his face by wire. Any second now it would begin to break apart, sliding off his face in chunks. That or the chunks would stay, but they would be pushed up and inside his face, lodging there, perhaps even entering his brain.

Blood flowed. He couldn't taste or smell anything else. It was like having a molten nickel lodged inside his head. It flowed over his lips and down the back of his throat in streams.

Then, after an indiscernible amount of time—but for the omnipresent night still brushing against the exterior of the Humvee's tinted windows—the kicking stopped.

Diren panted, practically wheezing. A layer of sweat gleamed on every visible part of his body, running over his tan, leathery skin like oil on the ground.

Sater coughed and sputtered, scattered specks of blood from his nose and mouth. It felt like he was breathing through a wet, sloppy noodle.

"Was that good for you, too?" Sater said. His voice sounded alien, contorted.

Immediate regret. He got another stomp to the face, boot heel making contact with the lower half of his face, rattling his jaw. He felt a shooting pain in his mouth, like being stabbed, and a fresh gout of blood. He spat onto the floor of the hatch, and white spots poking out of the red.

For a moment, he just stared, taking a mental snapshot of the bits of broken teeth. Then, he started laughing.

It was the kind of laughing fit he'd used to get into as a little kid, when his older sister was teasing him, wouldn't stop tickling him. The manic, uncontrollable kind. It just came out.

It didn't sound the same, though. It was guttural, sputtering. Like an engine turning over. Tiny flecks of red shotgunned around, hitting various parts of the hatch, landing on clothes, and gunmetal, and the scratchy fabric on the back of the car seat.

Diren's face twisted into the visual representation of a growl.

He opened his mouth, but whatever he was about to say, he didn't get a chance to say it. A bullet tore through the hatch door, punching a hole in the seat and splintering the windshield in an array of spidery cracks.

"Do I need to get up there and drive myself!?" Diren roared.

There was no answer, only the clamor of the engine as the driver slammed on the gas. The Humvee vibrated. An infinite conveyor belt of pine trees rolled past, melded together in a kaleidoscopic blur.

More gunshots. Sater could hear them zipping past, like little airplanes. Occasionally, they glanced off the exterior, thumping loudly. In Sater's head, they were making little sparks, like in the movies.

Sater erupted in another bout of laughter.

It was all so ridiculous.

Diren lurched forward, shoving the barrel of his shotgun into Sater's gut, punching the wind out of him. He held it there, pushing.

"Don't you worry, boy," Diren said. "You and your buddies aren't dying today. You've got your whole lives ahead of you. A life with the Wolves."

He pulled back, leaning on the seat again, seemingly at home with the situation. "Yeah, we're going to get along well. Real well."

Sater slumped sideways, struggling for breath. "Somehow...I doubt it..."

It was Diren's turn to laugh. "What a find! Our very own Bannerets. They even know how to use the Black Darts, too. There's two, right? Between the one your friend has on him and that guy in the wheelchair?"

Diren watched Sater, waiting for an answer. Didn't get one. Didn't need one.

"That's the next phase of our plan, you know," Diren said. "Retrieving the other Dart. One is good. Two is better. We learn how to use one, keep it safe. The other...well, I know a guy who says he can disassemble and reverse-engineer the thing."

Sater's gut did a loop-de-loop. Though maybe part of that was the bullet that had just pinged off the hatch, not far from his head.

More Dart's in circulation, huh? Great plan. Excellent.

"Let me get this straight," Sater said, propping himself up. "Someone convinced you to bring them a Black Dart?"

"Who do you think you're talking to?" Diren said. "An amateur? Diren's always two steps ahead. If not more. Look where you are."

"Being shot at by Federal Agents?" Sater said. *Also, did you just refer to yourself in the third person?*

As if on cue, a bullet ricocheted off the top of the car.

Diren's jaw clenched. He was tense, but it seemed like kicking the shit out of Sater had soothed him somewhat, kept him more level-headed. It had been a release. That was the feeling Sater had, anyway.

"Coming up on the target." Said someone in the passenger seat up front. "Should be a couple minutes."

Diren nodded, before turning back to Sater. "You don't give me enough credit, you know." He said. "You never have."

Diren was a brute force kind of guy. Literally. Rithium wasn't just a game, to him. He'd show up at your door, break into your house. Sater had always known that much. He was a criminal first, Rithium player a far second.

Perhaps because of this, it was hard to imagine Diren's problem-solving skills were particularly sophisticated, overall. Though, the events of today may have punctured a bit of a hole in that.

Because really, the man did have a point. He had showed up at the right place, at the right time. He hadn't managed to get Oscar as part of the deal— yet—but he seemed to have been prepared for that. He seemed to still have a plan.

"Running a crew isn't about being the smartest, or the toughest." Diren said. "It's about who you know. It's about making sure the people who *are* have your back. I learned this a long time ago."

He leaned back, setting the back of his head against the window, resting the shotgun on his leg. The driver seemed to have put some distance between us and the feds, and there hadn't been any gunshots for a good minute, now.

"Do you know how tall those vans are?" Diren pointed back, in the direction of the pursuing van down the road.

Sater only managed to take a deep breath, inhaling blood. It was getting harder and harder to breathe. Everything was swelling up.

"The top of the van is about..." He held up his hand flat, palm down. "Ten feet off the ground. Nine-point-twenty-five feet, actually." He lowered his hand, as if moving it down a scale that Sater couldn't see. "All the seats have the same height. If you calculate the average height of the teams, their heads come to about a foot below the roof."

"Average?" Sater said. He coughed. He was starting to feel light-headed. "Calculate? Those are some five-dollar words for you, Diren."

"Like I say," Diren said. "It's about who you know."

"Someone you know...is playing you..." Dark spots were popping in and out of Sater's vision.

Diren didn't seem phased. He pulled a phone out of his pocket, seemed to be checking something. Once he put the phone away, he turned toward the front of the car. "Slow it down. Just a little. I want our friend to see this."

He grabbed Sater by the collar, dragging him over to the hatch door window. "Don't pass out just yet. The fireworks are about to start."

CHAPTER 32

I ANGLE MY NECK back, staring upward. Oscar is calmly staring back, hands in his pockets, feet firmly planted on the side of the Opus Tower. He watches me, patiently. Expectantly.

Despite everything, it's so ridiculous, I almost burst out laughing. You'd think at this point, nothing would surprise me. But it does. Because games are supposed to have rules. They are simulations. They have a connective thread to reality.

There is nothing real about this. No in-game reason or mechanic explaining why or how this could be happening. This is true of Furling as well, but for some reason, this just hits different. The visual of it. Like seeing someone suddenly take advantage of an over-the-top glitch or cheat code.

"If you're really expecting me to join you up there," I say, "I think you're about to be disappointed."

Oscar cocks his head. "Hardly seems fair. For me to be defying the laws of physics while you're stuck on the ground, there."

"That's what I'm saying. I don't...remember how to do that."

"Oh." Oscar says. "Right. I keep forgetting. There's all these versions of you. Like layers. Timelines. But when I look at you, I just see...you."

My muscles are tight. I'm ready to draw at any second. Because this needs to be over. But at the same time, I have to ask.

"How did they do this?" I ask. "How did they make me forget?"

Oscar shrugs. "Does it matter? Do you really even want to know?"

I don't answer. He knows I do.

"Drugs." Oscars says. "Brainwashing. Bogus therapy sessions. And who knows what else. What do you think those facilities are all about? They lay the groundwork. They plant...triggers. Then, when it's time, they execute. Making people forget is just part of it. A way to cover their tracks."

It makes so much sense. But at the same time, it seems...wrong. Impossible.

"That's impossible." I say. "How could so many people—"

"Nobody knows anything." Oscar says. "God, we've had this conversation so many times before— It's all isolated. Cogs making other cogs turn, not having a full grasp of the nature of the machine. Engineers build the technology, without knowing what it's for. Workers administer pills based on what flower has been left in the room, whether it's a sunflower, or a rose. Therapists say what they're told to say, never clear on the full effects of what they're doing. Most patients don't really remember the sessions anyway, they're all so drugged up—"

"Except you." I say. "Somehow, you seem to know how this entire thing works. They don't erase your memory, because you're one of them. You're their lapdog—"

Suddenly, Oscar bursts out laughing. It's a harsh laugh, laced with dark humor, and contempt. "You're more right than you know. But not for the reasons you think."

I have no idea what he's talking about.

"They've tried." He says. "Some people are more prone to manipulation, because they manipulate themselves. You live in a world of your own making, Kit. You always have. You think it protects you, but it doesn't."

"What's that supposed to mean?"

Oscar shrugs. "Whatever. All you need to know is that the techniques don't work on me, for some reason. Maybe that's why I'm able to see how it works in the system. Whatever it is that blocks people from seeing it doesn't seem to work on me."

"What do you mean?" I say. "What do you mean, 'in the system'?"

Oscar lifts up the Dart at the end of his necklace, shakes it. "Why stop at hacking the game when you can hack the people, too."

I shake my head. "That doesn't make any sense."

"Look," Oscar says. "You're the one with massive gaps in his memory, asking *me* what's really going on." Then, "Not that I couldn't...reverse that. If it's really what you want. It would save us a lot of time."

It takes me a second to absorb what he's saying. What he's implying.

He wants a real fight. The last game we ever play, the two of us.

Or maybe he just wants his old, whole friend back. Even if it's just for a few minutes.

Assuming it's even possible. Assuming he's not trying to trick me, psyche me out.

"If that was actually possible," I say, "You would've already done it. If it's such a time-saver."

"I could have." Oscar says. "Plenty of times. I chose not to. Soon enough, you'll know why."

"How ominous."

"I was trying to protect you." I can see his throat bob as he swallows, hard. "But it looks like we're past that, now."

He flips forward, away from the tower, rolling his body.

I take a step back, drawing both my revolvers.

I should take the shot. He's vulnerable. Mid-trajectory. Perhaps even unsuspecting.

"Not that I couldn't...reverse that."

Since the beginning of this, all I've wanted is to remember. To understand. Instead, all I have are these vague shapes. Secondhand accounts of theories of my life. Stories I'm supposed to trust without ever really knowing for myself.

Oscar lands directly in front of me, close enough to touch. He frowns.

"Don't say I didn't warn you." He says.

Then, he reaches out and touches my forehead with the tip of his finger.

CHAPTER 33

SUDDENLY, THERE ARE TWO versions of me. The one who remembers, and the one who doesn't. One is quickly and irreversibly absorbing the other, like a twin in utero.

Memories flow, squirming, leeches latching onto my consciousness, making it so I—

—can't stop running, even months after Oscar's death; years, even. I run security detail for gangs who have managed to get their hands on cloudboxes. Security inside Rithium, that is, though I do help vet the people they bring into the fold. I develop a knack for detecting undercover Police, keeping them out. In return for my services, I usually get room and board. And Rithium access.

The last guy I work for—my longest stint working for a specific gang—is this guy named Lex. Lex is smart. He has lots of cloudboxes, running in lots of places. It's decentralized. Even when one of his places gets hit, the effect on his operation as a whole is minimal. For a while.

That's when the raids start to happen. The ones inside Rithium, that is. Cops coming in and disrupting meetings, compromising locations. Some of Lex' guys who get taken out stop showing up. At the time, we're not sure what that means. Everything's happening so fast.

This new cop starts showing up. Someone I don't recognize right away. He works hard to keep his identity hidden. From me, anyway.

He's good. Really good. Not only that, but he's doing things I didn't know were possible inside Rithium. He's breaking the rules. And every time I see him, he seems to be able to break Rithium just a little bit more, until—

—the raid happens, the real one, the one where Lex' entire operation gets shut down, and we are all carted away. There's a TV in the Police Station, and I see my face in the news, as well as the faces of my colleagues, Lex included.

It looks like I'm done-zo. They're going to make an example of us. It's all part of the narrative. I'm going to go away for a long time. I'm going to be in prison for a good chunk of my life. Will I be experiencing withdrawals the whole time? It's going to be murder. It's going to be—

—a deal. Some secret deal. The FBI sets the papers in front of me. All I have to do is sign them. I'm—

—one of them, now. They introduce me to my new partner. Only, I know who he is. He's my best friend in the world. I ran for years because I thought he was dead. Now, here he is, right in front of me. In Rithium, at least. He teaches me how to use the Dart, how to manipulate the game, how to do insane things—I can feel the muscle memory coming back to me, all the tricks and knowledge—and now, we get to live the way I always wanted to. Playing everyday. It—

—takes me a while to realize what it is the Black Guns do. What really scares me is I'm pretty sure Oscar already knows. He doesn't seem to care that—

—a new group, the Bannerets, has started to fight back, standing up to the FBI. The Feds send me to execute one of them, send a message.

I go to do the job, but I can't do it. I can't pull the trigger. I won't.

The target is Tanya's brother, though I don't know this at the time.

He asks me my name. I tell him.

At night, I lie awake in my Aberdale bed.

I've failed. I've gone against the Feds. There's nothing left to do but wait, until—

—I'm freed by the Bannerets. The first of two times the Bannerets will break me out of Aberdale.

For a few months, I go into hiding with them, live with them. They are genuine, compassionate people. They seem to care about me. They truly believe I'm one of them. Tanya's brother trusts me, and maybe that's why she trusts me, too. This is the first time I've ever felt believed in like this, cared about like this.

They start teasing Tanya and I, telling us we clearly like each other.

We make out on the back porch, in the glow of the light, while the rest of the gang laugh and talk inside.

Late at night, while everyone's asleep, I walk and think, staring up at the stars. I've become happy and complacent. I barely notice the black van pulling over, until it's up on the shoulder. I'm knocked onto the ground. I'm—

—unable to see anything. Something is covering my face. All I can hear is the rumbling sound of the van. That, and my own hoarse voice as I scream relentlessly into the dark. There's prick in the side of my neck, and I feel myself losing—

—consciousness. Being removed from a vehicle; different from the one I was in before. I'm being dragged, propelled. Doors open and close. I hear fans. Loud, buzzing lights.

Then, I'm dropped. *My face hits a cold, tiled floor. I get my knees and look up. I see a familiar face.*

It's Samuel. He's much the same as I remember him. Minus a couple fingers on one of his hands, a detail he seems to intentionally reveal to me right away, holding his hand up like a trophy. He doesn't look all that happy to see me.

He snaps his fingers, pointing. I'm lifted up, moved over to a wide window, what looks like a one-way mirror. On the other side is—

"No!" I drop my revolvers, fall backward, landing on my ass in the dirt. "Nononono—"

"You get it now, don't you?" Oscar says, crouching next to me. There's a harsh glint in his eyes, as if he's angry with himself, already regretting what he just did. "Now, don't you understand?"

CHAPTER 34

THE VANS PULLED FORWARD behind them, closing the distance, headlight beams widening in the dark. Muzzle lights flashed from the sides of the closest van, bullets flying, thundering.

Sater's forehead was pressed hard against the window, Diren's palm braced against the nape of his neck.

In his upper peripheral vision, Sater could see a spark of light; a bullet glancing off of something that the Humvee had just passed underneath, some kind of thick, taut, metal cable, stretched out across the road. It would have been hard to make out if you weren't looking for it, winding your way through the thick forest in the dead of night.

Sater swallowed painfully. Somewhere in the middle of being kicked he had bit down on his tongue, and it was starting to swell. But that was background noise. More importantly, the pursuing van was about to get a haircut, to put it mildly.

"Oh, *THIT*." Sater said.

The van made contact with the cable right in the middle of the windshield. Icy cracks split the glass, but only for the most infinitesimal fraction of a second, before the entire roof flipped backward and away from the van, as if sheared off with the world's most efficient can opener. It seemed to hang in the air for a second, caught by wind resistance, before rotating and bouncing off of the asphalt.

Rubber tires screeched, cutting the air, as the second van swerved, avoiding the flying roof, but still managing to hit the cable. The cable cut halfway through the length through the van before it came to a stop.

Sater felt his whole body being shoved against the back of the Humvee as if by an invisible hand as it made a hard brake.

Diren shoved Sater off to the side as he popped open the hatch. All the other car doors opened as well, as the Wolves jumped out.

Seconds later, as the Wolves disappeared into the dark, the gunshots started up again, lighting up the night like fireworks.

CHAPTER 35

"YOU KNOW WHAT YOU have to do now, don't you?" Oscar says. "You know what this means."

I shake my head. "No, I don't. I can fix it. I can make it work."

"You didn't kill the leader of the Bannerets—Tanya's brother—because you lost your memory." Oscar says. "They hadn't wiped it, yet. You know the real reason. It's because of what you saw. In that room."

It's like he's reading my thoughts. Traveling with me, down the dark tunnel of my mind.

"You've been shackled with this chain for a long time, Kit." Oscar says. "It's your story. It's who you are. You'll never be free—"

I scramble for my revolvers.

Oscar pivots, and his boot hits me across the face, knocking me sideways on the ground. I press my palms into the dirt, push myself up onto my knees, only to feel the barrels of both the Black Guns pressing down into my skull.

Somehow, I'm hyperventilating, my whole virtual body shaking.

"I made a mistake." Oscar says. "I see that, now. Just...look at you."

"I thought it was gonna be a fair fight?" I say. "I thought we were going to play."

"It was." Oscar says. I can feel the gunmetal trembling in his hands. "But I can't take the chance. I need to free you from this."

He laughs, a harsh noise that sounds almost like a bark. "Goodbye, old friend." He whispers, as if he's putting me to sleep.

I feel the slight vibration of his fingers beginning to clench in the triggerwell.

Something kicks in, like adrenaline. A determined spark of energy. My teeth click together.

I unfurl, furling in the air behind Oscar, just as his shots go off. I rotate in the air, leg lashing out, going for a sidekick to Oscar's head.

Oscar ducks, like it's a premonition. He swivels while I'm still in the air, aiming at me.

I furl again, putting some distance between us, but also forcing him to turn toward me, again. He's standing near my fallen revolvers, puppy-guarding them.

I activate my Action Skill as soon as I've reappeared, reaching for the hilt of my sword at the same time. I had a feeling about this before, but now I know for sure. I remember. I can use the Dart to manipulate the time-slow ability of my Action Skill. I can adjust the speed, control how much of the time-slow I use at once, distributing it in disparate bursts if I need to. The only thing I can't control is how long it takes for the time-slow to regenerate.

As I draw the sword, light flashes in my peripheral, sunlight glinting off of the half-drawn blade.

Oscar fires off a black bullet from each of the guns, a lingering bout of flame bursting from each barrel.

I side-step, moving into a low crouch. While I'm doing this, I turn my body, aligning the flat of my half-drawn blade.

I avoid one of the bullets entirely with the sidestep. The second bullet I manage to line up correctly, and it glances off the blade of my sword, sparking painfully.

I weave and duck, causing the next bullet to miss. By this point my sword is free. And the next bullet is on an unavoidable trajectory for my chest.

I slow time down to an excruciating crawl. Every second of energy I put into the sword-swing feels like wading through cement, but at the last second I manage to line it up, causing the bullet to ricochet off the blade, grazing my cheek.

I slide—letting time speed up again, to conserve Action—and swipe toward Oscar. He unfurls. I roll, snatching up the revolvers. I sheathe the sword, furling over to the roof of a building a ways away so I can get a lay of the land.

It takes me about a second to spot Oscar, once again standing sideways on the tower. He gives me a friendly wave.

I unfurl, refurling in the air across from him. I alter gravity, creating my own sort of gravity well that pulls me down against the tower, standing the side of it. It feels perfectly natural, though it does require some focus.

We both have our guns up, at the ready, arms extended.

"This is actually pretty fun." Oscar says, grinning. Then, "Well, what are you waiting for?"

I clamp down on the triggers, firing as fast as I can. I slow time down—way down—and watch as bullets collide, ricocheting, deflecting, altering each other's paths. It's a ballistic dance.

Suddenly, I'm out of bullets. I unfurl, reappearing on the flat top of the tower. It will be an easier environment for reloading, gravity-wise.

I fumble for the ammo pouch strapped to my belt. Just as I have it, Oscar appears in front of me, evaporating in reverse.

His boot hits me in the chest, knocking me backward into a fall. The pouch spills open, shells flying. I slow time way down. The rounds hover, glittering like satellites. I adjust my revolvers as I fall backward, sliding as many of the airborne rounds as I can into the cylinders.

I lock the cylinder wheels shut just as Oscar has his guns on me, just in time to deflect the incoming bullets with my own.

We unfurl and refurl, over and over, trying to get a one-up on each other, occasionally firing off shots that bounce off each other.

Suddenly, there's a loud crash near the base of the tower, and the entire structure begins to shake.

I teleport away from Oscar so I can take a second to see what's going on. I see dust and flying debris at the base of the tower, along with the flailing wings of the black dragon. One of the Bannerets is on top of it, gripping the hilt of a giant sword that's currently impaled in the back of the dragon's skull.

RIP.

The tower isn't just shaking, though. It's beginning to tilt. Slow at first, almost imperceptibly, like a slight swaying. Then, the laws of physics seem to take over, and the tower is in free fall. It's going to crash into the city.

Somewhere, I hear Oscar laughing. I run sideways along the edge of the tower, looking for him.

There's a whoosh of pressure behind me. Arms wrap around me, clamping my torso, trapping me. His laughter is my ear, so loud I can feel it popping; unless it's just the pressure from falling.

We're on the lower side. The tower, as well as gravity itself, is pushing us inexorably downwards, crushing us. We're upside down, though what's down feels like up. The cityscape is rushing up toward us, an upside-down city falling out of the sky.

I try to un-furl, but I can feel Oscar using his Dart to stop me, like a reverse-furling. Or something.

I strain against the pressure, trying to bust through it.

The city is incoming, seconds away.

Just when the rooftops are close enough to reach out and touch, I feel the pressure give. Both Oscar and I disappear, reappearing on a flat rooftop several blocks away—as far away as I can take us before he stops me again.

The force of the entire weight of the tower transfers, even after the teleportations, and we're sent sprawling, rolling. Mid-roll, I can feel the ground quaking, like a nuke just went off. A blast of air propels me forward, sending me airborne, roiling in a thick storm of dust and dirt and rocks and bits of wood.

Still flying, rolling and bouncing on the roof, I make out a form I'm apparently gaining on, tossed toward in the fog of debris. It's Oscar, bouncing across the rooftop in much the same way I am.

I lash out with my fist, hitting him in the back, in the middle of his spine. My body slams into his. I grab the cord of his Dart necklace at the back of his neck, fingers latching tight around it. I feel resistance, as it seems Oscar is pulling on the front of the necklace, trying to keep me from getting a better hold. There's a loud roar of sound that feels incredibly close, and I realize it's me, screaming.

Seconds pass as our bodies spin, airborne. At some point we must have rolled over the lip of the roof and are now flying free.

I'm on top of Oscar, pulling on the cord with both hands, my knee pressed into his back. The dust is so thick I can't see more than a couple feet in any direction.

A slanted, shingled roof appears like a ghostly apparition. We slam into and through the roofing. Somewhere in the impact, I hear the snap of Oscar's cord. Somewhere in the midst of flying bits of wood and clay, I see Oscar's Black Dart, knocked flying.

Oscar's hand reaches out, fingers just barely brushing it, pushing it out of reach as it falls.

We're in freefall in the inside of what appears to be a giant storage shed.

Oscar spins his body, struggling, trying to grab my Dart. I bring up my hands, deflecting his lunges, struggling against him.

We're falling fast, and not just toward the ground. There's a splintered length of wood jutting out of a thick support beam that appears to have been damaged by the towerfall. Oscar is unaware of it, completely focused on scrabbling for the Dart.

I wrap one hand around the Dart, protecting it. With my other hand, I grip Oscar by the shoulder, adjusting him underneath me, despite his struggles. I aim for the javelin-like hunk of wood.

There's a glint in Oscar's eyes, as if he can tell I'm up to something. He stops struggling and grabs me, fingers digging into my shoulders. Now I can't avoid the javelin without rotating Oscar's body as well. It's all or none. Fine by me. I just hold on even tighter.

There's a sickening squelch as the javelin pierces us both through the abdomen, abruptly halting our fall, like puppets yanked by their strings.

The pain is there, but it's more of a discomfort, really. The simworld's attempt to communicate injury without going overboard. It's unpleasant, but mostly in the same way a dream can be unpleasant. More of an attempt to simulate trauma than the real thing.

Oscar is a few feet below me on the javelin, arms and legs dangling away from his body, like a doll being lifted by a crane. It looks like he's just out of reach.

We're both panting and heaving. Occasionally wincing. The ground is still trembling slightly. I can hear various structures around the city crashing and crumbling, knocking into each other. The support beam we're attached to wobbles and sways precariously.

"Look..." Oscar says, between gasps. "Look what you did..."

I reach down and grab the shaft of the javelin with both hands. I pull, grunting. I can feel it sliding and scraping as it travels through me, catching on my intestines.

Oscar starts laughing. Not a maniacal, insane laugh. More like the kind of laugh that reminds me of staying up late with friends, being tired and hysterical.

I grit my teeth and continue pulling, facilitating my slow descent toward Oscar.

"This was...your idea...remember?" Oscar says, through the strained smile on his face.

"Which— which part?" I say, between grunts, focusing on my slow progress along the javelin.

"Playing...Rithium..."

Quite suddenly, his eyes go dead.

I can see my gun in Oscar's holster. I fumble for it, managing to pinch the handle with two of my fingers and get it out. As soon it's in my hand, it shimmers white, just like before.

I have it. It's done.

Now I can de-spawn. Now it's okay to—

But I can already feel my avatar dying, as everything starts to go black.

CHAPTER 36

"KIT! KIT!"

Someone's hands were on me, shaking me. Someone with a pulped, bloody face.

I sat up, instinctively jerking away.

"Tank GOT!" The person said. "I tink I'b about to pass out..."

I squinted at the figure. It was his hair that clued me in, as messy and disheveled as it was. "Sater?"

He collapsed next to me. "I tried to...I tried..."

His eyes went shut.

I reached out, slapping the side of his face. "Sater?"

Not good. He seemed badly injured. Possibly had a concussion. Clearly needed medical attention.

Yeah, just throw that onto the pile of things you need to worry about.

Gunshots sounded, lights flashing amidst the trees.

One thing at a time. Where the hell am I.

The back of a car.

Tanya was lying on her back next to me. She was twitching slightly, eyes fluttering behind the lids. I reached out, brushing the side of her face with my fingers. For some reason I was afraid to touch or move her. I had this feeling that she was in a precarious place, right on the precipice of death.

It would be just my luck to lose her now, after I'd somehow managed to regain my memories of her. Another cruel joke in a world that so far hadn't much held back with it's cruelty.

But at the same time, how cosmically fitting. To lose Tanya in virtually the same way that Oscar lost Jackie...

I shook myself, decided to get my bearings. I was in a hatch at the back of the car. There were five seats total in the car. All empty.

The keys were in the ignition.

I looked over at Sater and Tanya, lying next to each other in the hatch. I needed to get out of here, get these people to a hospital. But something was stopping me. The thing that I saw in that memory, behind the one-way mirror.

This might be my only chance...

I ran my hands around, feeling underneath the seats, across the dashboard, inside the glovebox. Then I remembered my time with Lex, and the types of places they'd used to stash firearms for safekeeping.

I opened the front passenger door and ran my hand across the metal panel where a child safety lock would be, until I came across a small hole. I stuck my finger in and pulled, opening a latch in the side of the door. I reached into the opening and pulled a glock-looking handgun, not unlike my Black Gun in Rithium. I slid out the mag, checking to make sure it was full, then shoved it back into place with a metallic *SNAP*.

In the hatch, I leaned down and gave Tanya a gentle kiss on the lips. Perhaps the last I would ever give her. I examined the contours of her face, trying to memorize them. Perhaps so that, no matter what, I would never forget again.

"I love you." I said, quiet as a whisper.

The only response was the loud, intermittent gunshots behind me. With effort, I tore myself away, and headed toward the flashing lights amid the trees.

CHAPTER 37

I MOVED SLOWLY AT first, head ducked low, half-expecting a bullet to tear through me at any moment, or to see the flash of a muzzle in the shadows nearby, signaling my imminent death.

It was overcast, but I could make out the shape of two vans a short ways down the winding road.

It seemed like there were two groups shooting at each other. The one taking cover behind one of the vans—who I assumed to be the Feds—and the ones taking cover in the trees.

I hunched and stepped carefully, only taking any potentially noisy movement under the cover of the gunshots echoing in the trees. I looped around, heading toward the group in the trees. I felt a need to get a handle on what this unknown element was. Who these people were. I needed to—

I froze, staring.

I was nearing the first van, and I could see it semi-clearly, or at least a detailed silhouette of it.

It looked as if someone had taken a giant can opener to it. The roof appeared to have been shredded off completely, leaving jagged sawtooth patterns in the frame. The windshield was completely shattered.

What the hell.

It was obvious, for more reasons than one, that I was walking in on something I didn't entirely understand.

The second van was where most of the gunfire was originating from, as well as centered on.

The van itself had crashed into some kind of structure. Seemingly the same thing that the first van had hit.

I had to squint for a couple seconds before making out that it was some kind of cable, suspended in the treeline. Likely anchored by a couple structures hiding in the trees, on either side of the road. I suspected there was a lot of concrete involved, and who knew what else. This was planned at least somewhat ahead of time.

Speculate later. Act now.

I moved in toward the group taking cover in the woods, coming up on their flank. Suddenly, I saw a shadow advancing toward them, weaving between trees.

I hit the ground, pressing my face into the dirt, just in time to hear the barrage of gunfire. It sounded like a fully automatic weapon, and it was cutting through everything. Bits of grass and dirt and tree bark went flying. Even with my face pressed down I could see the way the flashes lit up the surrounding area, almost like it was daytime.

Eventually, the gunfire died. This pause was followed by a final perfunctory burst of shots as if to make sure.

The area went dead quiet. I could hear the officer's footsteps—I had to assume that that's who it was, one of the SWAT team who'd managed to flank around—as he checked the area, making sure the threats were taken care of. His boots made loud crunch sounds as he stepped over pine needles and brambles. There was an eminent *click* as he turned on the flashlight attachment on his rifle. A massive cone of light extended, flooding the area, sweeping.

The light cast a long shadow of a man weaving between the trees. Kit could just make out the loose leather vest that seemed to flop and dangle as he ran.

Shots rang out again, spitting up dirt and aggressively pruning bits of underbrush. Chips of splitting bark shot out from the trunks of trees.

Finally, the shooting stopped, followed by a "*Shit*," from the officer.

The figure seemed to have escaped. For now.

The officer continued to stand there for a while, scanning with his light, searching for any other survivors.

I was still and quiet, but I could hear my heart pounding in my head, throbbing.

The light passed over where I was. If it had hit me just right, he should have been able to see me. But the searchlight passed over me and kept moving.

After what was probably a couple seconds—though, laying in the dark with my face pressed against the dirt, it felt like hours—the footsteps started up again, moving back toward the road.

"CLEAR!" The officer yelled.

One Mississippi, I thought, still laying there. *Two Mississippi...*

At some point, I needed to move.

The next step for the SWAT team would be to find Tanya, Sater and I, kill us, and take the Dart. I needed to head them off before then. But there was also something I needed to do first.

I needed to find Oscar.

I pushed myself up onto my knees, peeking into the semi-clearing by the roadway. I started to follow the officer back. Not directly behind him, but off to the side. I moved on all fours, creeping through the underbrush.

Turns out that was a good call, as the other members of the team shone lights on the officer as he drew close. The officer came to a stop a few steps away. They all just looked at each other, as if they were lost and unsure what to do now.

"What the hell was all of that?" One of the officers said. His voice was somewhat muted by the mask he wore, and to be honest it seemed like an extremely understated reaction, considering the circumstances. "What do we do now?"

There was a moment of awkward silence. They weren't moving as fast as I thought they would be. With most of them gone, maybe there was no clear chain of command. No clear idea of what was supposed to happen next.

A phone rang. A loud, generic ringtone.

The officers gave each other startled looks. Then they moved toward the van, opening doors, moving aside crushed glass with the butts of their rifles to clear the windows as they reached inside.

One of them pulled out a little flip phone, with a little screen on it that was glowing blue.

The one with the phone looked around at everyone else. He let his rifle hang by the strap so that he could use his other gloved hand to flip the phone open. He held it up to his ear.

"Hello?"

His demeanor went stiff, at attention. "Yes, sir." He went on to describe the situation, but he mostly used codewords and phrases I didn't understand.

For a good several seconds, he was quiet. Then, "Of course, Sir."

He closed the phone, put it in his pocket.

"Well?" Said one of the others.

The one with the phone shrugged. "Our orders are to terminate Peacelock, as well as the three Banneret members. Then, we apprehend the Dart."

My heart jumped, slamming against my ribcage. Was I already too late?

I continued to creep forward, not sure when exactly to make my move. Or what exactly that move would even be.

The four remaining SWAT team members moved out, heading toward the first van. Was that where they expected Oscar to be?

I followed along the side of the road, just inside the treeline.

As I did, contemplating what to do next, I couldn't help but wonder; are firearms in Rithium at all like in real life? Was my experience with guns in the simworld even remotely useful in this situation? How accurate was this pistol, even, at this range?

I had no frame of reference. I'd never fired a real gun in my life.

The officers, who had been jogging, came to a stop at the back of the van. One of them peeked inside. "He's in there."

He put his hand on the door to open it.

Before I even realized what I was doing, I shot him in the neck.

Blood splatted against the tinted back window of the van. The force of the shot shoved him forward. He slumped, and his body slid down onto the ground, smearing a ribbon of blood in its wake.

The other three officers spun, immediately crouching into position. I had already shot the second officer in the chest, moving down the officers in a row from left to right, like playing keys on a piano. By the time I was on the fourth officer he managed to let off a burst of shots in my direction. I dove, letting off a shot before I hit the ground that landed in the officer's chest, downing him.

Adrenaline fueled me as I jumped back up on my feet, feeling more than a little like Max Payne.

I ran up to the downed officers, taking turns aiming and shooting at each of them interchangeably. I was high on adrenaline, my actions propelled by quick, shallow breaths. I was aiming at no parts of the body in particular, though this was in an attempt to incapacitate them as much as I could, if not kill.

Eventually the slide smacked back, gun clicking impotently as I continued to squeeze the trigger. I looked at it for a second, then threw it. It bounced, sliding on the asphalt.

I was slowly starting to come back down, breathe normally. At the same time, there was something fixating about the array of bodies in front of me.

I had survived this encounter either out of luck, or surprise, or my skills with virtual guns somehow translating to real life. Honestly, I didn't really care which. What mattered, at this point, was that I was alive.

I stepped over the bodies, grabbed the van's back door, and pulled it open.

The door squeaked loudly as it swung wide.

I squinted, peering into the dark interior of the van. "Oz? Oz, are you there? Oz—"

It took a few seconds for my eyes to adjust to the sheer darkness inside the van. Eventually, I was able to make out the shadowy silhouette lying sideways on the floor, strapped against a bulky wheelchair.

I froze, soaking it in, slowly picking up on the finer details, the nuances of what I was seeing. The patchy, matted hair. The cold, grey eye. Realizing.

Nothing could have prepared me for it.

I crept up into the van. My hands fumbled, running along his torso, looking for the strap that held him against the chair. My fingers brushed the skin of his hands. He felt...cold.

Eventually, my fingers found the thick, plastic strap, just over his sternum. I clicked it open, pulled—only to find that it was stuck on something, wouldn't come free.

I crawled in closer on my hands and knees, trying to get a better look, only to touch something warm, sticky and wet that was soaking into the floor. And then I saw it. The shard of metal trapped in Oscar's chest, holding the strap in place.

I fell against him, pressing my face against his, listening to see if he was still breathing. I squeezed his wrist, feeling for a pulse. I squeezed the side of his neck, feeling for a pulse. Feeling nothing.

Time got weird after that. The next thing I knew I was carrying Oscar as I walked back up the road, stepping on—nearly slipping on—and over cubes of broken glass, around bodies strewn on the asphalt. A steady stream of blood dripped from my hand, the one I'd used to pull the metal out of my friend. My oldest friend.

There was an electric *thunk* sound, from off in the woods. Light blasted me, making me squint as I tried to look at the source. In my peripheral I could see the long, stretched shadows of trees, like tentacled limbs.

"Good work, Winter."

I halted midstep, recognizing the voice immediately.

Footsteps, as someone moved off to the side, into the road, out of the glare of the floodlights.

It was Samuel. The man from the arcade. The man from my recently rediscovered memories. Memories I almost wished I could blot out forever.

He was wearing a suit. And sunglasses, which I suppose made sense. I myself was still squinting, trying to watch him closely.

Oscar was limp and heavy in my arms. I held him close. It didn't seem right to put him down just yet, like a piece of luggage.

Samuel kept walking, closing the distance. He used his high-heeled boots to kick aside bits of broken glass and metal.

"I see you have what we need." Samuel said.

CHAPTER 38

I HELD UP OSCAR'S body. I could feel a tremor building, reverberating throughout my body. I was shaking with rage. "All this for a couple...pieces of plastic."

Samuel glanced around. "Not just pieces of plastic. Certainly not. But I take your meaning. It's all a bit extravagant isn't it?"

"Don't bother explaining your plan." I said. "I don't need to know how you knew this was going to happen. I honestly don't give a shit."

One of Samuel's eyebrows shot up. "Really? You're not even a little curious?"

I pulled Oscar close, holding him against me. In a way, it was still hard to imagine that all of this was actually happening. It felt like I was making a conscious effort just to hold onto the moment. Onto my own lucidity.

"What's the point of all this?" I said, barely realizing I was doing so.

"What people get wrong about 'conspiracies'," Samuel said, stepping over the body of an officer, "Is that there's this single, grand, definite plan. 'The Plan'. Which is absurd, of course. There's no 'Plan'."

He paused, for emphasis, before continuing.

"There are '*Plans*', Kit. Hundreds of them. More than I can keep track of. Plans within plans. Backups within backups. This was just one of the situations for which we had anticipated a favorable outcome. These may be the first of the government's Darts we manage to acquire, but they won't be the last. Especially once our RnD department gets a hold of them. Speaking of," He held out his hand. "The Darts?"

I had one of the Darts. The other one was still wrapped around Oscar's neck.

I looked at Samuel's outstretched hand, then back up at his face. "What's the backup if I don't hand them over?"

Samuel didn't answer. His body was a statue, hand still outstretched.

"You know," I said, "We're not all that different, you and I. Pieces in someone else's game. You don't even know why you're supposed to keep me alive."

Samuel's expression went sour. He withdrew his hand. "We're taking you in alive because you're going to work for us, now. And you know why."

He pulled a smartphone out of his pocket. He made a couple taps, then held it up so I could see the screen. Though I didn't need to. I already knew what it would be.

It was a livestream of the inside of a bare, concrete room. Someone was sitting on the floor, back against the wall. She had long, dark, matted hair. It was Jackie.

Seemingly satisfied by whatever reaction I was giving off, Samuel put the phone away.

"Now, let's stop wasting time. You're going to hand over the Darts. You're going to hand over yourself. You and your friends are coming with us."

I didn't move. I stood my ground, mulling it over. Everything was down to the wire, now. If there was another move to play, now was the time. Though such a possibility seemed slimmer by the second.

Such a poor deal. Trading three lives for the one. And what kind of a life would it be, for Jackie? It wasn't clear.

Still, I could feel the compulsion to do it. That weight, hanging from my neck, like a hundred-pound Dart.

I could fix things. Make them right, finally.

An ironic sentiment considering I was holding the broken remains of my best friend. A ridiculous one. But surely there was some truth to it.

A shaky semblance of a plan began to form in my head. Jigsaw pieces that, while from the wrong puzzle, just might fit.

It was a chance more than a plan, if I was honest with myself. But it was something.

"What happens to Jackie? If I cooperate?" I said.

"She lives." Samuel said. "Obviously. If you don't, she dies."

"You'll release her?" I said.

Samuel nodded, after a half-second of hesitation. "That was our deal, wasn't it?"

"Should I believe it?"

"Believe this." Samuel said. "Say no, and she's dead. I'll let you watch."

I suddenly felt tired. So tired. And not just because I was holding a dead man in my arms. Though I could have sworn I could feel Oscar's body growing more rigid by the minute, harder to hold.

The jig was up. This whole time I'd been running from my past, some part of me thinking I could stay ahead of it. But that long chain snaking out of the darkness in my dream—in a way, it was real. It was taut, suspended in the air. I was attached to it. All that motion and effort, only to be running in place.

I crouched down, carefully setting Oscar on the ground. For a moment, I pressed my face against his.

"Goodbye." I whispered in his ear.

I ran my fingers over his face, closing his eyelids. I gripped the Black Dart hanging from his neck and pulled, snapping the cord.

I stood. "You don't want to shoot me. You'd risk damaging the Darts." I didn't have to be able to see past the floodlights to know that there were gunmen there, trained on me.

"But I will." Samuel said.

"But you don't want to." I let that hang for a second. Then, "I'll come with you, Sam. But it's just going to be me. Leave my friends out of it."

Samuel shrugged. "They were secondary, anyway. You're the one they want."

I was somewhat surprised at this. But then I glanced at the stubs on Samuel's hand, where two fingers used to be. His employers didn't tolerate failure. Any option that would make things run smoother, allow him to hedge his bets, he would take. Short of letting me get away with the Darts, that is. That wasn't on the table. Even hitting me with some kind of tranquilizer would give me a window of time where I might find a way to break the Darts, or stumble, perhaps damaging them that way. Not to mention how much easier it is to kidnap and transport a willing participant.

Samuel motioned, signaling to one of the gunmen behind the floodlights to approach.

"Wait." I said.

Samuel held up a hand.

"Call an ambulance first. My friends are in the back of the Humvee."

Samuel nodded and snapped his fingers.

Someone holding a rifle jogged out from behind the floodlights and handed Samuel a little flip phone. He opened it and dialled three numbers. He looked directly at me as he spoke to the operator. The call lasted a couple of minutes. Once the essential information was relayed, he snapped the phone shut and tossed it over to the rifleman, who caught it and put it in his jacket pocket.

"Alright." Samuel said. "It's time."

"I have your word my friends aren't coming?"

"There's no time for that, anyway." Samuel said, just as the floodlights shut off, plunging us in darkness, save for a few flashlight beams in the woods, as well as the light attached to the gunman's rifle, trained on me. "We have minutes before that ambulance arrives. We're not clambering over this wreckage to get to your Bannerets. Not today. And before you ask, Jackie's being released as we speak. The order was already given. She won't be any use to us anyway, once we're through with you." He took a step closer. "You were always going to give yourself up, Kit. You might say it was...in the stars."

Somehow, I believed him. I exhaled, feeling a knot of tension release itself in my chest.

I'd done what I could. Jackie would be released, if Samuel held up his end of the deal. At the very least, I'd bought Tanya and Sater some time. I'd—

As the henchman with the light on his rifle stepped close, his arm whipped toward me, and I felt a prick in the side of my neck. Spots of oblivion infringed on my vision, black holes expanding in the already overwhelming dark.

CHAPTER 39

MY CONSCIOUSNESS RETURNED TO me slowly, by degrees, as my faculties steadily returned to me.

I was in a car. I could feel the slight tremor of the engine. The rock and sway as we made turns, navigated bumps and hills in the road.

I could feel the fabric of a bag over my head, smothering my vision with black, tightly woven thread. The bag was held in place by a ziptie, pulled—uncomfortably—tight around my neck.

The radio was on. Someone had it turned to a 90's hip-hop station.

Eventually the going became less bumpy as we smoothed out into a downward incline. There was one last bump after that, as the car leveled out. Suddenly the 90's rap took on an echoey quality, as if I could hear it on the outside of the car as well as in.

The car kept moving, turning a couple times. Then it stopped.

The engine cut out. So did the music.

It suddenly felt uncomfortably quiet. Someone on my left was breathing raspily, like he had a sore throat.

One of the doors opened. The car started *bing*ing, reminding the driver the keys were still in the ignition. Keys jangled, *snick*ing as they were removed, placed in the driver's pocket.

"Just take the bag off," one of the henchmen said. "It'll make this easier."

I felt a snap, and the pressure around my neck released. Someone grabbed the bag. Strands of my hair were caught in the fibers, and they yanked painfully as the fabric was pulled across my face, and over my head.

Someone shoved me out of the car.

We were in what appeared to be a massive, well-lit, underground garage. There were easily a hundred vehicles parked, with plenty of room for more. Thick, concrete support pillars were dotted throughout the lot, painted bright yellow.

"C'mon, let's go."

I was pushed, escorted by several henchman—I counted six—toward the outer wall. Cars passed us, weaving through the garage, some of them exiting through tunnel openings, heading toward some other part of the...complex? Whatever this was.

There was an elevator in the wall. One of the henchmen pressed the button, and the doors slid open. They pushed/pulled me into the elevator, sandwiching me inside.

Someone pressed one of ten buttons in the console, and the doors slid shut. Then, the elevator began to descend.

It occurred to me that I might never get to go above ground again for the rest of my life. Seemed like a reasonable enough assumption, at that point. No one built a fortress like this unless they were trying to keep people out. As well as keep certain things locked away inside.

I was beginning to think I was one of those things.

The doors opened to a hallway so long that looking down it gave a feeling of vertigo. I could hear the jumbled echoes of several different tense conversations. It was a lot like what I had imagined that the stock exchange was like. There were phones ringing. The sound of papers being shuffled, flipped through, stacked, and filed.

Some of the voices were english. Some were speaking in a language that sounded eastern-european—vaguely Russian.

I was pushed past door after door of what appeared to be office rooms. Every time I tried to get a good look I felt a hand on the back of my head, shoving me.

We stopped at one of the open doorways. One of the henchmen rapped on the doorframe.

Someone wearing a blue button-down shirt made his way over, at the same time yelling at someone across the room in that foreign language.

He turned toward us. "Yes?"

"We were told to drop a package off," said the one who'd rapped on the door, "But they didn't tell us where. I don't want to leave him in the wrong section."

The one in the blue shirt gave me the briefest of glances. "What are you, new here? Where's your CL?"

"We were separated. We had to split—"

"I don't give a shit." Blue shirt started backing away. "Processing's been moved to Floor Seven. Get out of here."

Back to the elevator, descending slowly for several seconds.

The doors opened to a startlingly grungy space. Poorly lit, with lots of dark corners and crevices. Bare, yellow lightbulbs hung in the walkways, some of them blinking feebly, as if at any second they could all go out, allowing the dark tide of shadows to have their way, overwhelming the place.

A cloying, musty stench—and perhaps taste—hung in the air. Somewhere, I could hear slow, steady droplets of water falling.

I was led to a dark room. Someone flipped a switch, and light washed the room, emanating from a bright rectangle in the ceiling that buzzed loudly.

There were three objects in the room. A chair, a stool, and a stand with an old tube TV on it.

The chair had restraining straps for the arms and legs. Similar to an electric chair, without the hat suspended over it.

As they pulled me toward the chair, I pulled back. I almost couldn't help it. I had made a conscious decision to hand myself over, but part of me wasn't having it, some primal part.

Eventually, they had me in the chair, and the straps in place.

I heard what almost sounded like flip-flop footsteps, echoing in the hallway outside the room. Most of the henchmen turned and left, passing a newcomer. Some guy who looked like he was in his mid forties. He wore an open bathrobe, revealing nothing but a pair of white underwear underneath. He wore glasses, and carried a clipboard. He had slippers on his feet, which explained the unusual sound of his footsteps. He also had a pen in his mouth, held horizontally between his lips, which he removed as soon as he turned toward me.

"This is the guy?"

There was no answer. I could feel the presence of the two henchmen who'd stayed behind on each side of me.

The guy in the bathrobe sat on the stool, rolling across the floor a little bit. He took turns looking from me to the clipboard, as if somehow confirming what he was reading, or using me visually to compartmentalize it. Occasionally he licked his thumb and turned the page, scrolling with his eyes.

"Oooookay." He said. He clicked his pen and scratched a few things down. "You can go ahead and prep him."

He continued to scratch on the clipboard.

I yelped as a needle stabbed into my forearm. I couldn't help but watch the syringe slowly empty, it's contents shoved into my bloodstream.

Within seconds, I started to feel woozy. My body felt...heavy.

"Okay." The guy with the clipboard said, looking up at me. "Let's begin."

CHAPTER 40

THINGS WERE STARTING TO get weird. Wrong.

This is it. I thought, somewhat woozily, the sedative already starting to kick in. *Pay close attention.*

Not that I would remember any of it. Not if what Oscar said was true.

How had he described it?

It was like hacking. If people were machines, these people had discovered the computer terminal that controlled them. Just how difficult a process this was, or why it was only being used on Rithium users, I didn't know.

Hacking people.

That was really what they were doing. wasn't it? Analogy or otherwise, it was about to happen. And it was going to work. It always did.

No, wait. That actually wasn't true. It had never worked on Oscar. At least, according to him.

The question was *how.* That is, why had the techniques never worked on Oscar, even though they had always worked on me. The answer to this question could not have been more pertinent. More-

More...

Import...ant...

My neck lolled. My head had become both heavy and light at the same time, difficult to hold up.

"Hey." The guy on the stool said, snapping his fingers. "Over here."

What...*what had Oscar...said?*

It seemed hard to remember, now. And it wasn't getting easier. My memories felt like they were quickly morphing into lines of computer code on an old monitor, scrolling across a black background, strange and indecipherable. Disconnected, even. Part of a word dump on a floppy disk that could be ejected at any second-

No! No it's not. It's me. These are my memories. They're...who I am.

Still, the dissociative sensation persisted.

I blinked a couple times, and suddenly the room started to twist and turn, reality at odds with itself. Everything began to torque and narrow and elongate, like a piece of chewed up gum being stretched out.

"Looks like it's working so far," The man on the stool said. His voice echoed strangely, which in a way made sense because he was sitting at the end of a long, twisted, and vaguely undulating tunnel.

I laughed. A series of sharp, cackling chuckles that reverbed in an unnatural, electronic sort of way; more the product of a DJ than the wind-tunnel echo.

The man on the stool was writing on his notepad, again. His pen scraped against the paper, and the sound carried like quill-scratches on the far side of a canyon.

When he'd finished taking his note, he laid the clipboard flat across his knee, and the thump of the wood against the bone of his knee was unbearably loud, like a mic being struck hard by an open palm.

Following this was a strange, reverberating feedback sound, building in both pitch and intensity, culminating in a cork-like *POP*.

And suddenly, I was standing outside my own body.

CHAPTER 41

FOR THE MOST PART, reality had reasserted itself. Except for the fact that everything had a slightly warped look to it, as if I was viewing the room through a fish-eye lens. That, and perhaps the fact that I was standing outside my own freaking body, but at this point who's counting?

Also, at this point, should I even be surprised?

So you spontaneously discovered a means of astral projection. Not the weirdest thing to happen today.

Okay, so it's pretty weird. What are you going to do about it?

Let's be real; it wasn't astral projection. I've never been much for meditation or spirituality, anyway. Such phenomenon can be reasonably attributed to drugs, anyway, right?

Yeah, it was obviously the drugs. Whatever they had put in me, just now. Not that this made me feel any more equipped to deal with the situation.

I couldn't move. I could feel my phantom body, and my vision was at about head height. But it was as if the signals traveling from my brain to my body were getting cut off midway.

I kept trying, though.

C'mon. Take a step. Do something.

Nothing.

While I struggled to move, my real self—in the chair—seemed like a happy camper. He was sitting up straight with an alert posture, his eyes on the Stool man.

I'm a freaking teacher's pet.

"We're going to show you some videos here today," Stoolman said, once again consulting the clipboard. "Should be interesting to see how you react to them. But before that, we have an interactive portion of the experience, for you. Are you ready, kid?"

In my mind's eye, I could see the opening to Spongebob Squarepants.

That line. 'Kid' instead of 'kids', but otherwise the same. Even spoken with the same rhythm and intonation. It had to be an intentional reference.

What a sick freak.

But my dissociated body—in the chair—was already nodding eagerly.

Aye-aye, Captain.

"I'm going to go through some phrases, and you're going to repeat them after me. Make sense?"

He flipped one of his stupid pages. "Ready?"

My body nodded again.

Stoolman made direct, confident eye-contact with my body as he spoke. "I am a product of my environment."

For some reason I had been expecting some kind of Winter Soldier style code phrase—a string of words that, though meaningless, would activate some dormant effect in my brain. What I was getting instead was not only an intelligible sentence, but a philosophy itself, and laced with meaning.

"I-" There was a slight hesitation, before my body continued. "I am a product of my environment."

No. I thought. *That's not right.*

It used to be. I was just a junkie, hopelessly addicted, with now way out of my condition. That was what I thought.

No one wants to feel like they're directly responsible for the bad things in their life.

Some things had been outside of my control, obviously. The car accident was just that—an accident. My parents had passed away in a mess of smoke and tangled metal. The result of some mistake, some careless driving maneuver obviously, whether on the part of my father or the driver he crashed into, or both. But I had just been a passenger, a shadow in the backseat, not a participant. I had not acted. But in a way, I had been acted upon.

Using sketchy brain-altering tech in the backroom of an arcade? Totally on me. I should have known, really. No matter how desperate I was for an escape. Some mistakes are just mistakes, and sometimes, even if it's deep down, you know it's the wrong move.

Same with roping my friend Oscar into it. Same with involving Jackie. Same with lying to Evelyn, day after day, week after week. Same with stealing her money, right out of her wallet, while she was busy making *me* dinner, caring for me, having taken me in under *her* roof.

When I started feeling the side effects from Rithium, I could have come clean at any time. I could have sought help. But I didn't. I wanted to stay in the escape. I didn't want to face reality.

But I could have.

And if I had, everything would have been different.

So no, it wasn't true. It just wasn't.

Just as I had this thought, my body twitched in the chair, as if something had just occurred to it.

"I do not act." Stoolman said, reciting the next line from his clipboard. "I am acted upon."

In a way, this was true. I had been held against my will and experimented on for several years, at times not even aware of the context, or the reason why. My mind was not my own. It could be twisted and manipulated, and had been. But did it have to be that way?

Suddenly I could remember. The words Oscar spoke to me, when I asked why the memory erasure hadn't worked on him.

"You live in a world of your own making, Kit. You always have. You think it protects you, but it doesn't."

"I do not...act..." my body said, but the words were slurred, as if it was struggling to get them out. "I am acted...upon." It twitched again, neck rolling sideways against the shoulder, as if to scratch an upper arm itch with its ear.

Stoolman nodded and flipped a page. He paused after reading the next phrase, as if for emphasis, and as if this one was especially important. "I have no agency."

I felt a sudden, impending sense of urgency, that this moment needed to count. I focused on my body, trying to exert my will over it.

My body didn't move. It was frozen, stuck between two equally assertive directives.

I strained, and I could feel myself moving, my hand—or what I perceived to be my hand—extending toward the chair, as if I was about to use the Force, or perform some psychokinetic trick.

I am not just some product of my environment, I thought, slowly, with emphasis on each word in my mind.

I am not some particle in a test tube. I may sometimes be acted upon, but I can act as well, and it is my actions that define me.

I decide who I am, and what I do. I have agency.

I'm no junkie. Not if I don't want to be.

And as much as I love Rithium, it doesn't define me.

I don't need it. I can walk away. I know that, now.

I will walk-

*****

I blinked. I had just tried to move my arm, like before, and found that I could not. Because it was strapped to the arm of the chair.

I was still lightheaded and a little woozy, but overall, reality seemed to be....well, real.

Stoolman seemed to be taking notice of my sudden and obvious lucidity.

His eyebrows scrunched together, his mouth dropping open into a confused 'O' shape, and the clipboard dropped, smacking dramatically against his bare knees.

He looked from each of the two henchmen on either side of me, as if it was their fault.

In my peripheral, I could see one of them shrugging.

"Why didn't you repeat the words?" Stoolman said, to himself more than me.

I laughed. A full and hearty laugh—not of despair, but of excitement and exultation.

I was free. Finally free. Even though I was restrained in a chair, surrounded by guards, several levels underground, I was still free.

Wasn't that a weird thing.

Stoolman adjusted his glasses, observing me curiously. "What the hell are you laughing at?"

"Is this..." I said between snickers, trying to catch my breath, "All of it?"

Stoolman cocked his head, not understanding.

"Plans..." I said, more to myself, remembering what Samuel had said. "...Within plans, within plans. So is this a plan, or a plan within a plan?"

Stoolman must have understood something of what I was saying, because his jaw locked.

I was finally starting to catch my breath. I grinned. "What I'm saying is, what's next? Whatcha got, Doc?"

The man on the stool looked from one henchmen on either side of me, to the other, as if they might know the answer. Then, he sighed. "Well, shit."

CHAPTER 42

S AMUEL EITHER WASN'T NERVOUS—YET—OR he was hiding it well. Then again, he *was* wearing a set of oversized aviator sunglasses, like a shield of anonymity obscuring the upper half of his face. Sunlight glinted off one corner of the gold rim, reminding me of the cross of light that appears in anime after a character has been knocked into the sky.

It was the first time I'd been outside in five days, judging by my schedule of meals. Two per day, it seemed like, with ten meals total. Steaming, freshly microwaved TV dinner trays, covered in a tarp of wilting plastic cover. But I was hungry enough to partake. I had the feeling that I would need to keep my energy up, and I trusted that feeling.

At one point, a doctor came in to remove the stitches on my arm. My forearm still hurt from the surgery, but it seemed like it was finally starting to heal up. And my captors wanted to make sure it did. They wanted me in good health.

It had either taken my Stoolman a long time to get a hold of Samuel, or he had just been stalling. In the meantime, between meals, I had been escorted out of my dingy, square-shaped cell and moved to one of the upper floors so that Stoolman could run some tests. None of which had yielded any result that Stoolman seemed to like.

During these tests, which usually seemed to involve watching strange videos or listening to recorded phrases with neurotransmitters stuck to the side of my head, I thought about Jackie.

If what Samuel had said was true, this organization—whatever it was—no longer had any reason to hold on to her. They had set her free, long before they dragged me into that strange facility. Where had they dropped her? How was she? Was it possible that she could be with her family, right now?

This thought, this possibility, gave me such a sense of relief and consolation that the idea of spending the rest of my life imprisoned hardly phased me. It was as if my purpose had finally been fulfilled. I'd done what I needed to do.

And yet.

I thought about my friends. The most important people in my life. Tanya, and Mason, and Sater.

They hadn't deserved what had happened—in the case of Mason, I still wasn't sure what exactly *had* happened, but I had a bad feeling about it— and I found myself resenting the idea that it had been for nothing. And not just because of the Darts. Somehow, some way. I needed to know if they had made it out okay.

Though I had begun to feel I would find out soon enough.

Either they had run out of tests or Samuel had run out of patience.

I was cuffed and escorted into the elevator.

The first thing I saw when the elevator door slid open was the sun and sky.

I had stepped out onto a wide patio with a waist-high wall of clear glass that served as a railing. That was when I noticed Samuel, seated on the other side of a small circular table, like one you might see outside a cafe, perhaps with a shade umbrella planted in its center.

One of my jailors removed my handcuffs and stood idly in front of the elevator, which signaled to me that there wasn't any particular means of escaping from here.

I didn't head over to Samuel directly, though I could tell he was waiting for me. I had no way of knowing the next time I would get a view like this.

Before me was a sweeping view of a hilly, wooded property. Tall, thick pines swayed gently, cutting into the skyline.

There was no sign of civilization beyond the facility itself, though I did spot a watchtower propped on a rocky outcropping, with a guard standing watch inside. Visibility was pretty spotty, even with all the zones surrounding the facility that had obviously been cleared and logged. Maybe that was part of the point.

"What do you think?" Samuel said.

Somewhat hesitantly, I turned toward him. "About what?" The sky was clear, and I had to squint to look at him.

"Our nifty little corner of the world." Samuel said. He didn't smile, or shrug, or cross his legs. He was motionless, his gaze fixed on me behind those immutable shades.

A curtain of silence fell between us. I didn't mind.

I turned back toward the property. Though I had no way of knowing where we were, it reminded me of Evelyn's property in Montana.

"The staff tells me you're being...uncooperative."

It had occurred to me during my long hours of solitary confinement that I was close to being completely disposable to these people.

Using Jackie or some other form of blackmail had never been a viable option, not in the long term. Not if the brainwashing didn't work, and they could conclusively prove it. I would always find a way to try and foil their plans. They knew that.

Perhaps the next step was torture. They'd wring what they could out of me before dropping me into an incineration chute. Or something. Do those exist? They do in the movies. Surely a place like this had to have one, right?

"You know," I said, turning back to face Samuel, "I've had some time to think about what happened back there. I think I've more or less pieced it together."

The moment sat for a couple seconds, as if Samuel was considering whether or not he liked the fact that I was controlling the flow of the conversation.

"Downstairs, during your processing?" He said, his posture relaxing somewhat as he reached for his mug of coffee on the table.

"Before that. During the operation." I walked over to the table, pulled back one of the chairs, and sat in it. "This wasn't just you and the Police, obviously. There was a third party. Someone you strung along. A gang leader, most likely. Someone bold. Someone you knew would already be inclined to make a bid for the Dart. You knew there was more than one Dart involved. There were two. You told him that if he cooperated, he could have one of them."

"An interesting theory." Samuel said, and took a sip of his coffee.

"Things went south, though. The Feds were more prepared than you thought they would be. Maybe your intel was wrong. Maybe there were two vans instead of one. Who knows. The whole thing was chaos. I'm not really clear on how it all went down."

"Does it matter?" Samuel said. "I was there to pick up the pieces."

I nodded. "That you were. Most of those gang members didn't make it out. But your team was completely unscathed. And you walked away with both Darts. Worked out nicely."

"You're too kind." Samuel said, cracking a smile for the first time.

"You've made yourself some new enemies. This group you manipulated are down a few men and without their due recompense."

"That's what happens when you botch a job." Samuel said, smile fading.

"Think they'll see it that way?" I said. "Part of why people like you and the Feds have been able to operate like this is because groups like the Wolves and the Bannerets have been busy dealing with each other. But what happens when they have the same enemy?"

Samuel set down his coffee cup. "Look around you. This place is remote. It's secure. No one knows where we are. And even if they did—"

I stood suddenly. I had just looked out at the watchtower and noticed that the guard was no longer standing there.

At that time, I couldn't have possibly known—for certain, at least—that there was a squad of well-trained killers out there, who had coordinated in stealthily dispatching the guard in that watchtower. I also couldn't have known that a man named Diren the Wolf was hiding in the hills, looking at me through a sniper rifle scope. At the time, I didn't even know he existed.

But I had a hunch. A strong one.

I stepped closer to Samuel, adjacent to him, leaning against the table.

Samuel stiffened in his chair, nervous at how close I was but too invested in his 'badass' front to react by moving himself. "What is it you think you're doing?"

"Giving you a choice." I said, looking down at him. "It's kind of a thing I'm into, now."

Samuel just looked up at me. "...what?"

"The Darts." I said. "We're going to show the world the truth. The irrefutable proof. We're going to blow this thing wide open. But for that, I need my Dart."

Samuel snorted. "You're not wrong. You *would* need it."

"You were so busy weaving your own web of manipulation. So used to being in control. You thought you knew everything. Every step of the process worked out. Every detail jotted. But you never imagined that the machinations used to control me might be used against you. It's a blind spot, really. A big one."

"It's time to negotiate—that's the nice way of putting it, anyway—and you've never been the best at bluffing, *Winter*." Samuel said, straightening the front of his suit jacket, brushing away some invisible bit of dust in the process. "You have nothing."

I took a couple steps backward, away from Samuel. I rapped on the table, pointed at Samuel's mug in the center of it, and gave a thumbs up. I took a few more steps away from the table.

Just when Samuel stood, impatient, the mug in the center of the table exploded.

Ceramic shrapnel shot outward in every direction.

Samuel fell backward on his ass, arms flailing, knocking over both his chair and the table in the process.

I stood there, hands in my jean pockets.

I heard the scuffling of the elevator guard's boots behind me, followed by another distant crack of a gunshot, and a *FFFFFFFFT* sound, and the thump of his body collapsing.

Hands still in my pockets, I took a few careful, ginger steps over to the fallen henchmen. There was a pool of bright blood quickly forming underneath him, like a bubble surrounding his body.

I bent over and picked up his handgun, which was still in his hip holster. It was loaded. The safety was off.

I walked toward Samuel, stopping to pick up his dropped aviators. I wiped a layer of chalky dust off of the lens with my shirt. I slid one of the temples into the neck of my shirt, causing the shades to hang there. The sun-heated metal was almost uncomfortably hot against my chest.

I came to a stop just a few paces away from Samuel, who was still on his back. His elbows dug into the roof, elevating his heaving, hyperventilating torso.

I crouched down so my face was closer to being level with his, though there was still a slight angle.

I wrenched the tracking chip out of my jean pocket—the one that had been surgically removed from my arm—and chucked it. It skidded, coming to a stop within arm's reach of Samuel.

"I half assumed I would have to get creative, hide it somewhere, like under my tongue. Or, you know, other areas. But by the time I thought of it, I realized, you hadn't had me searched. It was never part of the plan. You hadn't even conceived of it."

I leveled the gun at him.

He was twitching a little, perhaps from the effort of holding himself at that angle. Upright, but not so much as to maybe get the attention of the sniper, give them the wrong idea.

Whoever was out there, they had been watching, waiting for a moment like this one, even if they hadn't expected things to happen in precisely this way.

"Pull out your phone." I said. With my free hand, I pulled the shades off my shirt collar and put them on. "Give the order."

"What- what order?" Samuel said. His body had reacted quickly to the gunshots. His brain seemed to be in shock and hadn't yet caught up.

"I only need one Dart." I said. "Preferably mine. The one with the data on it."

"If- if I do that," Samuel said, stammering. "It won't matter, anyway. They'll shut us down-"

"You'll cross that bridge when you come to it, I'm sure." I said. "In the meantime..."

"Do...do you seriously believe they'll just let you leave?" Samuel said. "After all-"

"The brainwashing worked. This is all part of your plan to infiltrate the Bannerets. No one dares to stand in the way of that."

"Will...will they believe that?"

I stood, gun pointed down at him. "Guess we'll just have to give it a shot."

CHAPTER 43

THE MECHANICAL GATE ROLLED slowly open. Ahead was a pathway of gravel road that wound it's way amidst the trees.

The handgun from before was tucked in my jeans. There was the weighted pressure from the Black Dart in my pocket.

It was a weird feeling. I was in no rush. I felt no sense of panic or urgency. But there was a very real kind of fear. Not of Samuel, or the Feds, or anyone else. Not that.

Perhaps dread was the right word. Something was coming. Some impending finality. An abstract feeling at first. But as I walked, the pieces began to come together in my mind.

Despite accomplishing the kind of massive breakthrough I suspected was normally accomplished through years of intensive psychotherapy, I knew that this wasn't quite over. Not for me, or for anyone. As much as I would have liked it to be.

Somewhere along the line, I had believed it would be. Even without considering the implications of my own little character arc. All we had to do was beat the bad guys and get the thing. And life would go on. I would ride off into the sunset. Or Tanya would ride off with me.

*Some*body would ride off into the sunset, is where I'm going with this. But preferably me.

Preferably on a Harley. With Tanya's arms wrapped around my waist, cheek pressed against my upper back, her hair whipping wildly in the wind, like something out of an eighties flick.

Like any dream, I was able to suspend this idea for at least a brief moment in time. But when considered rationally, in the cold light of day, the absurdities become apparent.

First of all, I'd never ridden a motorcycle in my life.

More importantly—how to put this...

I killed her brother.

There it is. In plain black and white.

And thanks to Oscar, I could now remember doing it. His name was Liam, and I had known him, and been friends with him, and I could clearly recall the look of horror and surprise on his face when I put my gun up against his face and pulled the trigger.

Because I had chosen Jackie—and in a way, the ease of my own guilt—over him.

I stopped in the middle of my walk and put my hand up against a tree, suddenly feeling like I was about to be sick on the grass.

It was one thing to believe that a manipulated version of myself, one whose memories had been altered or erased, had committed murder in this way. It had been a disturbing revelation, in an unsettling, abstract sort of way.

But now I know the truth of it.

What *I*—the real me—had done.

And now that I'd come to terms with my own agency, convicted that my actions were my own...

Well, you see where that left me.

I wasn't quite done, yet.

Depressing. But in a way, not so bad. Because it meant there was just one more obstacle I had to overcome.

CHAPTER 44

I WALKED FOR ABOUT a half hour before coming across a Humvee that could not have looked more like the one that I'd woken up in a few days ago. It wasn't, though. The dead giveaway being a distinct lack of scrapes and bullet holes. In fact, it looked like it was right off the lot.

The windows were darkly tinted. Impossible to see what was inside.

Sitting on top of the Humvee was an older-looking guy—could've been in his fifties—holding a long-barreled sniper rifle. The man I would later be informed was Diren. He was wearing a dark tank top and seemed to have a considerable amount of muscle in his shoulders, arms, and chest.

That face, though. Yeesh. I was reminded more than a little of Argus Filch from Harry Potter, plus a little extra in the nose department.

"Quick thinking back there," Diren said, still perched on the roof of the car, the barrel of his rifle cradled in the crook of his elbow. "The plan was to call Samuel's cell, but it seems like you had things under control. I assume you have the Dart?"

I hesitated. A dozen questions flashed through my mind. One of them, for whatever reason, stood out. "Samuel's cell number? How did...you have something like that?"

Diren flashed a toothy grin. One those teeth—silver in color—glinted sharply, reflecting the sun. "Do you actually want to know?"

I frowned.

Diren laughed. He slid off the roof of the car and landed on his feet, boots crunching on the gravel. "Don't worry, kid. We're on the same side."

"That's good, I guess?"

"Hop in."

He strode around one side of the Humvee and popped one of the back passenger doors.

"Is that an order?" I said.

Diren shrugged. "Just take a look inside."

Mmm, yes. I have some candy for you in my van.

Still, while I did detect some bad juju from this man, it didn't seem to be directed at me. At that moment.

Not for the first time that day, I went with my gut. I peered into the open passenger door.

Inside, Tanya was leaning forward in the opposite passenger seat.

She regarded me with the same look as she had back in the garage, when I was in the chair. Studying and assessing. Looking for the guy she used to know, somewhere in there.

She seemed to find me, and the result was a small, somehow sad-looking smirk.

Not really sure what I expected.

It took me a second to notice Sater was in the front passenger seat, looking at me through the rearview mirror. His nose was bandaged, and there were some dark-purple blotches here and there on his face. Other than that, he looked like he was more or less okay.

"Sater," I said, feeling like some sort of verbal acknowledgment was obligated, unlike the looks that Tanya and I had just exchanged.

It's strange how sometimes less is so much more. Tanya and I could have talked for a half hour, and probably would not have gotten to the core of what was communicated in those brief looks.

Emotions were complicated. Identifying, expressing, and navigating them, even more so.

When Tanya had kissed me—if that even counts when you're in Rithium —she'd been in the throes of one fragment of those emotions. The part that still cared about me, despite everything that had happened.

But again, emotions are complicated.

Similarly to Tanya's brief smile, Sater gave me a curt nod. No smile. No other acknowledgments. And while some of this could be attributed to whatever painkillers he might have been on, I had a feeling that he wasn't ready to reconcile our friendship with what I had done. If he ever would be. He hated me.

And for good reason.

I glanced around the car. Any other operatives that had been out there in the woods must have traveled separately, because I didn't see them. It was just the four of us.

"I'm assuming Mason didn't want to come?" I said.

"Mason's dead," Sater said flatly, eyes ahead.

Before I could think of what to say to that, the car was already moving.

*****

"Please tell me you have the Dart with you." Sater said.

We'd left the gravel backroads behind and were speeding down a highway, thick woods closely encroaching either side of the road.

"Do you think we would have left if he didn't?" Diren said. "Would've sent him right back in there."

Wow. Good to know?

"Not just any Dart," I said. "My Dart." I pulled the black box out of my pocket. "Had it confirmed with their computer before I left."

Sater twisted himself in his seat and reached around with an open hand. I gave him the Dart.

As soon as it touched Sater's palm his fingers snapped over it and he wrenched it away, like a passive aggressive venus fly trap.

"Who's the friend?" I said. Again, not knowing who he was, at the time.

"Not a friend," Sater said.

"Associate?" Diren said, taking his eyes off the road long enough to look over at Sater, flashing a silver-toothed grin.

From the slant-eyed look Sater gave back, he seemed to take issue with this as well, but he didn't argue the point. "Whatever. Associate. Temporarily."

"So you've made some kind of deal?" I said.

"Let's just say that outing the Darts has become a mutually beneficial activity," Sater said.

"We're on our way to a safehouse right now," Diren said. "So we can do...whatever it is the nerds are going to do."

"We're going to pull the data," Sater said. "Unencrypt it. And leak it."

"Will it be enough?" I said.

It was hard to imagine a world where the government-funded Rithium facilities would get shut down, all across the country.

"It's a start," Sater said, voice softening. Now that this team had accomplished what they came to do, it was as if the tension was leaking out of him.

Sater met my eyes through the rear-view mirror. "Technically, I guess that's thanks to you," he said. "Thank you."

"Hello?" Diren said. "Me and mine are the ones doing the groundwork, here."

Sater scowled. "Once *this* heals up," he said, indicating his bandaged face, "I'll consider it. The degree of my thanks will be in inverse proportion to whatever facial scars are under these bandages."

"How well your face heals will be thanks to the medical professionals on my payroll," Diren said. "Besides, scars give you street cred. You should thank me, regardless."

Sater muttered something less than intelligible. I doubted it was *'Thank you'.*

"Right now, we just need to get to the safehouse," Tanya said. "From there, we can figure out what the next step is."

It took me a second to realize she was talking to me. And not just about the Feds. She had real hope in her eyes.

I'd seen that look before. Back when I'd first been rescued. Back when I was a Banneret. Back when Tanya and I had been in love.

I could only take it for a couple seconds before I had to look away.

"Maybe," I said, feeling a lump rise in my throat. "The next step comes before that."

Tanya tilted her head, questioningly. "Before what?"

"The safehouse," I said. "There's a stop I need to make."

"Nope," Diren said, shaking his head. "It's gonna be a straight trip. I don't want to worry about Samuel tailing us, or who knows what else."

"Samuel's too busy formulating an escape plan," I said. "At this point, he's just looking to survive. His bosses think my escape is all part of the plan. And our success might even become a distraction he can capitalize on in some way. Besides, this stop...it's in your best interest."

"How's that?" Diren said.

"I'm intent on it," I said. "There's something I need to do. And you're all gonna wish I'd done it before being exposed to the inner workings of your operation. The less I know, and the sooner I'm out, the better."

Sater glared at me through the mirror. "Would you just say what it is you're...saying?!"

"Jackie," I said. "She'll be nearby. Which exact hospital, I don't know, but with some digging—"

Tanya's expression cut me off before her words did. I could tell she was about to go full banshee mode.

It reminded me of while we were dating, when I had said that the Rithium would probably kill me one day. That it would probably kill all of us.

She hadn't liked that. Not at all.

It had taken me a while to realize at least some of the emotions behind that. By admitting that Rithium—something to which I was addicted and was important to me—would kill me one day, in a weird way I was making *it* more important than *her*.

Women want to be the ones to kill you. Not in a hitwoman sort of way. It's not like they wait til a pre-appointed time, grab a kitchen knife, and rip back the shower curtain. (At least, most don't.)

They play the long game. They hold you. They take care of you. Until one day, they realize you're gone, and they have to let you go.

Okay, so that's not quite the same thing. But I do feel like there's some crossover there.

"Have..." she said, through gritted teeth, "You learned...nothing!?"

"There'll be police there, Winter," Sater said. "They'll take you into custody!"

"That's part of the idea," I said.

I somehow heard the slap before I felt it. And it felt the same way it sounded. Like a wet fish high-fiving a concrete wall at the speed of light.

Part of me expected the entire vicinity to explode in a crescendo of window glass crystals, ruptured by the soundwaves emanating from the point of impact.

Which was, of course, a bit dramatic.

My face turned sideways from the hit, but the reaction was more out of surprise and mental shock than pain.

If Tanya had actually wanted to hurt me, she would have. But her reaction had been an emotional one.

Her lips were pressed tight together. Her eyes were moist and bloodshot-looking. Her chest heaved in slow, drawn-out movements, like she was making an effort to control her breathing.

I knew, in part, because I'd held her, and cuddled her, and slept next to her. I knew her normal patterns. Her rhythms of breathing. Even the rhythm of her heart.

What a weird thing to know. Such an intimate thing of which to be acutely aware.

"If you do this," Sater said. "You're a dead man." He spoke calmly and rationally, ignoring Tanya's outburst—or perhaps as a counterpoint to it. "You know that, right?"

"No, I don't," I said. "Just because there are crooked people in the FBI doesn't mean the entire justice system is corrupt. Besides, when we leak this information-"

"They'll be even more incentivised," Sater said, "To kill you! You'll be a key witness, in custody! You'll be playing right into their hands-"

"Well, I don't know what else to do!" I said. "Surely, somebody will need to testify. Why shouldn't it be me?" Then, after I thought about it for a second, "*Especially* me."

"I don't know what that means," Tanya said, so quiet it was almost a whisper.

"Yeah, you do," I said. "Everybody in this car knows."

"I don't know," Diren said, sounding kind of left out, as well as irritated.

"Don't do this," Tanya said. "I swear to God, if you-"

"Jesus *Christ*." Diren said.

The car swerved suddenly. The front of the car dipped forward. Dirt and grass flew up onto the windshield. Then the car dipped back, until the front was more elevated than the back, the entire vehicle slightly offkilter. We were parked along the ditch on the side of the road.

Diren spun around in his seat, scowling. "Freaking kids. *I'm* going to decide what we're going to do about this. I thought up a plan while you three were busy yapping."

"What...kind of plan?" Sater said.

"*The* plan," Diren said. "Diren's plan. I've already made up my mind. My ride, my rules."

"With all due respect-" I said.

"If you want out of my car, " Diren said. "The door's right there."

I decided I wanted to stay in the car.

CHAPTER 45

IT WAS AROUND TWO PM.

Tanya and I sat on a grassy incline, in the shade of a tree that swayed dramatically and cast blotchy, dancing shadows.

We were just a few paces from the blacktop at the top of the hill, where Diren had parked the car.

Below, we had a full view of the back end of the hospital building.

It wasn't the biggest hospital I'd ever seen. Certainly not as big as the one I woke up in after the car accident. But there were hundreds of hospital room windows visible from where we were sitting, spanning five floors in height.

Neither Tanya or I had said a word to each other during the rest of the drive. That silence was yet to be broken as we sat quietly, enjoying each other's company, but also dreading whatever was to come. Unwilling to exacerbate the already complicated situation with more words. Words uttered in passion, and perhaps regretted later.

Diren had walked down the street while he was on the phone with somebody. He moved with an assertive restlessness, as if by physical motion he was causing the world to turn, moving time forward. He was making things happen. Bringing plans into being.

Sater, too, had walked off. In his case, it was toward the gas station just down the street.

Tanya was leaning forward, her legs tucked in against her torso, the crooks of her elbows cradling her knees. Her hair hung in clumps and messy, tangled vines, pulled and tugged by the wind.

She wore jean shorts and a bright-colored Hello Kitty t-shirt.

She slumped until her chin was in the gap between her knees. "I miss him," she said.

"Mason?" I said.

She gave a half-nod, kind of like a shrug. "Him, too."

She didn't have to say who she was primarily referring to.

I had kept seeing his face, like an apparition, ever since that night when Oscar had returned my memories. All throughout my time at Samuel's facility.

I pulled my knees up to my chest, mirroring Tanya. Despite how sunny it was, there was something cold about that wind. Chilling.

I missed Liam too, though I dared not say so. I had no right to seek any kind of consolation.

Nor did I have any right to console *her*. To reach out and hold her. To share in her grief.

More than Liam, I missed Oscar. And the way that I missed Oscar, that intense feeling of loss and regret; maybe that was what was my window into understanding at least some of how Tanya felt.

In a way, I had killed Oscar, too. Not unlike how I had spent so much time believing I had in the past. Reality had rearranged itself in the image of my nightmares.

I tried to imagine what Oscar might say if he was here, now. But I couldn't. He was gone. No amount of coping mechanics would make it better, or give me any kind of real closure. At least for a long time.

"I'm sorry." I said.

I couldn't find anything to say on top of that. To extrapolate on what I'd done, to emphasize the awfulness, would be like smooth-talking. Dressing up the truth. Framing it. And that wasn't for me to do. No amount of self-deprecation would be any good.

Tanya squinted her wet eyelids, lips quivering as she stared out across the grass. "You knew Jackie a lot longer than you knew us. You felt trapped. You didn't have a choice."

"I might have." I said.

Tanya sniffed. She wiped her eyes with the palm of her hand. "You didn't believe you did. And that doesn't make it okay. But at least it makes some sort of sense.

"Losing Liam was the worst thing that ever happened to me. And I don't think I want to lose you, too. It's the last thing I want. But every time I look at you, I see it. I see it happening. I see you...*doing* it."

I didn't know how to respond to that. Perhaps I just knew that I shouldn't. It wasn't something to apologize for. Something to fix, or make better. It simply...was.

"I've done so many things I regret," I said. "I wish I could make things better, somehow. Find some kind of reset. But all I can think about is the things that I did. They hold me back. I can't...move forward."

My cheeks were hot with tears. I suddenly felt stupid for sharing. It seemed inappropriate.

Like, what? Was she supposed to tell me it was alright? That everything was going to be okay?

Stupid.

I wiped the tears off my face.

A seagull hovered in the air above the roof of the hospital, a white specter floating in a sea of blue.

"You have to try," Tanya said.

I turned toward Tanya, blinking, trying to get the blurriness out of my eyes. "Try...what?"

"To move forward," Tanya said. "Otherwise, what's the point?"

The seagull lowered slowly, alighting on the outer edge of the rooftop.

Boot steps on the blacktop signalled Sater's return. He was holding a case of Newports. He sat at the top of the hill—which surprised me, considering he was wearing fitted dress pants— and held the open case of cigarettes out toward us, offering.

Both Tanya and I shook our heads.

Sater put one of the cigarettes in his mouth. He put the case in the inner breast pocket of his dress jacket, pulled a lighter out of what appeared to be the same pocket, and lit up. As he smoked, strands of his otherwise slicked-back hair bobbed back and forth in the wind, like vaulting poles.

Diren returned, prompting Tanya and I to head back up toward the car.

The ganglord had a triumphant glint in his eyes.

"This is the one," he said. "She's here."

"And you know this...how?" Sater said.

Diren's look soured a little, as if he'd been hoping he wouldn't have to divulge the actual source of his information. "Facebook." He snapped his fingers expectantly in Sater's direction.

Sater returned this gesture with a glare that lasted a full ten seconds. Still, he handed Diren a cigarette.

Diren used his own lighter to light it.

"The parents of this 'Jackie' don't seem too intent on protecting their privacy," he said. "Or hers."

"Great," I said. "So...what's the plan?"

Diren exhaled a thick plume of smoke. He clasped the lit cigarette between two fingers. "This."

And then he punched me in the face.

*****

"What if..." I paused, stopping to hold my head back and temporarily stem the streams of blood emanating from my nostrils. We were just outside the automatic sliding door. "What if the Feds are here, waiting for us? Shouldn't we come up with some kind of...distraction?"

Diren shrugged. "What if they aren't?"

"What if- what?"

"Do you always over-think everything?"

That gave me pause. "Actually, yes. Yes, I do."

Diren already had me by the shoulder and was steering me inexorably toward the sliding door. Sater and Tanya tailed behind.

We were in the wake.

The door made a harsh beeping/honking sound as it swung open. The same sound when it closed behind us.

"Easy," I said, shrugging Diren off me. He had been practically dragging me forward by the nape of my hoodie—one that he had picked up at a Walmart, thinking it would help disguise my appearance, somehow. "I'm doing it, I'm doing it."

It was warm inside. Almost uncomfortably so.

As per my experience with hospitals, the ceiling lights were just a tad too bright, legitimately tempting me to put on the pair of shades that Diren had also acquired from Walmart. But having the hood up inside was almost sketchy enough. Putting on the sunglasses would positively identify me as some kind of fugitive. That, or perhaps lead the hospital staff to think I was on drugs of some kind, my pupils dilating painfully. That was a thing, right? I was pretty sure it was.

There were only a dozen or so people waiting in the lobby. Most of the seats were empty. None of those waiting seemed to be in pain or any particular hurry.

We approached the front desk together, outnumbering the clerk four-to-one.

She looked to be in her mid-forties, wearing purple scrubs. She had a long mop of hair that looked—and possibly smelled—like it had been recently permed.

Tanya went first, explaining that there had been an accident, and that she believed my nose might be broken. She also claimed to think that I might have a concussion.

As the clerk started to hand a form to Tanya, explaining how it worked, Sater cut in, asking loudly about parking validation.

While the clerk was focused on the two of them, I took that as my cue to begin slinking away.

As the conversation between Sater and the clerk escalated into what sounded like some kind of argument, Tanya leaned back and gave me a thumbs up.

"Good luck."

I needed to move quickly. Hopefully the others would cover for me, telling the clerk that I'd just gone to use the restroom, but I didn't want to take the chance.

In my mind's eye, I visualized the picture of Jackie that Diren had shown me; the one posted on Facebook. She had been in her hospital bed. There was a view of the window, and it was clear that she was on one of the upper floors, along the back end of the building. The side that Diren had parked next to, earlier.

I avoided the elevator, instead following the signs with stairs on them. This led me to the door leading to the stairwell. As I pushed the door release, there was a loud clicking sound, echoing in the stairwell. By the time the door had slowly snapped shut behind me, I was halfway to the second floor.

I peeked through the small window in the door to the second floor. Saw no one.

I pressed the door release. Slowly. I didn't want it to snap loudly, echoing in the hallway.

I pushed the door open enough to peek out, and listen. Somewhere around the corner down the hall, I could hear a nurse talking quietly.

Somewhere else, probably a couple corners away, a landline phone rang insistently.

I stepped into the hall and shut the door quietly behind me. I headed off down the hall, in the opposite direction of the talking nurse. I wiped my bleeding nose on the sleeve of my hoodie, which was thankfully dark-red in color.

It didn't take me long to find her, walking down the hallway that ran along the back of the building, carefully peeking into every room as I went.

I froze as I saw her, peering through the open door to her room. And my breath caught.

She was sitting up in her bed. There were dark circles under her eyes. But she was smiling.

I knew that look. I had felt it. Exhausted. Traumatized. Broken. But still, a part of me feeling like everything might be okay, after all.

Someone in the room said something, and she laughed. Which was my big tip-off that she wasn't alone.

Jackie's parents were in the room with her. They stood at the foot of the bed, talking with her. They had likely spent most of their waking hours in this room since the moment they were notified.

Honestly, I don't know how I could have expected anything else. Of course they would want to be with her. They wouldn't want to let her out of their sight. They wouldn't be leaving anytime soon.

I stood just out of sight of both Jackie and her parents, my hand on the doorframe.

This complicated things. Didn't it? It was different with her parents here. Things could get ugly. The situation could escalate in a way I might not be able to control.

Jackie's parents might not have known my exact degree of involvement in her disappearance. But the last time they'd seen either of their kids had been just before I'd left their house in the pickup.

Oscar.

My fingers flexed, nails scraping painfully across the metal frame.

They don't know. Do they?

They might still not. And even if they did, do they know it was you?

My body trembled, as if possessed.

I began to step backward, away from the doorway.

You don't have to do this, I thought. *It's not necessary. It's over. Isn't that enough?*

You don't NEED to do this.

But I stopped, just a couple paces away from the room. The shaking stopped, replaced with a sense of purpose and calm that flowed over me, protecting and caressing, like an aura.

I didn't *need* to do this. There was nothing forcing me. No shackles or chains. Not anymore.

But I *wanted* to.

I reached over. I knocked on the doorframe three times. And I walked into the room.

About Author

Jacob Hawes has been writing from a young age. Growing up on a small family hobby farm, his days were filled with make-believe adventures of fighting monsters and slaying the bad guy. This fueled his imagination and set him on a path of writing and a love of stories.

He continues to live in the pacific northwest with his wife Ama and beloved dog Yugo, spending free time reading fantasy and studying writing.